THE BALLROOM OF ROMANCE

The Ballroom of Romance

and Other Stories

WILLIAM TREVOR

THE BODLEY HEAD
LONDON SYDNEY
TORONTO

ACKNOWLEDGMENTS

These stories first appeared in the *London Mag-
azine, Transatlantic Review, Nova, Redbook,* the
Antioch Review, Winter's Tales, and *Penguin
Modern Short Stories*. The Story 'Going Home'
was first broadcast by BBC Radio Three as a
radio play.

© William Trevor 1972
ISBN 0 370 01468 5
Printed and bound in Great Britain for
The Bodley Head Ltd,
9 Bow Street, London WC2E 7AL
by Cox & Wyman Ltd,
London, Reading and Fakenham
Set in Intertype Plantin
First Published 1972
Reprinted 1972

CONTENTS

Access to the Children

Malcolmson, a fair, tallish man in a green tweed suit that required pressing, banged the driver's door of his ten-year-old Volvo and walked quickly away from the car, jangling the keys. He entered a block of flats that was titled – gold engraved letters on a granite slab – The Quadrant.

It was a Sunday afternoon in late October. Yellow-brown leaves patterned grass that was not for walking on. Some scurried on the steps that led to the building's glass entrance doors. Rain was about, Malcolmson considered.

At three o'clock precisely he rang the bell of his ex-wife's flat on the third floor. In response he heard at once the voices of his children and the sound of their running in the hall. 'Hullo,' he said when one of them, Deirdre, opened the door. 'Ready?'

They went with him, two little girls, Deirdre seven and Susie five. In the lift they told him that a foreign person, the day before, had been trapped in the lift from eleven o'clock in the morning until teatime. Food and cups of tea had been poked through a grating to this person, a Japanese businessman who occupied a flat at the top of the block. 'He didn't get the hang of an English lift,' said Deirdre. 'He could have died there,' said Susie.

In the Volvo he asked them if they'd like to go to the Zoo and they shook their heads firmly. On the last two Sundays he'd taken them to the Zoo, Susie reminded him in her specially polite, very quiet voice: you got tired of the Zoo, walking round and round, looking at all the same animals. She smiled at him to show she wasn't being ungrateful. She suggested that in a little while, after a month or so, they could go to the Zoo again, because there might be some new animals. Deirdre said that there wouldn't be, not after a month or so: why should there be? 'Some old animals might have died,' said Susie.

Malcolmson drove down the Edgware Road, with Hyde Park in mind.

'What have you done?' he asked.

'Only school,' said Susie.

'And the news cinema,' said Deirdre. 'Mummy took us to a news cinema. We saw a film about how they make wire.'

'A man kept talking to Mummy. He said she had nice hair.'

'The usherette told him to be quiet. He bought us ice-creams, but Mummy said we couldn't accept them.'

'He wanted to take Mummy to a dance.'

'We had to move to other seats.'

'What else have you done?'

'Only school,' said Susie. 'A boy was sick on Miss Bawden's desk.'

'After school stew.'

'It's raining,' said Susie.

He turned the windscreen-wipers on. He wondered if he should simply bring the girls to his flat and spend the afternoon watching television. He tried to remember what the Sunday film was. There often was something suitable for children on Sunday afternoons, old films with Deanna Durbin or Nelson Eddy and Jeanette MacDonald.

'Where're we going?' Susie asked.

'Where d'you want to go?'

'*A Hundred and One Dalmatians.*'

'Oh, please,' said Susie.

'But we've seen it. We've seen it five times.'

'Please, Daddy.'

He stopped the Volvo and bought a *What's On*. While he leafed through it they sat quietly, willing him to discover a cinema, anywhere in London, that was showing the film. He shook his head and started the Volvo again.

'Nothing else?' Deirdre asked.

'Nothing suitable.'

At Speakers' Corner they listened to a Jehovah's Witness and then to a woman talking about vivisection. 'How horrid,' said Deirdre. 'Is that true, Daddy?' He made a face. 'I suppose so,' he said.

In the drizzle they played a game among the trees, hiding and chasing one another. Once when they'd been playing this game a woman had brought a policeman up to him. She'd seen him approaching the girls, she said; the girls had been playing alone and he'd joined in. 'He's our daddy,' Susie had said, but the woman had still argued, claiming that he'd given them sweets so that they'd say that. 'Look at him,' the woman had insultingly said. 'He needs a shave.' Then she'd gone away, and the policeman had apologised.

'The boy who was sick was Nicholas Barnet,' Susie said. 'I think he could have died.'

A year and a half ago Malcolmson's wife, Elizabeth, had said he must choose between her and Diana. For weeks they had talked about it; she knowing that he was in love with Diana and was having some kind of an affair with her, he caught between the two of them, attempting the impossible in his effort not to hurt anyone. She had given him a chance to get over Diana, as she put it, but she couldn't go on for ever giving him a chance, no woman could. In the end, after the shock and the tears and the period of reasonableness, she became bitter. He didn't blame her: they'd been in the middle

9

of a happy marriage, nothing was wrong, nothing was lacking.

He'd met Diana on a train; he'd sat with her, talking for a long time, and after that his marriage didn't seem the same. In her bitterness Elizabeth said he was stupidly infatuated: he was behaving like a murderer: there was neither dignity nor humanity left in him. Diana she described as a flat-chested American nymphomaniac and predator, the worst type of woman in the world. She was beautiful herself, more beautiful than Diana, more gracious, warmer, and funnier: there was a sting of truth in what she said; he couldn't understand himself. In the very end, after they'd been morosely drinking gin and lime-juice, she'd suddenly shouted at him that he'd better pack his bags. He sat unhappily, gazing at the green bottle of Gordon's gin on the carpet between his chair and hers. She screamed; tears poured in a torrent from her eyes. 'For God's sake go away,' she cried, on her feet, turning away from him. She shook her head in a wild gesture, causing her long fair hair to move like a horse's mane. Her hands, clenched into fists, beat at his cheeks, making bruises that Diana afterwards tended.

For months after that he saw neither Elizabeth nor his children. He tried not to think about them. He and Diana took a flat in Barnes, near the river, and in time he became used to the absence of the children's noise in the mornings, and to Diana's cooking and her quick efficiency in little things, and the way she always remembered to pass on telephone messages, which was something that Elizabeth had always forgotten to do.

Then one day, a week or so before the divorce was due, Diana said she didn't think there was anything left between them. It hadn't worked, she said; nothing was quite right. Amazed and bewildered, he argued with her. He frowned at her, his eyes screwed up as though he couldn't properly see her. She was very poised, in a black dress, with a necklace at her throat, her hair pulled smooth and neatly tied. She'd met a man called Abbotforth, she said, and she went on talking about that, still standing.

'We could go to the Natural History Museum,' Deirdre said.

'Would you like to, Susie?'

'Certainly not,' said Susie.

They were sitting on a bench, watching a bird that Susie said was a yellow-hammer. Deirdre disagreed: at this time of year, she said, there were no yellow-hammers in England, she'd read it in a book. 'It's a little baby yellow-hammer,' said Susie. 'Miss Bawden said you see lots of them.'

The bird flew away. A man in a raincoat was approaching them, singing quietly. They began to giggle. 'Sure, maybe some day I'll go back to Ireland,' sang the man, 'if it's only at the closing of my day.' He stopped, noticing that they were watching him.

'Were you ever in Ireland?' he asked. The girls, still giggling, shook their heads. 'It's a great place,' said the man. He took a bottle of VP wine from his raincoat pocket and drank from it.

'Would you care for a swig, sir?' he said to Malcolmson, and Malcolmson thanked him and said he wouldn't. 'It would do the little misses no harm,' suggested the man. 'It's good, pure stuff.' Malcolmson shook his head. 'I was born in County Clare,' said the man, 'in 1928, the year of the Big Strike.' The girls, red in the face from containing their laughter, poked at one another with their elbows. 'Aren't they the great little misses?' said the man. 'Aren't they the fine credit to you, sir?'

In the Volvo on the way to Barnes they kept repeating that he was the funniest man they'd ever met. He was nicer than the man in the news cinema, Susie said. He was quite like him, though, Deirdre maintained: he was looking for company in just the same way, you could see it in his eyes. 'He was staggering,' Susie said. 'I thought he was going to die.'

Before the divorce he had telephoned Elizabeth, telling her that Diana had gone. She hadn't said anything, and she'd put the receiver down before he could say anything else. Then the divorce came through and the arrangement was that the children should remain with Elizabeth and that he should have reasonable access to them. It was an extraordinary expression, he considered: reasonable access.

The Sunday afternoons had begun then, the ringing of a doorbell that had once been his own doorbell, the children in the hall, the lift, the Volvo, tea in the flat where he and Diana had lived and where now he lived on his own. Sometimes, when he was collecting them, Elizabeth spoke to him, saying in a matter-of-fact way that Susie had a cold and should not be outside too much, or that Deirdre was being bad about practising her clarinet and would he please speak to her. He loved Elizabeth again; he said to himself that he had never not loved her; he wanted to say to her that she'd been right about Diana. But he didn't say anything, knowing that wounds had to heal.

Every week he longed more for Sunday to arrive. Occasionally he invented reasons for talking to her at the door of the flat, after the children had gone in. He asked questions about their progress at school, he wondered if there were ways in which he could help. It seemed unfair, he said, that she should have to bring them up single-handed like this; he made her promise to telephone him if a difficulty arose; and if ever she wanted to go out in the evenings and couldn't find a baby-sitter, he'd willingly drive over. He always hoped that if he talked for long enough the girls would become so noisy in their room that she'd be forced to ask him in so that she could quieten them, but the ploy never worked.

In the lift on the way down every Sunday evening he

thought she was more beautiful than any woman he'd ever seen, and he thought it was amazing that once she should have been his wife and should have borne him children, that once they had lain together and loved, and that he had let her go. Three weeks ago she had smiled at him in a way that was like the old way. He'd been sure of it, positive, in the lift on the way down.

He drove over Hammersmith Bridge, along Castelnau and into Barnes High Street. No one was about on the pavements; buses crept sluggishly through the damp afternoon.

'Miss Bawden's got a black boy-friend,' Susie said, 'called Eric Mantilla.'

'You should see Miss Bawden,' murmured Deirdre. 'She hasn't any breasts.'

'She has lovely breasts,' shouted Susie, 'and lovely jumpers and lovely skirts. She has a pair of earrings that once belonged to an Egyptian empress.'

'As flat as a pancake,' said Deirdre.

After Diana had gone he'd found it hard to concentrate. The managing director of the firm where he worked, a man with a stout red face called Sir Gerald Travers, had been sympathetic. He'd told him not to worry. Personal troubles, Sir Gerald had said, must naturally affect professional life; no one would be human if that didn't happen. But six months later, to Malcolmson's surprise, Sir Gerald had suddenly suggested to him that perhaps it would be better if he made a move. 'It's often so,' Sir Gerald had said, a soft smile gleaming between chubby cheeks. 'Professional life can be affected by the private side of things. You understand me, Malcolmson?' They valued him immensely, Sir Gerald said, and they'd be generous when the moment of departure came. A change was a tonic; Sir Gerald advised a little jaunt somewhere.

In reply to all that Malcolmson said that the upset in his

private life was now over; nor did he feel, he added, in need of recuperation. 'You'll easily find another berth,' Sir Gerald Travers replied, with a wide, confident smile. 'I think it would be better.'

Malcolmson had sought about for another job, but had not been immediately successful: there was a recession, people said. Soon it would be better, they added, and because of Sir Gerald's promised generosity Malcolmson found himself in a position to wait until things seemed brighter. It was always better, in any case, not to seem in a hurry.

He spent the mornings in the Red Lion, in Barnes, playing dominoes with an old-age pensioner, and when the pensioner didn't turn up owing to bronchial trouble Malcolmson would borrow a newspaper from the landlord. He slept in the afternoons and returned to the Red Lion later. Occasionally when he'd had a few drinks he'd find himself thinking about his children and their mother. He always found it pleasant then, thinking of them with a couple of drinks inside him.

'It's *The Last of the Mohicans*,' said Deirdre in the flat, and he guessed that she must have looked at the *Radio Times* earlier in the day. She'd known they'd end up like that, watching television. Were they bored on Sundays? he often wondered.

'Can't we have *The Golden Shot*?' demanded Susie, and Deirdre pointed out that it wasn't on yet. He left them watching Randolph Scott and Binnie Barnes, and went to prepare their tea in the kitchen.

On Saturdays he bought meringues and brandy-snaps in Frith's Patisserie. The elderly assistant smiled at him in a way that made him wonder if she knew what he wanted them for; it occurred to him once that she felt sorry for him. On Sunday mornings, listening to the omnibus edition of *The Archers*, he made Marmite sandwiches with brown bread and tomato sandwiches with white. They loved sandwiches, which was something he remembered from the past. He remembered parties, Deirdre's friends sitting around a table, small and silent, eating crisps and cheese puffs and leaving all the cake.

When *The Last of the Mohicans* came to an end they watched *Going for a Song* for five minutes before changing the channel for *The Golden Shot*. Then Deirdre turned the television off and they went to the kitchen to have tea. 'Wash your hands,' said Susie, and he heard her add that if a germ got into your food you could easily die. 'She kept referring to death,' he would say to Elizabeth when he left them back. 'D'you think she's worried about anything?' He imagined Elizabeth giving the smile she had given three weeks ago and then saying he'd better come in to discuss the matter.

'Goody,' said Susie, sitting down.

'I'd like to marry a man like that man in the park,' said Deirdre. 'It'd be much more interesting, married to a bloke like that.'

'He'd be always drunk.'

'He wasn't drunk, Susie. That's not being drunk.'

'He was drinking out of a bottle –'

'He was putting on a bit of flash, drinking out of a bottle and singing his little song. No harm in that, Susie.'

'I'd like to be married to Daddy.'

'You couldn't be married to Daddy.'

'Well, Richard then.'

'Ribena, Daddy. Please.'

He poured drops of Ribena into two mugs and filled them up with warm water. He had a definite feeling that today she'd ask him in, both of them pretending a worry over Susie's obsession with death. They'd sit together while the children splashed about in the bathroom; she'd offer him gin and lime-juice, their favourite drink, a drink known as a Gimlet, as once he'd told her. They'd drink it out of green glasses that they'd bought, years ago, in Italy. The girls would dry themselves and come and say good-night. They'd go to bed. He might tell them a story, or she would. 'Stay to supper,' she would say, and while she made risotto he would go to her and kiss her hair.

'I like his eyes,' said Susie. 'One's higher than another.'

'It couldn't be.'

'It is.'

'He couldn't see, Susie, if his eyes were like that. Every-one's eyes are – '

'He isn't always drunk like the man in the park.'

'Who?' he asked.

'Richard,' they said together, and Susie added: 'Irishmen are always drunk.'

'Daddy's an Irishman and Daddy's not always – '

'Who's Richard?'

'He's Susie's boy-friend.'

'I don't mind,' said Susie. 'I like him.'

'If he's there tonight, Susie, you're not to climb all over him.'

He left the kitchen and in the sitting-room he poured him-self some whisky. He sat with the glass cold between his hands, staring at the grey television screen. 'Sure, maybe some day I'll go back to Ireland,' Deirdre sang in the kitchen, and Susie laughed shrilly.

He imagined a dark-haired man, a cheerful man, intelligent and subtle, a man who came often to the flat, whom his chil-dren knew well and were already fond of. He imagined him as he had imagined himself ten minutes before, sitting with Elizabeth, drinking Gimlets from the green Italian glasses.

'Say good-night to Richard,' Elizabeth would say, and the girls would go to him and kiss him good-night.

'Who's Richard?' he asked, standing in the kitchen doorway.

'A friend,' said Deirdre, 'of Mummy's.'

'A nice friend?'

'Oh, yes.'

'I love him,' said Susie.

He returned to the sitting-room and quickly poured himself more whisky. Both of his hands were shaking. He drank quickly, and then poured and drank some more. On the pale carpet, close to the television set, there was a stain where Diana had spilt a cup of coffee. He hated now this memory of her, he hated her voice when it came back to him, and the memory of her body and her mind. And yet once he had been rendered lunatic with the passion of his love for her. He had loved her more than Elizabeth, and in his madness he had spoilt everything.

'Wash your hands,' said Susie, close to him. He hadn't heard them come into the room. He asked them, mechanically, if they'd had enough to eat. 'She hasn't washed her hands,' Susie said. 'I washed mine in the sink.'

He turned the television on. It was the girl ventriloquist Shari Lewis, with Lamb Chop and Charley Horse.

Well, he thought under the influence of the whisky, he had had his fling. He had played the pins with a flat-chested American nymphomaniac and predator, and he had lost all there was to lose. Now it was Elizabeth's turn: why shouldn't she have, for a time, the dark-haired Richard who took another man's children on to his knee and kissed them good-night? Wasn't it better that the score should be even before they all came together again?

He sat on the floor with his daughters on either side of him, his arms about them. In front of him was his glass of whisky.

They laughed at Lamb Chop and Charley Horse, and when the programme came to an end and the news came on he didn't want to let his daughters go. An electric fire glowed cosily. Wind blew the rain against the windows, the autumn evening was dark already.

He turned the television off. He finished the whisky in his glass and poured some more. 'Shall I tell you,' he said, 'about when Mummy and I were married?'

They listened while he did so. He told them about meeting Elizabeth in the first place, at somebody else's wedding, and of the days they had spent walking about together, and about the wet, cold afternoon on which they'd been married.

'February the twenty-fourth,' Deirdre said.

'Yes.'

'I'm going to be married in summer-time,' Susie said, 'when the cow-parsley's out.'

His birthday and Elizabeth's were on the same day, April 21st. He reminded the girls of that; he told them of the time he and Elizabeth had discovered they shared the date, a date shared also with Hitler and the Queen. They listened quite politely, but somehow didn't seem much interested.

They watched *What's in a Game?* He drank more. He wouldn't be able to drive them back. He'd pretend he couldn't start the Volvo and then he'd telephone for a taxi. It had happened once before that in a depression he'd begun to drink when they were with him on a Sunday afternoon. They'd been to Madame Tussaud's and the Planetarium, which Susie had said frightened her. In the flat, just as this time, while they were eating their sandwiches, he'd been overcome with the longing that they should all be together again. He'd begun to drink and in the end, while they watched television, he'd drunk quite a lot. When the time came to go he'd said that he couldn't find the keys of the Volvo and that they'd have to have a taxi. He'd spent five minutes brushing his teeth so that Elizabeth wouldn't smell the alcohol when she opened the door. He'd smiled at her with his well-brushed teeth but she, not then being over her bitterness, hadn't smiled back.

The girls put their coats on. Deirdre drank some Ribena; he had another small tot of whisky. And then, as they were leaving the flat, he suddenly felt he couldn't go through the farce of walking to the Volvo, putting the girls into it and then pretending he couldn't start it. 'I'm tired,' he said instead. 'Let's have a taxi.'

They watched the Penrhyn Male Voice Choir in *Songs of Praise* while they waited for it to arrive. He poured himself another drink, drank it slowly, and then went to the bathroom to brush his teeth. He remembered the time Deirdre had been born, in a maternity home in the country because they'd lived in the country then. Elizabeth had been concerned because she'd thought one of Deirdre's fingers was bent and had kept showing it to nurses who said they couldn't see anything the matter. He hadn't been able to see anything the matter either, nor had the doctor. 'She'll never be as beautiful as you,' he'd said and quite soon after that she'd stopped talking about the finger and had said he was nice to her. Susie had been born at home, very quickly, very easily.

The taxi arrived. 'Soon be Christmas,' said the taximan. 'You chaps looking forward to Santa Claus?' They giggled because he had called them chaps. 'Fifty-six more days,' said Susie.

He imagined them on Christmas Day, with the dark-haired Richard explaining the rules of a game he'd bought them. He imagined all four of them sitting down at Christmas dinner, and Richard asking the girls which they liked, the white or the brown of the turkey, and then cutting them small slices. He'd have brought, perhaps, champagne, because he was that kind of person. Deirdre would sip from his glass, not liking the taste. Susie would love it.

He counted in his mind: if Richard had been visiting the flat for, say, six weeks already and assuming that his love affair with Elizabeth had begun two weeks before his first visit, that left another four months to go, allowing the affair ran an average course of six months. It would therefore come to an end at the beginning of March. His own affair with Diana had lasted from April until September. 'Oh darling,' said Diana, suddenly in his mind, and his own voice replied to her, caressing her with words. He remembered the first time they had made love and the guilt that had hammered at him and the passion there had been between them. He imagined Elizabeth naked in Richard's naked arms, her eyes open, looking at him, her fingers touching the side of his face, her lips slightly smiling. He reached forward and pulled down the glass shutter. 'I need cigarettes,' he said. 'There's a pub in Shepherd's Bush Road, the Laurie Arms.'

He drank two large measures of whisky. He bought cigarettes and lit one, rolling the smoke around in his mouth to disguise the smell of the alcohol. As he returned to the taxi, he slipped on the wet pavement and almost lost his balance. He felt very drunk all of a sudden. Deirdre and Susie were telling the taximan about the man in Hyde Park.

He was aware that he walked unsteadily when they left the taxi and moved across the forecourt of the block of flats. In the hall, before they got into the lift, he lit another cigarette, rolling the smoke about his mouth. 'That poor Japanese man,' said Deirdre.

He rang the bell, and when Elizabeth opened the door the girls turned to him and thanked him. He took the cigarette from his mouth and kissed them. Elizabeth was smiling: if only she'd ask him in and give him a drink he wouldn't have to worry about the alcohol on his breath. He swore to himself that she was smiling as she'd smiled three weeks ago. 'Can I come in?' he asked, unable to keep the words back.

'In?' The smile was still there. She was looking at him quite closely. He released the smoke from his mouth. He tried to remember what it was he'd planned to say, and then it came to him.

'I'm worried about Susie,' he said in a quiet voice. 'She talked about death all the time.'

'Death?'

'Yes.'

'There's someone here actually,' she said, stepping back into the hall. 'But come in, certainly.'

In the sitting-room she introduced him to Richard who was, as he'd imagined, a dark-haired man. The sitting-room was much the same as it always had been. 'Have a drink,' Richard offered.

'D'you mind if we talk about Susie?' Elizabeth asked Richard. He said he'd put them to bed if she liked. She nodded. Richard went away.

'Well?'

He stood with the familiar green glass in his hand, gazing at her. He said:

'I haven't had gin and lime-juice since – '

'Yes. Look, I shouldn't worry about Susie. Children of that age often say odd things, you know – '

'I don't mind about Richard, Elizabeth, I think it's your due. I worked it out in the taxi. It's the end of October now – '

'My due?'

'Assuming your affair has been going on already for six weeks – '

'You're drunk.'

He closed one eye, focusing. He felt his body swaying and he said to himself that he must not fall now, that no matter what his body did his feet must remain firm on the carpet. He sipped from the green glass. She wasn't, he noticed, smiling any more.

'I'm actually not drunk,' he said. 'I'm actually sober. By the time our birthday comes round, Elizabeth, it'll all be over. On April the twenty-first we could have family tea.'

'What the hell are you talking about?'

'The future, Elizabeth. Of you and me and our children.'

'How much have you had to drink?'

'We tried to go to *A Hundred and One Dalmatians*, but it wasn't on anywhere.'

'So you drank instead. While the children –'

'We came here in a taxi-cab. They've had their usual tea, they've watched a bit of *The Last of the Mohicans* and a bit of *Going for a Song* and all of *The Golden Shot* and *The Shari Lewis Show* and –'

'You see them for a few hours and you have to go and get drunk –'

'I am not drunk, Elizabeth.'

He crossed the room as steadily as he could. He looked aggressively at her. He poured gin and lime-juice. He said:

'You have a right to your affair with Richard, I recognise that.'

'A *right*?'

'I love you, Elizabeth.'

'You loved Diana.'

'I have never not loved you. Diana was nothing – nothing, nothing at all.'

'She broke our marriage up.'

'No.'

'We're divorced.'

'I love you, Elizabeth.'

'Now listen to me –'

'I live from Sunday to Sunday. We're a family, Elizabeth;

you and me and them. It's ridiculous, all this. It's ridiculous
making Marmite sandwiches with brown bread and tomato
sandwiches with white. It's ridiculous buying meringues and
going five times to *A Hundred and One Dalmatians* and
going up the Post Office Tower until we're sick of the sight of
it, and watching drunks in Hyde Park and poking about at
the Zoo –'

'You have reasonable access –'

'Reasonable access, my God!' His voice rose. He felt sweat
on his forehead. Reasonable access, he shouted, was utterly
no good to him; reasonable access was meaningless and
stupid; a day would come when they wouldn't want to go with
him on Sunday afternoons, when there was nowhere left in
London that wasn't an unholy bore. What about reasonable
access then?

'Please be quiet.'

He sat down in the armchair that he had always sat in. She
said:

'You might marry again. And have other children.'

'I don't want other children. I have children already. I
want us all to live together as we used to –'

'Please listen to me –'

'I get a pain in my stomach in the middle of the night.
Then I wake up and can't go back to sleep. The children will
grow up and I'll grow old. I couldn't begin a whole new thing
all over again: I haven't the courage. Not after Diana. A
mistake like that alters everything.'

'I'm going to marry Richard.'

'Three weeks ago,' he said, as though he hadn't heard her,
'you smiled at me.'

'Smiled?'

'Like you used to, Elizabeth. Before –'

'You made a mistake,' she said, softly. 'I'm sorry.'

'I'm not saying don't go on with your affair with this man.

I'm not saying that, because I think in the circumstances it'd be a cheek. D'you understand me, Elizabeth?'

'Yes, I do. And I think you and I can be perfectly good friends. I don't feel sour about it any more: perhaps that's what you saw in my smile.'

'Have a six-month affair – '

'I'm in love with Richard.'

'That'll all pass into the atmosphere. It'll be nothing at all in a year's time – '

'No.'

'I love you, Elizabeth.'

They stood facing one another, not close. His body was still swaying. The liquid in his glass moved gently, slurping to the rim and then settling back again. Her eyes were on his face: it was thinner, she was thinking. Her fingers played with the edge of a cushion on the back of the sofa.

'On Saturdays,' he said, 'I buy the meringues and the brandy-snaps in Frith's Patisserie. On Sunday morning I make the sandwiches. Then I cook sausages and potatoes for my lunch, and after that I come over here.'

'Yes, yes – '

'I look forward all week to Sunday.'

'The children enjoy their outings, too.'

'Will you think about it?'

'About what?'

'About all being together again.'

'Oh, for heaven's sake.' She turned away from him. 'I wish you'd go now,' she said.

'Will you come out with me on our birthday?'

'I've told you.' Her voice was loud and angry, her cheeks were flushed. 'Can't you understand? I'm going to marry Richard. We'll be married within a month, when the girls have had time to get to know him a little better. By Christmas we'll be married.'

He shook his head in a way that annoyed her, seeming in his drunkenness to deny the truth of what she was saying. He tried to light a cigarette; matches dropped to the floor at his feet. He left them there.

It enraged her that he was sitting in an armchair in her flat with his eyelids drooping through drink and an unlighted cigarette in his hand and his matches spilt all over the floor. They were his children, but she wasn't his wife: he'd destroyed her as a wife, he'd insulted her, he'd left her to bleed and she had called him a murderer.

'Our birthday,' he said, smiling at her as though already she had agreed to join him on that day. 'And Hitler's and the Queen's.'

'On our birthday if I go out with anyone it'll be Richard.'

'Our birthday is beyond the time – '

'For God's sake, there is no beyond the time. I'm in love with another man – '

'No.'

'On our birthday,' she shouted at him, 'on the night of our birthday Richard will make love to me in the bed you slept in for nine years. You have access to the children. You can demand no more.'

He bent down and picked up a match. He struck it on the side of the empty box. The cigarette was bent. He lit it with a wobbling flame and dropped the used match on to the carpet. The dark-haired man, he saw, was in the room again. He'd come in, hearing her shouting like that. He was asking her if she was all right. She told him to go away. Her face was hard; bitterness was there again. She said, not looking at him:

'Everything was so happy. We had a happy marriage. For nine years we had a perfectly happy marriage.'

'We could – '

'Not ever.'

25

Again he shook his head in disagreement. Cigarette ash fell on to the green tweed of his suit. His eyes were narrowed, watching her, seemingly suspicious.

'We had a happy marriage,' she repeated, whispering the words, speaking to herself, still not looking at him. 'You met a woman on a train and that was that: you murdered our marriage. You left me to plead, as I am leaving you now. You have your Sunday access. There is that legality between us. Nothing more.'

'Please, Elizabeth – '

'Oh for God's sake, stop.' Her rage was all in her face now. Her lips quivered as though in the effort to hold back words that would not be denied. They came from her, more quietly but with greater bitterness. Her eyes roved over the green tweed suit of the man who once had been her husband, over his thin face and his hair that seemed, that day, not to have been brushed.

'You've gone to seed,' she said, hating herself for saying that, unable to prevent herself. 'You've gone to seed because you've lost your self-respect. I've watched you, week by week. The woman you met on a train took her toll of you and now in your seediness you want to creep back. Don't you know you're not the man I married?'

'Elizabeth – '

'You didn't have cigarette burns all over your clothes. You didn't smell of toothpaste when you should have smelt of drink. You stand there, pathetically, Sunday after Sunday, trying to keep a conversation going. D'you know what I feel?'

'I love – '

'I feel sorry for you.'

He shook his head. There was no need to feel sorry for him, he said, remembering suddenly the elderly assistant in Frith's Patisserie and remembering also, for some reason, the woman in Hyde Park who peculiarly had said that he wasn't shaved. He looked down at his clothes and saw the burn marks she had mentioned. 'We think it would be better,' said the voice of Sir Gerald Travers unexpectedly in his mind.

'I'll make some coffee,' said Elizabeth.

She left him. He had been cruel, and then Diana had been cruel, and now Elizabeth was cruel because it was her right and her instinct to be so. He recalled with vividness Diana's face in those first moments on the train, her eyes looking at him, her voice. 'You have lost all dignity,' Elizabeth had whispered, in the darkness, at night. 'I despise you for that.' He tried to stand up but found the effort beyond him. He raised the green glass to his lips. His eyes closed and when he opened them again he thought for a drunken moment that he was back in the past, in the middle of his happy marriage. He wiped at his face with a handkerchief.

He saw across the room the bottle of Gordon's gin so nicely matching the green glasses, and the lime-juice, a lighter shade of green. He made the journey, his legs striking the arms of chairs. There wasn't much gin in the bottle. He poured it all out; he added lime-juice, and drank it.

In the hall he could hear voices, his children's voices in the bathroom, Elizabeth and the man speaking quietly in the kitchen. 'Poor wretch,' Elizabeth was saying. He left the flat and descended to the ground floor.

The rain was falling heavily. He walked through it, thinking that it was better to go, quietly and without fuss. It would all work out; he knew it; he felt it definitely in his bones. He'd arrive on Sunday, a month or so before their birthday, and something in Elizabeth's face would tell him that the dark-haired man had gone for ever, as Diana had gone. By then he'd be established again, with better prospects than the red-faced Sir Gerald Travers had ever offered him. On their birthday they'd both apologise to one another, wiping the slate clean: they'd start again. As he crossed the Edgware Road to the public house in which he always spent an hour or so on Sunday nights, he heard his own voice murmuring that it was understandable that she should have taken it out on him, that she should have tried to hurt him by saying he'd gone to seed. Naturally, she'd say a thing like that; who could blame her after all she'd been through? At night in the flat in Barnes he watched television until the programmes closed down. He usually had a few drinks, and as often as not he dropped off to sleep with a cigarette between his fingers: that was how the burns occurred on his clothes.

He nodded to himself as he entered the saloon bar, thinking he'd been wise not to mention any of that to Elizabeth. It would only have annoyed her, having to listen to a lot of stuff about late-night television and cigarettes. Monday, Tuesday, Wednesday, he thought, Thursday, Friday. On Saturday he'd buy the meringues and brandy-snaps, and then it would be Sunday. He'd make the sandwiches listening to *The Archers*, and at three o'clock he'd ring the bell of the flat. He smiled in the saloon bar, thinking of that, seeing in his mind the faces of his children and the beautiful face of their mother. He'd planted an idea in Elizabeth's mind and even though she'd been a bit shirty she'd see when she thought about it that it was what she wanted, too.

He went on drinking gin and lime-juice, quietly laughing over being so upset when the children had first mentioned the dark-haired man who took them on to his knee. Gin and lime-juice was a Gimlet, he told the barmaid. She smiled at him. He was celebrating, he said, a day that was to come. It was ridiculous, he told her, that a woman casually met on a train should have created havoc, that now, at the end of it all, he should week by week butter bread for Marmite and tomato

sandwiches. 'D'you understand me?' he drunkenly asked the
barmaid. 'It's *too* ridiculous to be true – that man will go
because none of it makes sense the way it is.' The barmaid
smiled again and nodded. He bought her a glass of beer,
which was something he did every Sunday night. He wept as
he paid for it, and touched his cheeks with the tips of his
fingers to wipe away the tears. Every Sunday he wept, at the
end of the day, after he'd had his access. The barmaid raised
her glass, as always she did. They drank to the day that was to
come, when the error he had made would be wiped away,
when the happy marriage could continue. 'Ridiculous,' he
said. 'Of course it is.'

Nice Day at School

Eleanor lay awake, thinking in advance about the day. The face of Miss Whitehead came into her mind, the rather pointed nose, eyes set wide apart, a mouth that turned up at the corners and gave the impression that Miss Whitehead was constantly smiling, although it was a widely held view among the girls whom she taught that Miss Whitehead had little to smile over, having missed out. The face of Liz Jones came into Eleanor's mind also, a pretty, wild face with eyes that were almost black, and black hair hanging prettily down on either side of it, and full lips. Liz Jones claimed to have gipsy blood in her, and another girl, Mavis Temple, had once remarked to Eleanor that she thought Liz Jones's lips were negroid. 'A touch of the tar brush,' Mavis Temple had said. 'A seaman done her mum.' She'd said it three years ago, when the girls had all been eleven, in Miss Homber's class. Everything had been different then.

In the early morning gloom Eleanor considered the difference, regretting, as always, that it had come about. It had been nice in Miss Homber's class, the girls' first year at Springfield Comprehensive: they'd all had a crush on Miss Homber because Miss Homber, who'd since become Mrs George Spaxton and a mother, had been truly beautiful and intelligent. Miss Homber told them it was important to wash all the parts of the body once per day, including you knew where. Four girls brought letters of complaint after that and Miss Homber read them out to the class, commenting on the grammar and the spelling errors and causing the girls to become less carefree about what they repeated to their mums. 'Remember, you can give birth at thirteen,' Miss Homber warned, and she added that if a boy ever said he was too embarrassed to go into a chemist's for preventatives he could always get them in a slot machine that was situated in the Gents at Barclay's filling station on the Portsmouth Road, which was something her own boy-friend had told her.

It had been nice in those days because Eleanor didn't be-lieve that any boy would try stuff like that on when she was thirteen, and the girls of the first year all agreed that it sounded disgusting, a boy putting his thing up you. Even Liz Jones did, although she was constantly hanging about the boys of the estate and twice had had her knickers taken down in the middle of the estate playground. There were no boys at Springfield Comprehensive, which was just as well, Eleanor had always considered, because boys roughened up a school so.

But in spite of their physical absence boys had somehow penetrated and increasingly, as Eleanor passed up through the school, references to them infiltrated all conversation. At thirteen, in Miss Croft's class, Liz Jones confessed that a boy called Gareth Swayles had done her in the corner of the estate playground, at eleven o'clock one night. She'd been done standing up, she reported, leaning against the paling that sur-rounded the playground. She said it was fantastic.

Lying in bed, Eleanor remembered Liz Jones saying that and saying a few months later that a boy called Rogo Pollini was twice as good as Gareth Swayles, and later that a boy called Tich Ayling made Rogo Pollini seem totally laughable. Another girl, Susie Crumm, said that Rogo Pollini had told her that he'd never enjoyed it with Liz Jones because Liz Jones put him off with all her wriggling and pinching. Susie Crumm, at the time, had just been done by Rogo Pollini.

By the time they reached Class 2 it had become the fashion to have been done and most of the girls, even quiet Mavis Temple, had succumbed to it. Many had not cared for the experience and had not repeated it, but Liz Jones said that this was because they had got it from someone like Gareth Swayles, who was no better on the job than a dead horse. Eleanor hadn't ever been done nor did she wish to be, by Gareth Swayles or anyone else. Some of the girls said it had hurt them: she knew it would hurt her. And she'd heard that even if Gareth Swayles, or whoever it was, went to the slot machine in Barclay's filling station it sometimes happened that the preventative came asunder, a disaster that would be followed by weeks of worry. That, she knew, would be her fate too.

'Eleanor's prissy,' Liz Jones said every day now. 'Eleanor's prissy like poor prissy Whitehead.' Liz Jones went on about it all the time, hating Eleanor because she still had everything in store for her. Liz Jones had made everyone else think that Eleanor would grow into a Miss Whitehead, who was terrified of men, so Liz Jones said. Miss Whitehead had hairs on her chin and her upper lip that she didn't bother to do anything about. Quite often her breath wasn't fresh, which was unpleasant if she was leaning over you, explaining something.

Eleanor, who lived on the estate with her parents, hated being identified with Miss Whitehead and yet she felt, especially when she lay awake in the early morning, that there was something in Liz Jones's taunting. 'Eleanor's waiting for Mr Right,' Liz Jones would say. 'Whitehead waited forever.' Miss Whitehead, Liz Jones said, never had a fellow for long because she wouldn't give herself wholly and in this day and age a girl had to be sensible and natural over a matter like that. Everyone agreed that this was probably so because there was no doubt about it that in her time Miss Whitehead had been pretty. 'It happens to you,' Liz Jones said, 'left solitary like that: you grow hairs on your face; you get stomach trouble that makes your breath bad. Nervous frustration, see.'

Eleanor gazed across her small bedroom, moving her eyes from the pink of the wall to her school uniform, grey and purple, hanging over the back of a chair. In the room there was a teddy-bear she'd had since she was three, and a gramophone, and records by the New Seekers and the Pioneers and Diana Ross, and photographs of such performers. In her vague, uninterested manner her mother said she thought it awful that Eleanor should waste her money on these possessions, but Eleanor explained that everyone at Springfield Comprehensive did so and that she herself did not consider it a waste of money.

'You up?' Eleanor heard her mother calling now, and she replied that she was. She got out of bed and looked at herself in a looking-glass on her dressing-table. Her night-dress was white with small sprigs of violets on it. Her hair had a reddish tinge, her face was long and thin and was not afflicted with spots, as were a few of the faces of her companions at Springfield Comprehensive. Her prettiness was delicate, and she thought as she examined it now that Liz Jones was definitely right in her insinuations: it was a prettiness that could easily disappear overnight. Hairs would appear on her chin and her upper lip, a soft down at first, later becoming harsher. 'Your sight, you know,' an oculist would worriedly remark to her, and tell her she must wear glasses. Her teeth would lose their gleam. She'd have trouble with dandruff.

Eleanor slipped her night-dress over her head and looked at her naked body. She didn't herself see much beauty in it, but she knew that the breasts were the right size for the hips, that arms and legs nicely complemented each other. She dressed and went into the kitchen, where her father was making tea and her mother was reading the *Daily Express*.

Her father hadn't been to bed all night. He slept during the day, being employed by night as a doorman in a night-club called Margo's, in Shepherd Market. Once upon a time her father had been a wrestler, but in 1961 he'd injured his back in a bout with a Japanese and had since been unfit for the ring. Being a doorman of a night-club kept him in touch, so he claimed, with the glamorous world he'd been used to in the past. He often saw familiar faces, he reported, going in and out of Margo's, faces that once had been his audience. Eleanor felt embarrassed when he talked like that, being unable to believe much of what he said.

'You're in for a scorcher,' he said now, placing a pot of tea on the blue formica of the table. 'No end to the heatwave, they can't see.'

He was a large, red-faced man with closely cut grey hair and no lobe to his right ear. He'd put on weight since he'd left the wrestling ring and although he moved slowly now, as though in some way compensating for years of nimbleness on the taut canvas, he was still, in a physical sense, a formidable opponent, as occasional trouble-makers at the night-club had painfully discovered.

Eleanor knocked Special K into a dish and added milk and sugar.

'That's a lovely young girl,' her father said. 'Mia Farrow. She was in last night, Eleanor.'

His breakfast-time conversation was always the same. Princess Margaret had shaken him by the hand and Anthony Armstrong-Jones had asked if he might take his photograph for a book about London he was doing. The Burtons came regularly, and Rex Harrison, and the Canadian Prime Minister whenever he was in London. Her father had a way of looking at Eleanor when he made such statements, his eyes screwed up, almost lost in the puffed red flesh of his face: he stared unblinkingly and beadily, as if defying her to reply that she didn't for a moment accept that Princess Margaret's hand had ever lain in his or that Anthony Armstrong-Jones had addressed him.

'Faceful of innocence,' he said. 'Just a faceful of innocence, Eleanor. "Good-night, Miss Farrow," I said, and she turned the little face to me and said to call her Mia.'

Eleanor nodded. Her mother's eyes were fixed on the *Daily Express*, moving from news item to news item, her lips occasionally moving also as she read. 'Liz Jones,' Eleanor wanted to say. 'Could you complain to the school about Liz Jones?' She wanted to tell them about the fashion in Class 2, about Miss Whitehead, and how everyone was afraid of Liz Jones. She imagined her voice speaking across the breakfast table, to her father who was still in his doorman's uniform and her mother who mightn't even hear her. There'd be embarrassment as her father listened, her own face would be as hot as fire. He'd turn his head away in the end, like the time she'd had to ask him for money to buy sanitary towels.

'Lovely little fingers,' he said, 'like a baby's fingers, Eleanor. Little wisps of things. She touched me with the tips.'

'Who?' demanded her mother, suddenly sharp, looking up. 'Eh, then?'

'Mia Farrow,' he said. 'She was down in Margo's last night. Sweetest thing; sweetest little face.'

'Ah, yes, Peyton Place,' her mother said, and Eleanor's father nodded.

Her mother had spectacles with swept-up, elaborately bejewelled frames. The jewels were made of glass, but they glittered, especially in strong sunlight, just like what Eleanor imagined diamonds must glitter like. Her mother, constantly smoking, had hair which she dyed so that it appeared to be black. She was a thin woman with bones that stuck out awkwardly at the joints, seeming as though they might at any moment break through the surface of taut, anaemic skin. In

Eleanor's opinion her mother had suffered, and once she had had a dream in which her mother was fat and married to someone else, a man, as far as Eleanor could make out, who ran a vegetable shop.

Her mother always had breakfast in her night-dress and an old fawn-coloured dressing-gown, her ankles below it as white as paper, her feet stuck into tattered slippers. After breakfast, she would return to bed with Eleanor's father, obliging him, Eleanor knew, as she had obliged him all her life. During the school holidays, and on Saturdays and Sundays when Eleanor was still in the flat, her mother continued to oblige him: in the bedroom he made the same kind of noise as he'd made in the wrestling ring. The Prince of Hackney he'd been known as.

Her mother was a shadow. Married to a man who ran a vegetable shop or to any other kind of man except the one she'd chosen, Eleanor believed she'd have been different: she'd have had more children, she'd have been a proper person with proper flesh on her bones, a person you could feel for. As she was, you could hardly take her seriously. She sat there in her night-clothes, waiting for the man she'd married to rise from the table and go into their bedroom so that she might follow. Afterwards she cleared up the breakfast things and washed them, while he slept. She shopped in the Express Dairy Supermarket, dropping cigarette ash over tins of soup and peas and packets of crisps, and at half-past eleven she sat in the corner of the downstairs lounge of the Northumberland Arms and drank a measure of gin and water, sometimes two.

'Listen to this,' her mother said in her wheezy voice. She quoted a piece about a fifty-five-year-old woman, a Miss Margaret Sugden, who had been trapped in a bath for two days and three nights. *'It ended,'* read Eleanor's mother, *'with two burly policemen – eyes carefully averted – lifting her out. It took them half an hour of gentle levering, for Miss*

36

Sugden, a well-rounded sixteen stone, was helplessly stuck.'

He laughed. Her mother stubbed her cigarette out on her saucer and lit a fresh one. Her mother never ate anything at breakfast-time. She drank three cups of tea and smoked the same number of cigarettes. He liked a large breakfast, eggs and bacon, fried bread, a chop sometimes.

'History's longest soak,' her mother said, still quoting from the *Daily Express*. Her father laughed again.

Eleanor rose and carried the dish she'd eaten her Special K out of to the sink, with her cup and her saucer. She rinsed them under the hot tap and stacked them on the red, plastic-covered rack to dry. Her mother spoke in amazed tones when she read pieces out of the newspaper, surprised by the activities of people and animals, never amused by them. Some part of her had been smashed to pieces.

She said good-bye to both of them. Her mother kissed her as she always did. Winking, her father told her not to take any wooden dollars, an advice that was as regular and as mechanical as her mother's embrace.

'Netball is it?' her mother vaguely asked, not looking up from the newspaper. There wasn't netball, Eleanor explained, as she'd explained before, in the summer term: she wouldn't be late back.

She left the flat and descended three flights of concrete stairs. She passed the garages and then the estate's playground, where Liz Jones had first of all been done. 'Good-morning, Eleanor,' a woman said to her, an Irish woman called Mrs Breen. 'Isn't it a great day?'

Eleanor smiled. The weather was lovely, she said. Mrs Breen was a lackadaisical woman, middle-aged and fat, the mother of eight children. On the estate it was said that she was no better than she should be, that one of her sons, who had a dark tinge in his pallor, was the child of a West Indian

railway porter. Another of Mrs Breen's children and suspect
also, a girl of Eleanor's age called Dolly who was reputed to be
the daughter of Susie Crumm's father. In the dream Eleanor
had had in which her own mother was fat rather than thin it
had seemed that her mother had somehow become Mrs Breen,
because in spite of everything Mrs Breen was a happy woman.
Her husband had a look of happiness about him also, as did all
the Breen children, no matter where they'd come from. They
regularly went to Mass, all together in a family outing, and
even if Mrs Breen occasionally obliged Susie Crumm's father
and others it hadn't taken the same toll of her as the obliging
of Eleanor's father by her mother had. For years, ever since
she'd listened to Liz Jones telling the class the full facts of
life, Eleanor had been puzzled by the form the facts apparently took when different people were involved. She'd accepted quite easily the stories about Mrs Breen and had
thought no less of the woman, but when Dolly Breen had said,
about a month ago, that she'd been done by Rogo Pollini,
Eleanor had felt upset, not caring to imagine the occasion, as
she didn't care to imagine the occasion that took place every
morning after breakfast in her parents' bedroom. Mrs Breen
didn't matter because she was somehow remote, like one of
the people her mother read about in the *Daily Express* or one
of the celebrities her father told lies about: Mrs Breen didn't
concern her, but Dolly Breen and Rogo Pollini did because
they were close to her, being the same as she was and of the
same generation. And her parents concerned her because they
were close to her also. You could no longer avoid any of it
when you thought of Dolly Breen and Rogo Pollini, or your
parents.

She passed a row of shops, Len Parrish the baker, a dry
cleaner's, the Express Dairy Supermarket, the newsagent's
and post office, the off-licence attached to the Northumberland
Arms. Girls in the grey and purple uniform of Springfield

Comprehensive alighted in numbers from a bus. A youth whistled at her. 'Hi, Eleanor,' said Gareth Swayles, coming up behind her. In a friendly manner he put his hand on her back, low down, so that as though by accident he could in a moment slip it over her buttocks.

There's a new boy in Grimes the buitcher's, Liz Jones wrote on a piece of paper. *He's not on the estate at all.* She folded the paper and addressed it to Eleanor. She passed it along the row of desks.

'*Je l'ai vu qui travaillait dans la cour,*' said Miss Whitehead.

I saw him in Grimes, Eleanor wrote. *Funny-looking fish.* She passed the note back and Liz Jones read it and showed it to her neighbour, Thelma Joseph. *Typical Eleanor,* Liz Jones wrote and Thelma Joseph giggled slightly.

'*Un anglais qui passait ses vacances en France,*' said Miss Whitehead.

Miss Whitehead lived in Esher, in a bed-sitting-room. Girls had sometimes visited her there and those who had done so described for others what Miss Whitehead's residence was like. It was very clean and comfortable and neat. White paint shone on the window ledges and the skirting-boards, lace curtains hung close to sparkling glass. On the mantelpiece there were ornaments in delicate ceramic, Highland sheep and cockerels, and a chimney sweep with his brushes on his back. A clock ticked on the mantelpiece, and in the fireplace – no longer used – Miss Whitehead had stood a vase of dried flowers. Her bed was in a recess, not at all obtrusive in the room, a narrow divan covered in cheerful chintz.

'*Le pêcheur,*' said Miss Whitehead, '*est un homme qui* ... Eleanor?'

'*Pêche?*'

'*Très bien. Et la blanchisseuse est une femme qui . . . ?*'
'*Lave le linge.*'

Liz Jones said it must be extraordinary to be Miss White-head, never to have felt a man's hand on you. *Gareth Swayles said he'd give it to her,* she'd written on one of the notes she was constantly passing round the class. *Imagine Swayles in bed with Whitehead!*

'*La mère n'aime pas le fromage,*' said Miss Whitehead, and Liz Jones passed another note to Eleanor. *The new boy in Grimes is called Denny Price,* it said. *He wants to do you.*

'Eleanor,' said Miss Whitehead.

She looked up from the elaborately looped handwriting of Liz Jones. In their bedroom her father would be making the noises he used to make in the wrestling ring. Her mother would be lying there. Once, when she was small, she'd gone in by mistake and her father had been standing without his clothes on. Her mother had pulled a sheet up to cover her own nakedness.

'Why are you writing notes, Eleanor?'

'She didn't, Miss Whitehead,' Liz Jones said. 'I sent her – '

'Thank you, Elizabeth. Eleanor?'

'I'm sorry, Miss Whitehead.'

'Were you writing notes, Eleanor?'

'No, I – '

'I sent her the note, Miss Whitehead. It's a private matter–'

'Not private in *my* class, Elizabeth. Pass me the note, Eleanor.'

Liz Jones was sniggering: Eleanor knew that she'd wanted this to happen. Miss Whitehead would read the note out, which was her rule when a note was found.

'The new boy in Grimes is called Denny Price,' Miss Whitehead said. 'He wants to do you.'

The class laughed, a muffled sound because the girls' heads were bent over their desks.

40

'He wants to have sexual relations with Eleanor,' Liz Jones explained, giggling more openly. 'Eleanor's a – '

'Thank you, Elizabeth. The future tense, Elizabeth: *s'asseoir*.'

Her voice grated in the classroom. Her voice had become unattractive also, Eleanor thought, because she'd never let herself be loved. In her clean bed-sitting-room she might weep tonight, recalling the insolence of Liz Jones. She'd punish Liz Jones when the bell went, the way she always inflicted punishment. She'd call her name out and while the others left the room she'd keep the girl longer than was necessary, setting her a piece of poetry to write out ten times and explaining, as if talking to an infant, that notes and conversation about sexual matters were not permitted in her classroom. She'd imply that she didn't believe that the boy in Grimes' had said what Liz Jones had reported he'd said. She'd pretend it was all a fantasy, that no girl from Springfield Comprehensive had ever been done in the playground of the estate or anywhere else. It was easy for Miss Whitehead, Eleanor thought, escaping to her bed-sitting-room in Esher.

'It's your bloody fault,' Liz Jones said afterwards in the washroom. 'If you weren't such a curate's bitch – '

'Oh, for heaven's sake, shut up about it!' Eleanor cried.

'Denny Price wants to give you his nine inches – '

'I don't want his bloody nine inches. I don't want anything to do with him.'

'You're under-sexed, Eleanor. What's wrong with Denny Price?'

'He's peculiar-looking. There's something the matter with his head.'

'Will you listen to this!' Liz Jones cried, and the girls who'd gathered round tittered. 'What's his head got to do with it for God's sake? It's not his head that's going to–' She broke off, laughing, and all the girls laughed also, even though several of them didn't at all care for Liz Jones.

'You'll end like Whitehead,' Liz Jones said. 'Doing yourself in Esher.' The likes of Whitehead, she added, gave you a sickness in your kidneys. Eleanor had the same way of walking as Whitehead had, which was a way that dried-up virgins acquired because they were afraid to walk any other way in case a man touched their dried-up bottoms.

Eleanor went away, moving through the girls of other classes, across the washroom.

'Liz Jones is a nasty little tit,' a girl called Eileen Reid whispered, and Joan Moate, a fair-haired girl with a hint of acne, agreed. But Liz Jones couldn't hear them. Liz Jones was still laughing, leaning against a wash-basin with a cigarette in her mouth.

For lunch that day at Springfield Comprehensive there was stew and processed potatoes and carrots, with blancmange afterwards, chocolate and strawberry.

'Don't take no notice,' Susie Crumm said to Eleanor. The way Liz Jones went on, she added, it wouldn't suprise her to hear that she'd contracted syphilis.

'What's it like, Susie?' Eleanor asked.

'Syphilis? You get lesions. If you're a girl you can't tell sometimes. Fellas get them all over their equipment – '

'No, I mean what's it like being done?'

' 'Sall right. Nice really. But not like Jones goes for it. Not all the bloody time.'

They ate spoonfuls of blancmange, sucking it through their teeth.

' 'Sall right,' Susie Crumm repeated when she'd finished. ' 'Sall right for an occasion.'

Eleanor nodded. She wanted to say that she'd prefer to

42

keep it for her wedding night, but she knew that if she said that she'd lose Susie Crumm's sympathy. She wanted it to be special, not just a woman lying down waiting for a man to finish taking his clothes off; not just a fumbling in the dark of the estate playground, or something behind the North-umberland Arms, where Eileen Reid had been done.

'My dad said he'd gut any fella that laid a finger on me,' Susie Crumm said.

'Jones's said the same.'

'He done Mrs Breen. Jones's dad.'

'They've all done Mrs Breen.' For a moment she wanted to tell the truth: to add that Susie Crumm's dad had done Mrs Breen also, that Dolly Breen was Susie's half-sister.

'You've got a moustache growing on you,' Liz Jones said, coming up behind her and whispering into her hair.

The afternoon of that day passed without incident at Springfield Comprehensive, while on the estate Eleanor's father slept. He dreamed that he was wrestling again. Be-tween his knees he could feel the ribs of Eddie Rodriguez; the crowd was calling out, urging him to give Eddie Rodriguez the final works. Two yards away, in the kitchen, Eleanor's mother prepared a meal. She cut cod into pieces, and sliced potatoes for chips. He liked a crisply fried meal at half-past six before watching a bit of television. She liked cod and chips herself, with tinned peas, and bread and butter and apricot jam, and Danish pastries and tea, and maybe a tin of pears. She'd bought a tin of pears in the Express Dairy: they might as well have them with a tin of Carnation cream. She'd get everything ready and then she'd run an iron over his uniform, sponging off any spots there were. She thought about *Cross-roads* on the television, wondering what would happen in the episode today.

'I'd remind you that the school photographs will be taken on Tuesday,' Miss Whitehead said. 'Clean white blouses, please.'

They would all be there: Eleanor, Liz Jones, Susie Crumm, Eileen Reid, Joan Moate, Mavis Temple, and all the others: forty smiling faces, and Miss Whitehead standing at the end of the middle row. If you kept the photograph it would be a memory for ever, another record of the days at Springfield Comprehensive. 'Who's that with the bow legs?' her father had asked a few years ago, pointing at Miss Homber.

'Anyone incorrectly dressed on Tuesday,' Miss Whitehead said, 'will forfeit her place in the photo.'

The bell rang for the end of school. 'Forfeit her bloody knickers,' said Liz Jones just before Miss Whitehead left the classroom.

The girls dispersed, going off in twos and threes, swinging the brief-cases that contained their school books.

'Walk with you?' Susie Crumm suggested to Eleanor, and together they left the classrooms and the school. 'Baking, i'n' it?' Susie Crumm remarked.

They walked slowly, past concrete buildings, the Eagle Star Insurance Company, Barclays Bank, the Halifax Building Society. Windows were open, the air was chalky dry. Two girls in front of them had taken off their shoes but now, finding the pavement too hot to walk on, had paused to put them on again. The two girls shrieked, leaning on one another. Women pushed prams around them, irritation in their faces.

'I want to get fixed in a Saxone,' Susie Crumm said. 'Can't wait to leave that bloody place.'

An *Evening Standard* van swerved in front of a bus, causing the bus-driver to shout and blow his horn. In the cab of the van the driver's mate raised two fingers in a gesture of disdain.

'I fancy selling shoes,' Susie Crumm said. 'Fashion shoes

type of thing. You get them at cost if you work in a Saxone.'

Eleanor imagined the slow preparation of the evening meal in her parents' flat, and the awakening of her father. He'd get up and shave himself, standing in the bathroom in his vest, braces hanging down, his flies half open. Her mother spent ages getting the evening meal, breaking off to see to his uniform and then returning to the food. He couldn't bear not being a wrestler any more.

'What you going to do, Eleanor?'

She shook her head. She didn't know what she was going to do. All she wanted was to get away from the estate and from Springfield Comprehensive. She wondered what it would be like to work in the Eagle Star Insurance Company, but at the moment that didn't seem important. What was important was the exact present, the afternoon of a certain day, a day that was like others except for the extreme heat. She'd go back and there the two of them would be, and in her mind there'd be the face of Miss Whitehead and the voice of Liz Jones. She'd do her homework and then there'd be *Crossroads* on the TV and then the fried meal and the washing-up and more TV, and then he'd go, saying it was time she was in bed. 'See you in the morning,' he'd say and soon after he'd gone they'd both go to bed, and she'd lie there thinking of being married in white lace in a church, to a delicate man who wouldn't hurt her, who'd love the virginal innocence that had been kept all these years for him alone. She'd go away in a two-piece suit on an autumn afternoon when the leaves in London were yellow-brown. She'd fly with a man whose fingers were long and thin and gentle, who'd hold her hand in the aeroplane, Air France to Biarritz. And afterwards she'd come back to a flat where the curtains were the colour of lavender, the same as the walls, where gas fires glowed and there were rugs on natural-wood floors, and the telephone was pale blue.

'What's matter?' Susie Crumm asked.

'Nothing.'

They walked past Len Parrish the baker, the dry cleaner's, the Express Dairy Supermarket, the newsagent's and post office, the off-licence attached to the Northumberland Arms.

'There's that fella,' Susie Crumm said. 'Denny Price.'

His head was awkwardly placed on his neck, cocked to one side. His hair was red and long, his face small in the midst of it. He had brown eyes and thick, blubbery lips.

'Hullo,' he said.

Susie Crumm giggled.

'Like a fag?' he said, holding out a packet of Anchor. 'Smoke, do you, girls?'

Susie Crumm giggled again, and then abruptly ceased. 'Oh God!' she said, her hand stretched out for a cigarette. She was looking over Denny Price's shoulder at a man in blue denim overalls. The man, seeing her in that moment, sharply called at her to come to him.

'Stuff him,' she said before she smiled and obeyed.

'Her dad,' said Denny Price, pleased that she had gone. 'You want a fag, Eleanor?'

She shook her head, walking on. He dropped into step with her.

'I know your name,' he said. 'I asked Liz Jones.'

'Yes.'

'I'm Denny Price. I work in Grimes'.'

'Yes.'

'You're at the Comprehensive.'

'Yes.'

She felt his fingers on her arm, squeezing it just above the elbow. 'Let's go for a walk,' he said. 'Come down by the river, Eleanor.'

She shook her head again and then, quite suddenly, she didn't care what happened. What harm was there in walking by the river with a boy from Grimes'? She looked at the fingers that were still caressing her arm. All day long they had handled meat; the fingernails were bitten away, the flesh was red from scouring. Wasn't it silly, like an advertisement, to imagine that a man would come one day to marry her in white lace in a church and take her, Air France, to Biarritz?

'We'll take a bus to the bridge,' he said. 'A thirty-seven.'

He sat close to her, paying her fare, pressing a cigarette on her. She took it and he lit it for her. His eyes were foxy, she noticed; she could see the desire in them.

'I saw you a week back,' he said.

They walked by the river, away from the bridge, along the tow-path. He put his arm around her, squeezing a handful of underclothes and flesh. 'Let's sit down here,' he said.

They sat on the grass, watching barges going by and schoolboys rowing. In the distance traffic moved, gleaming, on the bridge they'd walked from. 'God,' he said, 'you have fantastic breasts.'

His hands were on them and he was pushing her back on to the grass. She felt his lips on her face, and his teeth and his tongue, and saliva. One hand moved down her body. She felt it under her skirt, on the bare flesh of her thigh, and then on her stomach. It was like an animal, a rat gnawing at her, prodding her and poking. There was no one about; he was muttering, his voice thickly slurred. 'Take down your knickers,' he said.

She pushed at him and for a moment he released his hold, imagining she was about to undo some of her clothing. Instead she ran away, tearing along the tow-path, saying to herself that if he caught up with her she'd hit him with the brief-case that contained her school books.

But he didn't follow her and when she looked back he was lying where she had left him, stretched out as though wounded on the grass.

Her father talked of who might come that night to Margo's. He mentioned Princess Margaret. Princess Margaret had seen him wrestling, or if it hadn't been Princess Margaret it had been a face almost identical to hers. The Burtons might come tonight; you never knew when the Burtons were going to pop in.

Her mother placed the fried fish, with chips and peas, in front of him. She never really listened to him when he went on about the night-club because her mind was full of what had happened on *Crossroads*. She put her cigarette on a saucer on the draining-board, not extinguishing it. She remembered the news items she'd read at breakfast-time and wondered about them all over again.

Tomorrow would be worse, Eleanor thought. Even at this very moment Denny Price's blubber lips might be relating the incident to Liz Jones, how Eleanor had almost let him and then had drawn back. 'I went down by the river with a boy,' she wanted to say. 'I wanted to get done because it's the Class 2 fashion. I'm tired of being mocked by Liz Jones.' She could say it with her eyes cast down, her fork fiddling with a piece of cod on her plate. She wouldn't have to see the embarrassment in her father's face, like she'd seen it when she'd asked for money for sanitary towels. Her mother wouldn't hear at first, but she'd go on saying it, repeating herself until her mother did hear. She longed for the facts to be there in the room, how it disgusted her to imagine her father taking off his uniform in the mornings, and Rogo Pollini doing Dolly Breen. She wanted to say she'd been disgusted when Denny Price had told her to take down her knickers.

'Extraordinary, that woman,' her mother said. 'Fancy two days stuck in a bath.'

Her father laughed. It could be exaggerated, he said: you couldn't believe everything you read, not even in the news-papers.

'Extraordinary,' her mother murmured.

Her mother was trapped, married to him, obliging him so that she'd receive housekeeping money out of which she could save for her morning glass of gin. He was trapped himself, going out every night in a doorman's uniform, the Prince of Hackney with a bad back. He crushed her mother because he'd been crushed himself. How could either of them be expected to bother if she spoke of being mocked, and then asked them questions, seeking reassurance?

They wouldn't know what to say – even if she helped them by explaining that she knew there was no man with delicate hands who'd take her away when the leaves in London were yellow-brown, that there were only the blubber lips of Denny Price and the smell of meat that came off him, and Susie Crumm's father doing Mrs Breen, and Liz Jones's father doing her also, and the West Indian railway porter, and Mr Breen not aware of a thing. They wouldn't know what she was talking about if she said that Miss Whitehead had divorced herself from all of it by lying solitary at night in a room in Esher where everything was clean and neat. It was better to be Miss Whitehead than a woman who was a victim of a man's bad back. In her gleaming room Miss Whitehead was more successful in her pretence than either of them was in theirs. Miss Whitehead was complete and alone, having discarded what she wished to discard, accepting now that there was no Mr Right.

'Nice day at school?' her mother inquired suddenly in her vague manner, as though mistily aware of a duty.

Eleanor looked up from her fish and regarded both of them at once. She smiled, forcing herself to, feeling sorry for them because they were trapped by each other; because for them it was too late to escape to a room in which everything was clean.

The Ballroom of Romance

On Sundays, or on Mondays if he couldn't make it and often he couldn't, Sunday being his busy day, Canon O'Connell arrived at the farm in order to hold a private service with Bridie's father, who couldn't get about any more, having had a leg amputated after gangrene had set in. They'd had a pony and cart then and Bridie's mother had been alive: it hadn't been difficult for the two of them to help her father on to the cart in order to make the journey to Mass. But two years later the pony had gone lame and eventually had to be destroyed; not long after that her mother had died. 'Don't worry about it at all,' Canon O'Connell had said, referring to the difficulty of transporting her father to Mass. 'I'll slip up by the week, Bridie.'

The milk lorry called daily for the single churn of milk, Mr Driscoll delivered groceries and meal in his van, and took away the eggs that Bridie had collected during the week. Since Canon O'Connell had made his offer, in 1953, Bridie's father hadn't left the farm.

As well as Mass on Sundays and her weekly visits to a wayside dance-hall Bridie went shopping once every month, cycling to the town early on a Friday afternoon. She bought things for herself, material for a dress, knitting wool, stockings, a newspaper, and paper-backed Wild West novels for her father. She talked in the shops to some of the girls she'd been at school with, girls who had married shop-assistants or shop-keepers, or had become assistants themselves. Most of them had families of their own by now. 'You're lucky to be peaceful in the hills,' they said to Bridie, 'instead of stuck in a hole like this.' They had a tired look, most of them, from pregnancies and their efforts to organise and control their large families.

As she cycled back to the hills on a Friday Bridie often felt that they truly envied her her life, and she found it surprising that they should do so. If it hadn't been for her father she'd have wanted to work in the town also, in the tinned meat factory maybe, or in a shop. The town had a cinema called the Electric, and a fish-and-chip shop where people met at night, eating chips out of newspaper on the pavement outside. In the evenings, sitting in the farmhouse with her father, she often thought about the town, imagining the shop-windows lit up to display their goods and the sweet-shops still open so that people could purchase chocolates or fruit to take with them to the Electric cinema. But the town was eleven miles away, which was too far to cycle, there and back, for an evening's entertainment.

'It's a terrible thing for you, girl,' her father used to say, genuinely troubled, 'tied up to a one-legged man.' He would sigh heavily, hobbling back from the fields, where he managed as best he could. 'If your mother hadn't died,' he'd say, not finishing the sentence.

If her mother hadn't died her mother could have looked after him and the scant acres he owned, her mother could somehow have lifted the milk-churn on to the collection plat-form and attended to the few hens and the cows. 'I'd be dead without the girl to assist me,' she'd heard her father saying to Canon O'Connell, and Canon O'Connell replied that he was certainly lucky to have her.

'Amn't I as happy here as anywhere?' she'd say herself, but her father knew she was pretending and was saddened because the weight of circumstances had so harshly interfered with her life.

Although her father still called her a girl, Bridie was thirty-six. She was tall and strong: the skin of her fingers and her palms were stained, and harsh to touch. The labour they'd experienced had found its way into them, as though juices had come out of vegetation and pigment out of soil: since childhood she'd torn away the rough scotch grass that grew each spring among her father's mangolds and sugar beet; since childhood she'd harvested potatoes in August, her hands daily rooting in the ground she loosened and turned. Wind had toughened the flesh of her face, sun had browned it; her neck and nose were lean, her lips touched with early wrinkles.

But on Saturday nights Bridie forgot the scotch grass and the soil. In different dresses she cycled to the dance-hall, encouraged to make the journey by her father. 'Doesn't it do you good, girl?' he'd say, as though he imagined she begrudged herself the pleasure. 'Why wouldn't you enjoy yourself?' She'd cook him his tea and then he'd settle down with the wireless, or maybe a Wild West novel. In time, while still she danced, he'd stoke the fire up and hobble his way upstairs to bed.

The dance-hall, owned by Mr Justin Dwyer, was miles from anywhere, a lone building by the roadside with treeless boglands all around and a gravel expanse in front of it. On pink pebbled cement its title was painted in an azure blue that matched the depth of the background shade yet stood out well, unfussily proclaiming *The Ballroom of Romance*. Above these letters four coloured bulbs – in red, green, orange and mauve – were lit at appropriate times, an indication that the evening rendezvous was open for business. Only the façade of the building was pink, the other walls being a more ordinary grey. And inside, except for pink swing-doors, everything was blue.

On Saturday nights Mr Justin Dwyer, a small, thin man, unlocked the metal grid that protected his property and drew it back, creating an open mouth from which music would later pour. He helped his wife to carry crates of lemonade and packets of biscuits from their car, and then took up a position in the tiny vestibule between the drawn-back grid and the pink swing-doors. He sat at a card-table, with money and tickets spread out before him. He'd made a fortune, people said: he owned other ballrooms also.

People came on bicycles or in old motor-cars, country people like Bridie from remote hill farms and villages. People who did not often see other people met there, girls and boys, men and women. They paid Mr Dwyer and passed into his dance-hall, where shadows were cast on pale-blue walls and light from a crystal bowl was dim. The band, known as the Romantic Jazz Band, was composed of clarinet, drums and piano. The drummer sometimes sang.

Bridie had been going to the dance-hall since first she left the Presentation Nuns, before her mother's death. She didn't mind the journey, which was seven miles there and seven back: she'd travelled as far every day to the Presentation Nuns on the same bicycle, which had once been the property of her mother, an old Rudge purchased originally in 1936. On Sundays she cycled six miles to Mass, but she never minded either: she'd grown quite used to all that.

'How're you, Bridie?' inquired Mr Justin Dwyer when she arrived in a new scarlet dress one autumn evening in 1971. She said she was all right and in reply to Mr Dwyer's second query she said that her father was all right also. 'I'll go up one of these days,' promised Mr Dwyer, which was a promise he'd been making for twenty years.

She paid the entrance fee and passed through the pink swing-doors. The Romantic Jazz Band was playing a familiar melody of the past, *The Destiny Waltz*. In spite of the band's

53

title, jazz was not ever played in the ballroom: Mr Dwyer did not personally care for that kind of music, nor had he cared for various dance movements that had come and gone over the years. Jiving, rock and roll, twisting, and other such variations had all been resisted by Mr Dwyer, who believed that a ballroom should be, as much as possible, a dignified place. The Romantic Jazz Band consisted of Mr Maloney, Mr Swanton, and Dano Ryan on drums. They were three middle-aged men who drove out from the town in Mr Maloney's car, amateur performers who were employed otherwise by the tinned-meat factory, the Electricity Supply Board, and the County Council.

'How're you, Bridie?' inquired Dano Ryan as she passed him on her way to the cloakroom. He was idle for a moment with his drums, *The Destiny Waltz* not calling for much attention from him.

'I'm all right, Dano,' she said. 'Are you fit yourself? Are the eyes better?' The week before he'd told her that he'd developed a watering of the eyes that must have been some kind of cold or other. He'd woken up with it in the morning and it had persisted until the afternoon: it was a new experience, he'd told her, adding that he'd never had a day's illness or discomfort in his life.

'I think I need glasses,' he said now, and as she passed into the cloakroom she imagined him in glasses, repairing the roads, as he was employed to do by the County Council. You hardly ever saw a road-mender with glasses, she reflected, and she wondered if all the dust that was inherent in his work had perhaps affected his eyes.

'How're you, Bridie?' a girl called Eenie Mackie said in the cloakroom, a girl who'd left the Presentation Nuns only a year ago.

'That's a lovely dress, Eenie,' Bridie said. 'Is it nylon, that?'

'Tricel actually. Drip-dry.'

Bridie took off her coat and hung it on a hook. There was a small wash-basin in the cloakroom above which hung a discoloured oval mirror. Used tissues and pieces of cotton-wool, cigarette-butts and matches covered the concrete floor. Lengths of green-painted timber partitioned off a lavatory in a corner.

'Jeez, you're looking great, Bridie,' Madge Dowding remarked, waiting for her turn at the mirror. She moved towards it as she spoke, taking off a pair of spectacles before endeavouring to apply make-up to the lashes of her eye. She stared myopically into the oval mirror, humming while the other girls became restive.

'Will you hurry up, for God's sake!' shouted Eenie Mackie. 'We're standing here all night, Madge.'

Madge Dowding was the only one who was older than Bridie. She was thirty-nine, although often she said she was younger. The girls sniggered about that, saying that Madge Dowding should accept her condition – her age and her squint and her poor complexion – and not make herself ridiculous going out after men. What man would be bothered with the like of her anyway? Madge Dowding would do better to give herself over to do Saturday-night work for the Legion of Mary: wasn't Canon O'Connell always looking for aid?

'Is that fellow there?' she asked now, moving away from the mirror. 'The guy with the long arms. Did anyone see him outside?'

'He's dancing with Cat Bolger,' one of the girls replied. 'She has herself glued to him.'

'Lover boy,' remarked Patty Byrne, and everyone laughed because the person referred to was hardly a boy any more, being over fifty it was said, a bachelor who came only occasionally to the dance-hall.

Madge Dowding left the cloakroom rapidly, not bothering

to pretend she wasn't anxious about the conjunction of Cat Bolger and the man with the long arms. Two sharp spots of red had come into her cheeks, and when she stumbled in her haste the girls in the cloakroom laughed. A younger girl would have pretended to be casual.

Bridie chatted, waiting for the mirror. Some girls, not wishing to be delayed, used the mirrors of their compacts. Then in twos and threes, occasionally singly, they left the cloakroom and took their places on upright wooden chairs at one end of the dance-hall, waiting to be asked to dance. Mr Maloney, Mr Swanton and Dano Ryan played *Harvest Moon* and *I Wonder Who's Kissing Her Now* and *I'll Be Around*.

Bridie danced. Her father would be falling asleep by the fire; the wireless, tuned in to Radio Eireann, would be murmuring in the background. Already he'd have listened to *Faith and Order* and *Spot the Talent*. His Wild West novel, *Three Rode Fast* by Jake Matall, would have dropped from his single knee on to the flagged floor. He would wake with a jerk as he did every night and, forgetting what night it was, might be surprised not to see her, for usually she was sitting there at the table, mending clothes or washing eggs. 'Is it time for the News?' he'd automatically say.

Dust and cigarette smoke formed a haze beneath the crystal bowl, feet thudded, girls shrieked and laughed, some of them dancing together for want of a male partner. The music was loud, the musicians had taken off their jackets. Vigorously they played a number of tunes from *State Fair* and then, more romantically, *Just One of Those Things*. The tempo increased for a Paul Jones, after which Bridie found herself with a youth who told her he was saving up to emigrate, the nation in his opinion being finished. 'I'm up in the hills with the uncle,' he said, 'labouring fourteen hours a day. Is it any life for a young fellow?' She knew his uncle, a hill farmer whose stony acres were separated from her father's by one other farm only. 'He has me gutted with work,' the youth told her. 'Is there sense in it at all, Bridie?'

At ten o'clock there was a stir, occasioned by the arrival of three middle-aged bachelors who'd cycled over from Carey's public house. They shouted and whistled, greeting other people across the dancing area. They smelt of stout and sweat and whiskey.

Every Saturday at just this time they arrived, and, having sold them their tickets, Mr Dwyer folded up his card-table and locked the tin box that held the evening's takings: his ballroom was complete.

'How're you, Bridie?' one of the bachelors, known as Bowser Egan, inquired. Another one, Tim Daly, asked Patty Byrne how she was. 'Will we take the floor?' Eyes Horgan suggested to Madge Dowding, already pressing the front of his navy-blue suit against the net of her dress. Bridie danced with Bowser Egan, who said she was looking great.

The bachelors would never marry, the girls of the dance-hall considered: they were wedded already, to stout and whiskey and laziness, to three old mothers somewhere up in the hills. The man with the long arms didn't drink but he was the same in all other ways: he had the same look of a bachelor, a quality in his face.

'Great,' Bowser Egan said, feather-stepping in an inaccurate and inebriated manner. 'You're a great little dancer, Bridie.'

'Will you lay off that!' cried Madge Dowding, her voice shrill above the sound of the music. Eyes Horgan had slipped two fingers into the back of her dress and was now pretending they'd got there by accident. He smiled blearily, his huge red face streaming with perspiration, the eyes which gave him his nickname protuberant and bloodshot.

'Watch your step with that one,' Bowser Egan called out, laughing so that spittle sprayed on to Bridie's face. Eenie

Mackie, who was also dancing near the incident, laughed also and winked at Bridie. Dano Ryan left his drums and sang. 'Oh, how I miss your gentle kiss,' he crooned, 'and long to hold you tight.'

Nobody knew the name of the man with the long arms. The only words he'd ever been known to speak in the Ballroom of Romance were the words that formed his invitation to dance. He was a shy man who stood alone when he wasn't performing on the dance-floor. He rode away on his bicycle afterwards, not saying good-night to anyone.

'Cat has your man leppin' tonight,' Tim Daly remarked to Patty Byrne, for the liveliness that Cat Bolger had introduced into foxtrot and waltz was noticeable.

'I think of you only,' sang Dano Ryan. 'Only wishing, wishing you were by my side.'

Dano Ryan would have done, Bridie often thought, because he was a different kind of bachelor: he had a lonely look about him, as if he'd become tired of being on his own. Every week she thought he would have done, and during the week her mind regularly returned to that thought. Dano Ryan would have done because she felt he wouldn't mind coming to live in the farmhouse while her one-legged father was still about the place. Three could live as cheaply as two where Dano Ryan was concerned because giving up the wages he earned as a road-worker would be balanced by the saving made on what he paid for lodgings. Once, at the end of an evening, she'd pretended that there was a puncture in the back wheel of her bicycle and he'd concerned himself with it while Mr Maloney and Mr Swanton waited for him in Mr Maloney's car. He'd blown the tyre up with the car pump and had said he thought it would hold.

It was well known in the dance-hall that she fancied her chances with Dano Ryan. But it was well known also that Dano Ryan had got into a set way of life and had remained in it for quite some years. He lodged with a widow called Mrs Griffin and Mrs Griffin's mentally affected son, in a cottage on the outskirts of the town. He was said to be good to the affected child, buying him sweets and taking him out for rides on the cross-bar of his bicycle. He gave an hour or two of his time every week to the Church of Our Lady Queen of Heaven, and he was loyal to Mr Dwyer. He performed in the two other rural dance-halls that Mr Dwyer owned, rejecting advances from the town's more sophisticated dance-hall, even though it was more conveniently situated for him and the fee was more substantial than that paid by Mr Dwyer. But Mr Dwyer had discovered Dano Ryan and Dano had not forgotten it, just as Mr Maloney and Mr Swanton had not forgotten their discovery by Mr Dwyer either.

'Would we take a lemonade?' Bowser Egan suggested. 'And a packet of biscuits, Bridie?'

No alcoholic liquor was ever served in the Ballroom of Romance, the premises not being licensed for this added stimulant. Mr Dwyer in fact had never sought a licence for any of his premises, knowing that romance and alcohol were difficult commodities to mix, especially in a dignified ballroom. Behind where the girls sat on the wooden chairs Mr Dwyer's wife, a small stout woman, served the bottles of lemonade, with straws, and the biscuits and the crisps. She talked busily while doing so, mainly about the turkeys she kept. She'd once told Bridie that she thought of them as children.

'Thanks,' Bridie said, and Bowser Egan led her to the trestle table. Soon it would be the intermission: soon the three members of the band would cross the floor also for refreshment. She thought up questions to ask Dano Ryan.

When first she'd danced in the Ballroom of Romance, when she was just sixteen, Dano Ryan had been there also, four years older than she was, playing the drums for Mr

Maloney as he played them now. She'd hardly noticed him
then because of his not being one of the dancers: he was part
of the ballroom's scenery, like the trestle table and the lemonade bottles, and Mrs Dwyer and Mr Dwyer. The youths
who'd danced with her then in their Saturday-night blue suits
had later disappeared into the town, or to Dublin or Britain,
leaving behind them those who became the middle-aged
bachelors of the hills. There'd been a boy called Patrick
Grady whom she had loved in those days. Week after week
she'd ridden away from the Ballroom of Romance with the
image of his face in her mind, a thin face, pale beneath black
hair. It had been different, dancing with Patrick Grady, and
she'd felt that he found it different dancing with her, although
he'd never said so. At night she'd dreamed of him and in the
daytime too, while she helped her mother in the kitchen or her
father with the cows. Week by week she'd returned to the
ballroom, smiling on its pink façade and dancing then in the
arms of Patrick Grady. Often they'd stood together drinking
lemonade, not saying anything, not knowing what to say. She
knew he loved her, and she believed then that he would lead
her one day from the dim, romantic ballroom, from its blue-
ness and its pinkness and its crystal bowl of light and its
music. She believed he would lead her into sunshine, to the
town and the Church of Our Lady Queen of Heaven, to
marriage and smiling faces. But someone else had got Patrick
Grady, a girl from the town who'd never danced in the wayside ballroom. She'd scooped up Patrick Grady when he
didn't have a chance.

Bridie had wept, hearing that. By night she'd lain in her
bed in the farmhouse, quietly crying, the tears rolling into her
hair and making the pillow damp. When she woke in the early
morning the thought was still naggingly with her and it remained with her by day, replacing her daytime dreams of
happiness. Someone told her later on that he'd crossed to

Britain, to Wolverhampton, with the girl he'd married, and she imagined him there, in a place she wasn't able properly to visualise, labouring in a factory, his children being born and acquiring the accent of the area. The Ballroom of Romance wasn't the same without him, and when no one else stood out for her particularly over the years and when no one offered her marriage, she found herself wondering about Dano Ryan. If you couldn't have love, the next best thing was surely a decent man.

Bowser Egan hardly fell into that category, nor did Tim Daly. And it was plain to everyone that Cat Bolger and Madge Dowding were wasting their time over the man with the long arms. Madge Dowding was already a figure of fun in the ballroom, the way she ran after the bachelors; Cat Bolger would end up the same if she wasn't careful. One way or another it wasn't difficult to be a figure of fun in the ballroom, and you didn't have to be as old as Madge Dowding: a girl who'd just left the Presentation Nuns had once asked Eyes Horgan what he had in his trouser pocket and he told her it was a penknife. She'd repeated this afterwards in the cloak-room, how she'd requested Eyes Horgan not to dance so close to her because his penknife was sticking into her. 'Jeez, aren't you the right baby!' Patty Byrne had shouted delightedly; everyone had laughed, knowing that Eyes Horgan only came to the ballroom for stuff like that. He was no use to any girl.

'Two lemonades, Mrs Dwyer,' Bowser Egan said, 'and two packets of Kerry Creams. Is Kerry Creams all right, Bridie?'

She nodded, smiling. Kerry Creams would be fine, she said.

'Well, Bridie, isn't that the great outfit you have!' Mrs Dwyer remarked. 'Doesn't the red suit her, Bowser?'

By the swing-doors stood Mr Dwyer, smoking a cigarette that he held cupped in his left hand. His small eyes noted all developments. He had been aware of Madge Dowding's anxiety when Eyes Horgan had inserted two fingers into the back opening of her dress. He had looked away, not caring for the incident, but had it developed further he would have spoken to Eyes Horgan, as he had on other occasions. Some of the younger lads didn't know any better and would dance very close to their partners, who generally were too embarrassed to do anything about it, being young themselves. But that, in Mr Dwyer's opinion, was a different kettle of fish altogether because they were decent young lads who'd in no time at all be doing a steady line with a girl and would end up as he had himself with Mrs Dwyer, in the same house with her, sleeping in a bed with her, firmly married. It was the middle-aged bachelors who required the watching: they came down from the hills like mountain goats, released from their mammies and from the smell of animals and soil. Mr Dwyer continued to watch Eyes Horgan, wondering how drunk he was.

Dano Ryan's song came to an end, Mr Swanton laid down his clarinet, Mr Maloney rose from the piano. Dano Ryan wiped sweat from his face and the three men slowly moved towards Mrs Dwyer's trestle table.

'Jeez, you have powerful legs,' Eyes Horgan whispered to Madge Dowding, but Madge Dowding's attention was on the man with the long arms, who had left Cat Bolger's side and was proceeding in the direction of the men's lavatory. He never took refreshments. She moved, herself, towards the men's lavatory, to take up a position outside it, but Eyes Horgan followed her. 'Would you take a lemonade, Madge?' he asked. He had a small bottle of whiskey on him: if they went into a corner they could add a drop of it to the lemonade. She didn't drink spirits, she reminded him, and he went away.

'Excuse me a minute,' Bowser Egan said, putting down his bottle of lemonade. He crossed the floor to the lavatory. He too, Bridie knew, would have a small bottle of whiskey on him. She watched while Dano Ryan, listening to a story Mr Maloney was telling, paused in the centre of the ballroom, his head bent to hear what was being said. He was a big man, heavily made, with black hair that was slightly touched with grey, and big hands. He laughed when Mr Maloney came to the end of his story and then bent his head again, in order to listen to a story told by Mr Swanton.

'Are you on your own, Bridie?' Cat Bolger asked, and Bridie said she was waiting for Bowser Egan. 'I think I'll have a lemonade,' Cat Bolger said.

Younger boys and girls stood with their arms still around one another, queueing up for refreshments. Boys who hadn't danced at all, being nervous because they didn't know any steps, stood in groups, smoking and making jokes. Girls who hadn't been danced with yet talked to one another, their eyes wandering. Some of them sucked at straws in lemonade bottles.

Bridie, still watching Dano Ryan, imagined him wearing the glasses he'd referred to, sitting in the farmhouse kitchen, reading one of her father's Wild West novels. She imagined the three of them eating a meal she'd prepared, fried eggs and rashers and fried potato-cakes and tea and bread and butter and jam, brown bread and soda and shop bread. She imagined Dano Ryan leaving the kitchen in the morning to go out to the fields in order to weed the mangolds, and her father hobbling off behind him, and the two men working together. She saw hay being cut, Dano Ryan with the scythe that she'd learned to use herself, her father using a rake as best he could. She saw herself, because of the extra help, being able to attend to things in the farmhouse, things she'd never had time for because of the cows and the hens and the fields. There were bedroom curtains that needed repairing where the net had ripped, and wallpaper that had become loose and needed to be stuck up with flour paste. The scullery required white-washing.

The night he'd blown up the tyre of her bicycle she'd thought he was going to kiss her. He'd crouched on the ground in the darkness with his ear to the tyre, listening for escaping air. When he could hear none he'd straightened up and said he thought she'd be all right on the bicycle. His face had been quite close to hers and she'd smiled at him. At that moment, unfortunately, Mr Maloney had blown an impatient blast on the horn of his motor-car.

Often she'd been kissed by Bowser Egan, on the nights when he insisted on riding part of the way home with her. They had to dismount in order to push their bicycles up a hill and the first time he'd accompanied her he'd contrived to fall against her, steadying himself by putting a hand on her shoulder. The next thing she was aware of was the moist quality of his lips and the sound of his bicycle as it clattered noisily on the road. He'd suggested then, regaining his breath, that they should go into a field.

That was nine years ago. In the intervening passage of time she'd been kissed as well, in similar circumstances, by Eyes Horgan and Tim Daly. She'd gone into fields with them and permitted them to put their arms about her while heavily they breathed. At one time or another she had imagined marriage with one or other of them, seeing them in the farmhouse with her father, even though the fantasies were unlikely.

Bridie stood with Cat Bolger, knowing that it would be some time before Bowser Egan came out of the lavatory. Mr Maloney, Mr Swanton and Dano Ryan approached, Mr Maloney insisting that he would fetch three bottles of lemonade from the trestle table.

'You sang the last one beautifully,' Bridie said to Dano Ryan. 'Isn't it a beautiful song?'

Mr Swanton said it was the finest song ever written, and

Cat Bolger said she preferred *Danny Boy*, which in her opinion was the finest song ever written.

'Take a suck of that,' said Mr Maloney, handing Dano Ryan and Mr Swanton bottles of lemonade. 'How's Bridie tonight? Is your father well, Bridie?'

Her father was all right, she said.

'I hear they're starting a cement factory,' said Mr Maloney. 'Did anyone hear talk of that? They're after striking some commodity in the earth that makes good cement. Ten feet down, over at Kilmalough.'

'It'll bring employment,' said Mr Swanton. 'It's employment that's necessary in this area.'

'Canon O'Connell was on about it,' Mr Maloney said. 'There's Yankee money involved.'

'Will the Yanks come over?' inquired Cat Bolger. 'Will they run it themselves, Mr Maloney?'

Mr Maloney, intent on his lemonade, didn't hear the questions and Cat Bolger didn't repeat them.

'There's stuff called Optrex,' Bridie said quietly to Dano Ryan, 'that my father took the time he had a cold in his eyes. Maybe Optrex would settle the watering, Dano.'

'Ah sure, it doesn't worry me that much –'

'It's terrible, anything wrong with the eyes. You wouldn't want to take a chance. You'd get Optrex in a chemist, Dano, and a little bowl with it so that you can bathe the eyes.'

Her father's eyes had become red-rimmed and unsightly to look at. She'd gone into Riordan's Medical Hall in the town and had explained what the trouble was, and Mr Riordan had recommended Optrex. She told this to Dano Ryan, adding that her father had had no trouble with his eyes since. Dano Ryan nodded.

'Did you hear that, Mrs Dwyer?' Mr Maloney called out. 'A cement factory for Kilmalough.'

Mrs Dwyer wagged her head, placing empty bottles in a

crate. She'd heard references to the cement factory, she said: it was the best news for a long time.

'Kilmalough'll never know itself,' her husband commented, joining her in her task with the empty lemonade bottles.

' 'Twill bring prosperity certainly,' said Mr Swanton. 'I was saying just there, Justin, that employment's what's necessary.'

'Sure, won't the Yanks – ' began Cat Bolger, but Mr Maloney interrupted her.

'The Yanks'll be in at the top, Cat, or maybe not here at all – maybe only inserting money into it. It'll be local labour entirely.'

'You'll not marry a Yank, Cat,' said Mr Swanton, loudly laughing. 'You can't catch those fellows.'

'Haven't you plenty of homemade bachelors?' suggested Mr Maloney. He laughed also, throwing away the straw he was sucking through and tipping the bottle into his mouth. Cat Bolger told him to get on with himself. She moved towards the men's lavatory and took up a position outside it, not speaking to Madge Dowding, who was still standing there.

'Keep a watch on Eyes Horgan,' Mrs Dwyer warned her husband, which was advice she gave him at this time every Saturday night, knowing that Eyes Horgan was drinking in the lavatory. When he was drunk Eyes Horgan was the most difficult of the bachelors.

'I have a drop of it left, Dano,' Bridie said quietly. 'I could bring it over on Saturday. The eye stuff.'

'Ah, don't worry yourself, Bridie – '

'No trouble at all. Honestly now – '

'Mrs Griffin has me fixed up for a test with Dr Cready. The old eyes are no worry, only when I'm reading the paper or at the pictures. Mrs Griffin says I'm only straining them due to lack of glasses.'

66

He looked away while he said that, and she knew at once that Mrs Griffin was arranging to marry him. She felt it instinctively: Mrs Griffin was going to marry him because she was afraid that if he moved away from her cottage, to get married to someone else, she'd find it hard to replace him with another lodger who'd be good to her affected son. He'd become a father to Mrs Griffin's affected son, to whom already he was kind. It was a natural outcome, for Mrs Griffin had all the chances, seeing him every night and morning and not having to make do with weekly encounters in a ballroom.

She thought of Patrick Grady, seeing in her mind his pale, thin face. She might be the mother of four of his children now, or seven or eight maybe. She might be living in Wolverhampton, going out to the pictures in the evenings, instead of looking after a one-legged man. If the weight of circumstances hadn't intervened she wouldn't be standing in a wayside ballroom, mourning the marriage of a road-mender she didn't love. For a moment she thought she might cry, standing there thinking of Patrick Grady in Wolverhampton. In her life, on the farm and in the house, there was no place for tears. Tears were a luxury, like flowers would be in the fields where the mangolds grew, or fresh whitewash in the scullery. It wouldn't have been fair ever to have wept in the kitchen while her father sat listening to *Spot the Talent*: her father had more right to weep, having lost a leg. He suffered in a greater way, yet he remained kind and concerned for her.

In the Ballroom of Romance she felt behind her eyes the tears that it would have been improper to release in the presence of her father. She wanted to let them go, to feel them streaming on her cheeks, to receive the sympathy of Dano Ryan and of everyone else. She wanted them all to listen to her while she told them about Patrick Grady who was now in Wolverhampton and about the death of her mother and her own life since. She wanted Dano Ryan to put his arm around her so that she could lean her head against it. She wanted him to look at her in his decent way and to stroke with his road-mender's fingers the backs of her hands. She might wake in a bed with him and imagine for a moment that he was Patrick Grady. She might bathe his eyes and pretend.

'Back to business,' said Mr Maloney, leading his band across the floor to their instruments.

'Tell your father I was asking for him,' Dano Ryan said. She smiled and she promised, as though nothing had happened, that she would tell her father that.

She danced with Tim Daly and then again with the youth who'd said he intended to emigrate. She saw Madge Dowding moving swiftly towards the man with the long arms as he came out of the lavatory, moving faster than Cat Bolger. Eyes Horgan approached Cat Bolger. Dancing with her, he spoke earnestly, attempting to persuade her to permit him to ride part of the way home with her. He was unaware of the jealousy that was coming from her as she watched Madge Dowding holding close to her the man with the long arms while they performed a quickstep. Cat Bolger was in her thirties also.

'Get away out of that,' said Bowser Egan, cutting in on the youth who was dancing with Bridie. 'Go home to your mammy, boy.' He took her into his arms, saying again that she was looking great tonight. 'Did you hear about the cement factory?' he said. 'Isn't it great for Kilmalough?'

She agreed. She said what Mr Swanton and Mr Maloney had said: that the cement factory would bring employment to the neighbourhood.

'Will I ride home with you a bit, Bridie?' Bowser Egan suggested, and she pretended not to hear him. 'Aren't you my girl, Bridie, and always have been?' he said, a statement that made no sense at all.

His voice went on whispering at her, saying he would

marry her tomorrow only his mother wouldn't permit another woman in the house. She knew what it was like herself, he reminded her, having a parent to look after: you couldn't leave them to rot, you had to honour your father and your mother.

She danced to *The Bells Are Ringing*, moving her legs in time with Bowser Egan's while over his shoulder she watched Dano Ryan softly striking one of his smaller drums. Mrs Griffin had got him even though she was nearly fifty, with no looks at all, a lumpish woman with lumpish legs and arms. Mrs Griffin had got him just as the girl had got Patrick Grady.

The music ceased, Bowser Egan held her hard against him, trying to touch her face with his. Around them, people whistled and clapped: the evening had come to an end. She walked away from Bowser Egan, knowing that not ever again would she dance in the Ballroom of Romance. She'd been a figure of fun, trying to promote a relationship with a middle-aged County Council labourer, as ridiculous as Madge Dowding dancing on beyond her time.

'I'm waiting outside for you, Cat,' Eyes Horgan called out, lighting a cigarette as he made for the swing-doors.

Already the man with the long arms – made long, so they said, from carrying rocks off his land – had left the ballroom. Others were moving briskly. Mr Dwyer was tidying the chairs.

In the cloakroom the girls put on their coats and said they'd see one another at Mass the next day. Madge Dowding hurried. 'Are you O.K., Bridie?' Patty Byrne asked and Bridie said she was. She smiled at little Patty Byrne, wondering if a day would come for the younger girl also, if one day she'd decide that she was a figure of fun in a wayside ballroom.

'Good-night so,' Bridie said, leaving the cloakroom, and

the girls who were still chatting there wished her good-night. Outside the cloakroom she paused for a moment. Mr Dwyer was still tidying the chairs, picking up empty lemonade bottles from the floor, setting the chairs in a neat row. His wife was sweeping the floor. 'Good-night, Bridie,' Mr Dwyer said. 'Good-night, Bridie,' his wife said.

Extra lights had been switched on so that the Dwyers could see what they were doing. In the glare the blue walls of the ballroom seemed tatty, marked with hair-oil where men had leaned against them, inscribed with names and initials and hearts with arrows through them. The crystal bowl gave out a light that was ineffective in the glare; the bowl was broken here and there, which wasn't noticeable when the other lights weren't on.

'Good-night so,' Bridie said to the Dwyers. She passed through the swing-doors and descended the three concrete steps on the gravel expanse in front of the ballroom. People were gathered on the gravel, talking in groups, standing with their bicycles. She saw Madge Dowding going off with Tim Daly. A youth rode away with a girl on the cross-bar of his bicycle. The engines of motor-cars started.

'Good-night, Bridie,' Dano Ryan said.

'Good-night, Dano,' she said.

She walked across the gravel towards her bicycle, hearing Mr Maloney, somewhere behind her, repeating that no matter how you looked at it the cement factory would be a great thing for Kilmalough. She heard the bang of a car-door and knew it was Mr Swanton banging the door of Mr Maloney's car because he always gave it the same loud bang. Two other doors banged as she reached her bicycle and then the engine started up and the headlights went on. She touched the two tyres of the bicycle to make certain she hadn't a puncture. The wheels of Mr Maloney's car traversed the gravel and were silent when they reached the road.

'Good-night, Bridie,' someone called, and she replied, pushing her bicycle towards the road.

'Will I ride a little way with you?' Bowser Egan asked.

They rode together and when they arrived at the hill for which it was necessary to dismount she looked back and saw in the distance the four coloured bulbs that decorated the façade of the Ballroom of Romance. As she watched the lights went out, and she imagined Mr Dwyer pulling the metal grid across the front of his property and locking the two padlocks that secured it. His wife would be waiting with the evening's takings, sitting in the front of their car.

'D'you know what it is, Bridie,' said Bowser Egan, 'you were never looking better than tonight.' He took from a pocket of his suit the small bottle of whiskey he had. He uncorked it and drank some and then handed it to her. She took it and drank. 'Sure, why wouldn't you?' he said, surprised to see her drinking because she never had in his company before. It was an unpleasant taste, she considered, a taste she'd experienced only twice before, when she'd taken whiskey as a remedy for toothache. 'What harm would it do you?' Bowser Egan said as she raised the bottle again to her lips. He reached out a hand for it, though, suddenly concerned lest she should consume a greater share than he wished her to.

She watched him drinking more expertly than she had. He would always be drinking, she thought. He'd be lazy and useless, sitting in the kitchen with the *Irish Press*. He'd waste money buying a second-hand motor-car in order to drive into the town to go to the public houses on fair-days.

'She's shook these days,' he said, referring to his mother. 'She'll hardly last two years, I'm thinking.' He threw the empty whiskey bottle into the ditch and lit a cigarette. They pushed their bicycles. He said:

'When she goes, Bridie, I'll sell the bloody place up. I'll sell the pigs and the whole damn one and twopence worth.' He paused in order to raise the cigarette to his lips. He drew in smoke and exhaled it. 'With the cash that I'll get I could improve some place else, Bridie.'

They reached a gate on the left-hand side of the road and automatically they pushed their bicycles towards it and leaned them against it. He climbed over the gate into the field and she climbed after him. 'Will we sit down here, Bridie?' he said, offering the suggestion as one that had just occurred to him, as though they'd entered the field for some other purpose.

'We could improve a place like your own one,' he said, putting his right arm around her shoulders. 'Have you a kiss in you, Bridie?' He kissed her, exerting pressure with his teeth. When his mother died he would sell his farm and spend the money in the town. After that he would think of getting married because he'd have nowhere to go, because he'd want a fire to sit at and a woman to cook food for him. He kissed her again, his lips hot, the sweat on his cheeks sticking to her. 'God, you're great at kissing,' he said.

She rose, saying it was time to go, and they climbed over the gate again. 'There's nothing like a Saturday,' he said. 'Good-night to you so, Bridie.'

He mounted his bicycle and rode down the hill, and she pushed hers to the top and then mounted it also. She rode through the night as on Saturday nights for years she had ridden and never would ride again because she'd reached a certain age. She would wait now and in time Bowser Egan would seek her out because his mother would have died. Her father would probably have died also by then. She would marry Bowser Egan because it would be lonesome being by herself in the farmhouse.

The Forty-seventh Saturday

Mavie awoke and remembered at once that it was Saturday. She lay for a while, alone with that thought, considering it and relishing it. Then she thought of details: the ingredients of a lunch, the cleaning of the kitchen floor, the tidying of her bedroom. She rose and reached for her dressing-gown. In the kitchen she found a small pad of paper and wrote in pencil these words: *mackerel, parmesan cheese, garlic.* Then she drew back the curtains, placed a filled kettle over a gas jet and shook cornflakes on to a plate.

Some hours later, about mid-day, Mr McCarthy stood thoughtfully in a wine-shop. He sighed, and then said:

'*Vin rosé.* The larger size. Is it a litre? I don't know what it's called.'

'Jumbo *vin rosé,*' the assistant murmured, ignoring the demands of the accented word. 'Fourteen and seven.'

It was not a wine-shop in which Mr McCarthy had ever before made a purchase. He paused, his hand inside his jacket, the tips of his fingers touching the leather of his wallet.

'Fourteen and seven?'

The assistant, perceiving clearly that Mr McCarthy had arrested the action with which he had planned to draw money from within his clothes, took no notice. He blew on the glass of the bottle because the bottle was dusty. Whistling thickly with tongue and lips, he tore a piece of brown paper and proceeded to wrap with it. He placed the parcel in a carrier bag.

'I thought it was ten shillings that size,' Mr McCarthy said. 'I have got it in another place for ten shillings.'

The assistant stared at him, incredulous.

'I buy a lot of *vin rosé*,' Mr McCarthy explained.

The assistant, a man of thirty-five with a face that was pock-marked, spoke no word but stared on. In his mind he was already retailing the incident to his superior when, an hour or so later, that person should return. He scrutinised Mr McCarthy, so that when the time came he might lend authority to his tale with an accurate description of the man who had demanded *vin rosé* and then had argued about the charged price. He saw before him a middle-aged man of medium height, with a hat and spectacles and a moustache.

'Well, I haven't time to argue.' Mr McCarthy handed the man a pound note and received his change. 'Threepence short, that is,' he said; and the assistant explained:

'The carrier bag. It's necessary nowadays to charge. You understand?'

But Mr McCarthy lifted the wine out of the bag, saying that the brown paper wrapping was quite sufficient, and the assistant handed him a threepenny piece.

'I take a taxi,' Mr McCarthy explained. 'It's no hardship to carry.'

In the flat Mavie laid two mackerel on the smoking fat of the frying-pan and sniffed the air. A plastic apron covered her navy-blue, rather old-fashioned suit. Her fair hair, recently released from curling-pins, quivered splendidly about her head; her bosom heaved as she drew the tasty air into her lungs. She walked from the stove to the kitchen table, seeking a glass of medium dry sherry that a minute or two previously she had poured and placed somewhere.

'Ta-ra-ta-ta-ta-ta-ta-ta, ta-ta-ta-ta-ta-ta,' tuned Mr McCarthy in his taxi-cab, trying to put from his mind the extra four and sevenpence that he had been obliged to spend on the wine. 'A basement place,' he called to the driver. 'You'll know it by a motor-cycle and side-car parked outside.' The driver made no response.

'Motor-bike and side-car,' repeated Mr McCarthy. 'Parked by a lamp-post, number twenty-one. D'you understand?'

'Twenty-one, Roeway Road,' said the driver. 'We'll endeavour.'

Mr McCarthy closed his eyes and stretched his legs stiffly in front of him. He thought of Mavie, as was suitable at that moment. He saw her standing by the edge of the kitchen table, with a cigarette protruding from the left-hand extremity of her mouth and the thumb and forefinger of her right hand grasping a glass which contained sherry and which bore, painted around it on the outside, two thin lines, one in red, the other in gold. It was the forty-seventh time that Mr McCarthy had made this mid-day journey, in a taxi-cab with a bottle of wine.

'Doesn't he want you to dress up?' the girls had asked when first she had told them. 'Pith helmets, chukka boots?' Mavie had found that funny. She had laughed and said: 'Dress up? Rather the opposite!' But that was at the very beginning of the affair, before she had fallen so deeply in love with him.

'Hullo.' Mavie, holding the sherry glass before her, struck a pose in the basement kitchen. She had taken off her plastic apron.

'Hullo, Mavie.' He held out the bottle, his hat still upon his head, his soft raincoat creased and seeming unclean. 'I've brought some wine. A little wine. I thought it would cheer us up.' He had let himself in, for the door was always on the latch. He had clicked the Yale catch behind him, as he had long since learned she liked him to do, so that no disturbances might later take place. 'I don't care for disturbances,' Mavie had said on the fifth occasion: an embarrassing time, when a coal-heaver, mistaking the basement for the basement next door, had walked into her bedroom with a sack on his back to find Mr McCarthy and herself playing about on the covers of her bed.

'My, my, you're looking sweet.' He removed his hat and overcoat and cast his eye about for a corkscrew. It was his policy on these visits to prime himself beforehand with two measures of brandy and, having made his entry, to take an immediate glass of *vin rosé*. He did not care for Mavie's sherry. *British sherry* was how the label described it; a qualification that put Mr McCarthy off.

'I love that costume.' He had said this before, referring to Mavie's navy-blue coat and skirt. In reply she had once or twice pointed out that it had been, originally, the property of her sister Linda.

Mr McCarthy could smell the fish. He could sense the atmosphere rich with mackerel and the perfumed mist with which Mavie had sprayed the room.

'I'm doing a nice fresh mackerel in a custard sauce,' Mavie announced, moving towards the stove. She had been closely embraced by Mr McCarthy, who was now a little shaken, caught between the promise of the embrace and the thought of mackerel in a sauce. He imagined he must have heard incorrectly: he could not believe that the sauce was a custard one. 'Custard!' he said. 'Custard?'

Mavie stirred the contents of a bowl. She remembered the first time: she had made an omelette; the mushrooms with which she had filled it had not cooked properly and Mr McCarthy had remarked upon the fact. She could have wept, watching him move the mushrooms to the side of his plate. 'Have them on toast,' she had cried. 'I'll cook them a bit more, love, and you can have them on a nice piece of toast.' But he had shaken his head, and then, to show that all was well, he had taken her into his arms and had at once begun to unzip her skirt.

'Custard?' said Mr McCarthy again, aware of some revulsion in his bowels.

'A garlic custard sauce. I read it in that column.'

'My dear, I'd as soon have a lightly boiled egg. This wretched old trouble again.'

'Oh, you poor thing. But fish is as easy to digest. A small helping. I'd have steamed had I known. You poor soul. Sit down, for heaven's sake.'

He was thinking that he would vomit if he had to lift a single forkful of mackerel and garlic custard sauce to his lips. He would feel a retching at the back of his throat and before another second passed there would be an accident.

'Love, I should have told you: I am off fish in any shape or form. The latest thing, I am on a diet of soft-boiled eggs. I'm a terrible trouble to you, Mavie love.'

She came to where he was sitting, drinking his way through the wine, and kissed him. She said not to worry about anything.

Mr McCarthy had told Mavie more lies than he had ever told anyone else. He had invented trouble with his stomach so that he could insist upon simple food, even though Mavie, forgetfully or hopefully, always cooked more elaborately. He had invented a Saturday appointment at four o'clock every week so that no dawdling would be required of him after he had exacted what he had come to look upon as his due. He had invented a wife and two children so that Mavie might not get ideas above her station.

'Brush your teeth, Mavie, like a good girl.' Mr McCarthy was being practical, fearful of the garlic. He spoke with confidence, knowing that Mavie would see it as reasonable that she should brush her teeth before the moments of love.

While she was in the bathroom he hummed a tune and

reflected on his continuing good fortune. He drank more wine and when Mavie returned bade her drink some, too. It could only happen on Saturdays because the girl whom Mavie shared the flat with, Eithne, went away for the week-ends.

'Well, this is pleasant,' said Mr McCarthy, sitting her on his knee, stroking her navy-blue clothes. She sat there, a little heavy for him, swinging her legs until her shoes slipped off.

This Saturday was Mavie's birthday. Today she was twenty-seven, while Mr McCarthy remained at fifty-two. She had, the night before and for several other nights and days, considered the fact, wondering whether or not to make any-thing of it, wondering whether or not to let Mr McCarthy know. She had thought, the Saturday before, that it might seem a little pushing to say that it was her birthday in a week; it might seem that her words contained the suggestion that Mr McCarthy should arm himself with a present or should contrive to transform the day into a special occasion. She thought ecstatically of his arriving at the house with a wrapped box and sitting down and saying: 'What lovely mackerel!' and putting it to her then that since this was her twenty-seventh birthday he would arrange to spend the whole afternoon and the night as well. 'We shall take to the West End later on,' Mr McCarthy had said in Mavie's mind, 'and shall go to a show, that thing at the Palladium. I have the tickets in my wallet.'

'What terrible old weather it is,' said Mr McCarthy. 'You wouldn't know whether you're coming or going.'

Mavie made a noise of agreement. She remembered other birthdays: a year she had been given a kite, the time that her cake, its flavour chosen by her, had not succeeded in the oven and had come to the table lumpy and grey, disguised with hundreds and thousands. She had cried, and her mother had picked up a teaspoon and rapped her knuckles. 'After the show,' said Mr McCarthy, 'what about a spot of dinner in a little place I've heard of? And then liqueurs before we return in style to your little nest.' As he spoke Mr McCarthy nuzzled her neck, and Mavie realised that he was, in fact, nuzzling her neck, though he was not speaking.

'Today is a special day,' said Mavie. 'It's a very special November day.'

Mr McCarthy laughed. 'Every Saturday is a special day for me. Every Saturday is outlined in red on my heart.' And he initiated some horseplay which prevented Mavie from explaining.

Born beneath the sign of Scorpio, she was meant to be strong, fearless and enterprising. As a child she had often been in trouble, not because of naughtiness but because she had been dreamy about her work. She dreamed now, dominated by an image of Mr McCarthy rushing out of a sudden for flowers. She saw him returning, blooms everywhere, saying he had telephoned to put off his Saturday appointment and had telephoned his home to say he had been called away on vital business. She felt his hands seeking the outline of her ribs, a thing he liked to do. They lay in silence for a while, and increasingly she felt low and sad.

'How lovely you are,' murmured Mr McCarthy. 'Oh, Mavie, Mavie.'

She squeezed the length of pale flesh that was Mr McCarthy's arm. She thought suddenly of the day the coal-heaver had arrived and felt her neck going red at the memory. She remembered the first day, rolling down her stockings and seeing her lover watching her, he already naked, standing still and seeming puzzled, near the electric fire. She had not been a virgin that day, but in the meanwhile she had not once been unfaithful to him.

'Tell me you love me,' Mavie cried, forgetting about her birthday, abruptly caught up in a new emotion. 'Tell me now; it worries me sometimes.'

'Of course it does. Of course I do. I'm all for you, Mavie, as I've said a thousand times.'

'It's not that I doubt you, honey, only sometimes between one Saturday and another I feel a depression. It's impossible to say. I mean, it's hard to put into words. Have you got a fag?'

Mr McCarthy shook his head on the pillow. She knew he did not smoke: why then did she ask? It was like the custard sauce all over again. When he went to the trouble of inventing stomach trouble, you'd think she'd take the trouble to remember it.

'You don't smoke. I always ask and you always don't say anything and I always remember then. Am I very irritating to you, honey? Tell me you love me. Tell me I'm not irritating to you.'

'Mavie.'

'You don't like me today. I feel it. Jesus, I'm sorry about the mackerel. Tell the truth now, you don't like me today.'

'Oh yes, I do. I love you. I love you.'

'You don't like me.' She spoke as though she had not heard his protestations; she spaced the words carefully, giving the same emphasis to each.

'I love you,' said Mr McCarthy. 'Indeed I do.'

She shook her head, and rose and walked to the kitchen, where she found cigarettes and matches.

'My Mavie,' said Mr McCarthy from the bed, assuring himself that he was not finished yet, that he had not fully exacted his pleasurable due. 'Mavie, my young heart,' he murmured, and he began to laugh, thinking that merriment in the atmosphere would cheer matters up. 'Shall I do a little dance for you?'

Mavie, cigarette aglow, pulled the sheets around her as Mr McCarthy vacated the bed and stood, his arms outstretched, on the centre of the floor. He began to dance, as on many occasions before he had danced, swaying about without much tempo. When first he had performed in this way for her he had explained that his dance was an expression of his passion, representing, so he said, roses and presents of jewellery and lamé gowns. Once Mr McCarthy had asked Mavie to take the braces off his trousers and strike him with them while he acted out his dance. He was guilty, he said, because in their life together there were neither roses nor jewels nor restaurant dinners. But Mavie, shocked that he should feel like that, had refused his request, saying there was no cause for punishment. Sulkily, he had maintained otherwise, though he had not ever again suggested chastisement.

'How's that?' said Mr McCarthy, ending with a gesture. Mavie said nothing. She threw back the bed-clothes and Mr McCarthy strode jauntily towards her, a smile shaping beneath his moustache.

'I often wonder about her,' Mavie said a moment later. 'It's only natural. You can't help that.'

Mr McCarthy said: 'My wife's a hard case. She's well able to take care of herself. I'm on a leash where the wife is concerned.'

'I don't even know her name.'

'Oh, Mavie, Mavie. Isn't Mrs McCarthy enough?'

'I'm jealous. I'm sorry, honey.'

'No bother, Mavie. No bother, love.'

'I see her as a black-haired woman. Tall and sturdy. Would you rather we didn't speak of her?'

'It would be easier, certainly.'

'I'm sorry, honey.'

'No bother.'

'It's only jealousy. The green-eyed monster.'

'No need to be jealous, Mavie. No need at all. There's no love lost between Mrs McCarthy and myself. We never go together nowadays.'

'What sign is she under?'

'Sign, love?'

'Sagittarius? Leo? When's her birthday?'

Mr McCarthy's small eyes screwed up.

He looked through the lashes. He said:

'The twenty-ninth of March.'

'You make an occasion of it, do you? In the home, with the children around? You all give her presents, I suppose. Is there a special cake?'

'The wife likes a jam-roll. She buys one at Lyons.'

'And the children get her little gifts? Things from Woolworth's?'

'Something like that.'

'When I was little I used to buy presents in Woolworth's. My dad used to take me by the hand. I suppose you did, too. And your wife.'

'Yes, love, I suppose so.'

'I often think of your wife. I can't help it. I see her in my mind's eye.'

'She's a big woman,' said Mr McCarthy meditatively. 'Bigger than you, Mavie. A big, dark woman – more than that I won't say.'

'Oh, honey, I never meant to pry.'

'It's not prying I mind, Mavie. No, you're not prying. It's just that I don't wish to soil the hour.'

When Mr McCarthy had said that, he heard the words echoing in his mind as words occasionally do. *I don't wish to soil the hour*. Mavie was silent, feeling the words to be beautiful. *I don't wish to soil the hour*, she thought. She drew her finger-nails along the taut skin of Mr McCarthy's thigh. 'Oh God,' said Mr McCarthy.

She knew that when he left, at twenty to four, she would sit alone in her dressing-gown and weep. She would wash the dirty dishes from lunch and she would wash his lovingly: she would wash and dry his egg-cup and be aware that it was his. She knew that that was absurd, but she knew that it would happen because it had happened before. She did not think it odd, as Mr McCarthy had often thought, that she, so pretty and still young, should love so passionately a man of fifty-two. She adored every shred of him; she longed for his presence and the touch of his hand. 'Oh, my honey, my honey,' cried Mavie, throwing her body on the body of Mr McCarthy and wrapping him up in her plump limbs.

At half-past three Mr McCarthy, who had dropped into a light doze, woke to the awareness of a parched throat and a desire for tea. He sighed and caressed the fair hair that lay on the pillow beside him.

'I'll make a cup of tea,' said Mavie.

'*Merci*,' whispered Mr McCarthy.

They drank tea in the kitchen while Mr McCarthy buttoned his waistcoat and drew on his socks. 'I've bought a bow tie,' he confided, 'though I'm still a little shy in it. Maybe next week I'll try it out on you.'

'You could ask me anything under the sun and I'd do it for you. You could ask me anything, I love you that much.'

Hearing this, Mr McCarthy paused in the lacing of a boot. He thought of his braces, taut now about his shoulders; he thought of a foot fetish he had read about in the public library.

'I love you that much,' whispered Mavie.

'And I you,' said Mr McCarthy.

'I dream of you at nights.'

'I dream of you, my dear.'

Mavie sighed and looked over her shoulder, ill at ease. 'I cannot think of you dreaming of me.'

'I dream of you in my narrow twin bed, with the dark-haired woman in the twin beside it.'

'Don't speak like that. Don't talk to me of the bedroom.'

'I'm sorry.'

'I can't bear the thought of the twin beds in that room. I've told you before, honey.'

'Oh, Mavie, Mavie, if we could be together.'

'I love you that much.'

For a moment there was silence in the kitchen. Then, having tilted his cup to drain it of tea, Mr McCarthy rose to go.

As he crossed the floor his eyes fell on a birthday card propped up on the mantelshelf. It registered with him at once that the day was Mavie's birthday, and for a moment he considered remarking on that fact. Then he remembered the time and he kissed her on the head, his usual form of farewell. 'The forty-seventh time,' he murmured. 'Today was the forty-seventh.'

She walked with him along the passage to the door of the flat. She watched him mount the basement steps and watched his legs move briskly by the railings above. His footsteps died away and she returned to the kitchen and poured herself a cup of tea. She thought of him keeping his Saturday appointment, a business appointment he had always called it, and afterwards returning on a bus to his suburb. She saw him entering a door, opening it with a latchkey, being greeted by a dog and two children and the big, dark woman who was his wife. The dog barked loudly and the woman shrilled abuse, upbraiding her husband for a misdemeanour or some piece of forgetfulness or some small deceit discovered. She could feel his tiredness as he stood in his own hall, the latchkey still poised between his fingers, like a man at bay. Her eyes closed as she held that image in her mind; tears slipped from beneath their lids.

The bus let Mr McCarthy down at an Odeon cinema. He moved rapidly, checking his watch against a brightly lit clock that hung out over a shop. He was reckoning as he walked that there was time to have another cup of tea, with a Danish pastry perhaps, because he felt quite peckish. Afterwards, as always on a Saturday, he'd go to the pictures.

A Happy Family

On the evening of Tuesday, May 24th, 1962, I returned home in the usual way. I remember sitting in the number 73 bus, thinking of the day as I had spent it and thinking of the house I was about to enter. It was a fine evening, warm and mellow, the air heavy with the smell of London. The bus crossed Hammersmith Bridge, moving quite quickly towards the leafy avenues beyond. The houses of the suburbs were gayer in that evening's sunshine, pleasanter abodes than often they seemed.

'Hullo,' I said in the hall of ours, speaking to my daughter Bridget, a child of one, who happened to be loitering there. She was wearing her night-dress, and she didn't look sleepy. 'Aren't you going to bed?' I said, and Bridget looked at me as if she had forgotten that I was closely related to her. I could hear Anna and Christopher in the bathroom, talking loudly and rapidly, and I could hear Elizabeth's voice urging them to wash themselves properly and be quick about it. 'She's fourteen stone, Miss MacAdam is,' Christopher was saying. 'Isn't she, Anna?' Miss MacAdam was a woman who taught at their school, a woman about whom we had come to know a lot. 'She can't swim,' said Anna.

Looking back now, such exchanges come easily to my mind. Bits of conversations float to the surface without much of a continuing pattern and without any significance that I can see. I suppose we were a happy family: someone examining us might possibly have written that down on a report sheet, the way these things are done. Yet what I recall most vividly now when I think of us as a family are images and occasions that for Elizabeth and me were neither happy nor unhappy. I remember animals at the Zoo coming forward for the offerings of our children, smelling of confinement rather than the jungle, seeming fierce and hard-done-by. I remember birthday parties on warm afternoons, the figures of children moving swiftly from the garden to the house, creatures who might have been bored, with paper hats on their heads or in their hands, seeking adventure in forbidden rooms. I remember dawdling walks, arguments that came to involve all of us, and other days when everything went well.

I used to leave the house at half-past eight every morning, and often during the day I imagined what my wife's day must be like. She told me, of course. She told me about how ill-tempered our children had been, or how tractable; about how the time had passed in other ways, whom she had met and spoken to, who had come to tea or whom she had visited. I imagined her in summer having lunch in the garden when it was warm, dozing afterwards and being woken up by Bridget. In turn, she would ask me how the hours had gone for me and I would say a thing or two about their passing, about the people who had filled them. 'Miss Madden is leaving us,' I can hear myself saying. 'Off to Buenos Aires for some reason.' In my memory of this, I seem to be repeating the information. 'Off to Buenos Aires,' I appear to be saying. 'Off to Buenos Aires. Miss Madden.' And a little later I am saying it again, adding that Miss Madden would be missed. Elizabeth's head is nodding, agreeing that that will indeed be so. 'I fell asleep in the garden,' Elizabeth is murmuring in this small vision. 'Bridget woke me up.'

My wife was pretty when I married her, and as the years passed it seemed to me that she took on a greater beauty. I believed that this was some reflection of her contentment, and she may even have believed it herself. Had she suddenly said otherwise, I'd have been puzzled; as puzzled as I was, and as she was, on the evening of May 24th, when she told me about Mr Higgs. She sat before me then, sipping at a glass of sherry that I'd poured her and remembering all the details: all that Mr Higgs had said and all that she had said in reply.

She had been listening to a story on the radio and making coffee. Christopher and Anna were at school; in the garden Bridget was asleep in her pram. When the telephone rang Elizabeth walked towards it slowly, still listening to the wireless. When she said 'Hullo' she heard the coins drop at the other end and a man's voice said: 'Mrs Farrel?'

Elizabeth said yes, she was Mrs Farrel, and the man said: 'My name is Higgs.'

His voice was ordinary, a little uneducated, the kind of voice that is always drifting over the telephone.

'A very good friend,' said Mr Higgs.

'Good-morning,' said Elizabeth in her matter-of-fact way. 'Are you selling something, Mr Higgs?'

'In a sense, Mrs Farrel, in a sense. You might call it selling. Do I peddle salvation?'

'Oh, I am not religious in the least – '

'It may be your trouble, Mrs Farrel.'

'Yes, well – '

'You are Elizabeth Farrel. You have three children.'

'Mr Higgs – '

'Your father was a Captain Maugham. Born 1892, died 1959. He lost a leg in action and never forgave himself for it. You attended his funeral, but were glad that he was dead, since he had a way of upsetting your children. Your mother, seventy-four a week ago, lives near St Albans and is unhappy. You have two sisters and a brother.'

'Mr Higgs, what do you want?'

'Nothing. I don't want anything. What do you want, Mrs Farrel?'

'Look here, Mr Higgs – '

'D'you remember your tenth birthday? D'you remember what it felt like being a little girl of ten, in a white dress spotted with forget-me-not, and a blue ribbon tying back your hair? You were taken on a picnic. "You're ten years old," your father said. "Now tell us what you're going to do with yourself." "She must cut the chocolate cake first," your mother cried, and so you cut the cake and then stood up and announced the trend of your ambitions. Your brother Ralph laughed and was scolded by your father. D'you remember at all?'

Elizabeth did remember. She remembered playing hide-and-seek with her sisters after tea; she remembered Ralph climbing a tree and finding himself unable to get down again; she remembered her parents quarrelling, as they invariably did, all the way home.

'Do I know you, Mr Higgs? How do you manage to have these details of my childhood?'

Mr Higgs laughed. It wasn't a nasty laugh. It sounded even reassuring, as if Mr Higgs meant no harm.

On the evening of May 24th we sat for a long time wondering who the odd individual could be and what he was after. Elizabeth seemed nervously elated and naturally more than a little intrigued. I, on the other hand, was rather upset by this Mr Higgs and his deep mine of information. 'If he rings again,' I said, 'threaten him with the police.'

'Good morning, Mrs Farrel.'

'Mr Higgs?'

'My dear.'

'Well then, Mr Higgs, explain.'

'Ho, ho, Mrs Farrel, there's a sharpness for you. Explain? Why, if I explained I'd be out of business in no time at all. "So that's it," you'd say, and ring off, just like I was a salesman or a Jehovah's Witness.'

'Mr Higgs – '

'You was a little girl of ten, Mrs Farrel. You was out on a picnic. Remember?'

'How did you know all that?'

'Why shouldn't I know, for heaven's sake? Listen now, Mrs Farrel. Did you think then what you would be today? Did you see yourself married to a man and mothering his children? Have you come to a sticky end, or otherwise?'

'A sticky end?'

'You clean his house, you prepare his meals, you take his opinions. You hear on the radio some news of passing importance, some bomb exploded, some army recalled. Who does the thinking, Mrs Farrel? You react as he does. You've lost your identity. Did you think of that that day when you were ten? Your children will be ten one day. They'll stand before you at ten years of age, first the girl, then the boy. What of their futures, Mrs Farrel? Shall they make something of themselves? Shall they fail and be miserable? Shall they be unnatural and unhappy, or sick in some way, or perhaps too stupid? Or shall they all three of them be richly successful? Are you successful, Mrs Farrel? You are your husband's instrument. You were different at ten, Mrs Farrel. How about your children? Soon it'll be your turn to take on the talking. I'll listen like I was paid for it.'

I was aware of considerable pique when Elizabeth reported all this to me. I protested that I was not given to forcing my opinions on others, and Elizabeth said I wasn't either. 'Clearly, he's queer in the head,' I said. I paused, thinking about that, then said: 'Could he be someone like a window-cleaner to whom you once perhaps talked of your childhood? Although I can't see you doing it.'

Elizabeth shook her head; she said she didn't remember talking to a window-cleaner about her childhood, or about anything very much. We'd had the same window-cleaners for almost seven years, she reminded me: two honest, respectable men who arrived at the house every six weeks in a Ford motor-car. 'Well, he must be someone,' I said. 'Someone you've talked to. I mean, it's not guesswork.'

'Maybe he's wicked,' said Elizabeth. 'Maybe he's a small wicked man with very white skin, driven by some force he doesn't understand. Perhaps he's one of those painters who came last year to paint the hall. There was a little man – '

'That little man's name was Mr Gipe. I remember that well. "Gipe," he said, walking into the hall and saying it would be a long job. "Gipe, sir; an unusual name." '

'He could be calling himself Higgs. He could have read through my letters. And my old diaries. Perhaps Mr Gipe expected a tip.'

'The hall cost ninety pounds.'

'I know, but it didn't all go to Mr Gipe. Perhaps nobody tips poor Mr Gipe and perhaps now he's telephoning all the wives, having read through their letters and their private diaries. He telephones to taunt them and to cause trouble, being an evil man. Perhaps Mr Gipe is possessed of a devil.'

I frowned and shook my head. 'Not at all,' I said. 'It's a voice from the past. It's someone who really did know you when you were ten, and knows all that's happened since.'

'More likely Mr Gipe,' said Elizabeth, 'guided from Hell.'

'Daddy, am I asleep?'

I looked at her wide eyes, big and blue and clear, perfect replicas of her mother's. I loved Anna best of all of them; I suppose because she reminded me so much of Elizabeth.

'No, darling, you're not asleep. If you were asleep you couldn't be talking to me, now could you?'

'I could be dreaming, Daddy. Couldn't I be dreaming?'

'Yes, I suppose you could.'

'But I'm not, am I?'

I shook my head. 'No, Anna, you're not dreaming.'

She sighed. 'I'm glad. I wouldn't like to be dreaming. I wouldn't like to suddenly wake up.'

It was Sunday afternoon and we had driven into the country. We did it almost every Sunday when the weather was fine and warm. The children enjoyed it and so in a way did we, even though the woods we went to were rather tatty, too near London to seem real, too untidy with sweet-papers to be attractive. Still, it was a way of entertaining them.

'Elizabeth.'

She was sitting on a tree-stump, her eyes half-closed. On a rug at her feet Bridget was playing with some wooden beads. I sat beside her and put my arm about her shoulders.

'Elizabeth.'

She jumped a little. 'Hullo, darling. I was almost asleep.'

'You were thinking about Mr Higgs.'

'Oh, I wasn't. My mind was a blank; I was about to drop off. I can do it now, sitting upright like this.'

'Anna asked me if she was dreaming.'

'Where is she?'

'Playing with Christopher.'

'They'll begin to fight. They don't play any more. Why do they perpetually fight?'

I said it was just a phase, but Elizabeth said she thought they would always fight now. The scratching and snarling would turn to argument as they grew older and when they became adults they wouldn't ever see one another. They would say that they had nothing in common, and would admit to others that they really rather disliked one another and always had. Elizabeth said she could see them: Christopher married to an unsuitable woman, and Anna as a girl who lived promiscuously and did not marry at all. Anna would become a heavy drinker of whisky and would smoke slim cigars at forty.

'Heavens,' I said, staring at her, and then looking at the small figure of Anna. 'Why on earth are you saying all that?'

'Well, it's true. I mean, it's what I imagine. I can see Anna in a harsh red suit, getting drunk at a cocktail party. I can see Christopher being miserable – '

'This is your Mr Higgs again. Look, the police can arrange to have the telephone tapped. It's sheer nonsense that some raving lunatic should be allowed to go on like that.'

'Mr Higgs! Mr Higgs! What's Mr Higgs got to do with it? You've got him on the brain.'

Elizabeth walked away. She left me sitting there with her frightening images of our children. Out of the corner of my eye I saw that Bridget was eating a piece of wood. I took it from her. Anna was saying: 'Daddy, Christopher hurt me.'

'Why?'

'I don't know. He just hurt me.'

'How did he hurt you?'

'He pushed me and I fell.' She began to cry, so I comforted her. I called Christopher and told him he mustn't push Anna. They ran off to play again and a moment later Anna was saying: 'Daddy, Christopher pushed me.'

'Christopher, you mustn't push Anna. And you shouldn't have to be told everything twice.'

'I didn't push her. She fell.'

Anna put her thumb in her mouth. I glanced through the

trees to see where Elizabeth had got to, but there was no sign
of her. I made the children sit on the rug and told them a
story. They didn't like it much. They never did like my
stories: Elizabeth's were so much better.

'I'm sorry.' She stood looking down on us, as tall and
beautiful as a goddess.

'You look like a goddess,' I said.

'What's a goddess?' Anna asked, and Christopher said:
'Why's Mummy sorry?'

'A goddess is a beautiful lady. Mummy's sorry because she
left me to look after you. And it's time to go home.'

'Oh, oh, oh, I must find Mambi first,' Anna cried anxiously.
Mambi was a faithful friend who accompanied her everywhere she went, but who was, at the moment of departure,
almost always lost.

We walked to the car. Anna said: 'Mambi was at the top of
an old tree. Mambi's a goddess too. Daddy, do you *have* to be
beautiful to be a goddess?'

'I suppose so.'

'Then Mambi can't be.'

'Isn't Mambi beautiful?'

'Usually she is. Only she's not now.'

'Why isn't she now?'

'Because all her hair came off in the tree.'

The car heaved and wobbled all the way home as Christopher and Anna banged about in the back. When they fought
we shouted at them, and then they sulked and there was a
mile or so of peace. Anna began to cry as I turned into the
garage. Mambi, she said, was cold without her hair. Elizabeth
explained about wigs.

I woke up in the middle of that night, thinking about Mr
Higgs. I kept seeing the man as a shrimpish little thing, like

the manager of the shop where we hired our television set. He had a black moustache, like a length of thread stuck across his upper lip. I knew it was wrong, I knew this wasn't Mr Higgs at all; and then, all of a sudden, I began to think about Elizabeth's brother, Ralph.

A generation ago Ralph would have been called a remittance man. Just about the time we were married old Captain Maugham had packed him off to a farm in Kenya after an incident with a hotel receptionist and the hotel's account books. But caring for nothing in Kenya, Ralph had made his way to Cairo, and from Cairo on the long-distance telephone he had greeted the Captain with a request for financial aid. He didn't get it, and then the war broke out and Ralph disappeared. Whenever we thought of him we imagined that he was up to the most reprehensible racket he could lay his hands on. If he was, we never found out about it. All we did know was that after the war he again telephoned the Captain, and the odd thing was that he was still in Cairo. 'I have lost an arm,' Captain Maugham told him testily. 'And I,' said Ralph, 'have lost the empire of my soul.' He was given to this kind of decorated statement; it interefered so much with his conversation that most of the time you didn't know what he was talking about. But the Captain sent him some money and an agreement was drawn up by which Ralph, on receipt of a monthly cheque, promised not to return to England during his father's lifetime. Then the Captain died and Ralph was back. I gave him fifty pounds and all in all he probably cleaned up quite well. Ralph wasn't the sort of person to write letters; we had no idea where he was now. As a schoolboy, and even later, he was a great one for playing practical jokes. He was certainly a good enough mimic to create a Mr Higgs. Just for fun, I wondered? Or in some kind of bitterness? Or did he in some ingenious way hope to extract money?

The following morning I telephoned Elizabeth's sisters.

Daphne knew nothing about where Ralph was, what he was doing or anything about him. She said she hoped he wasn't coming back to England because it had cost her fifty pounds the last time. Margaret, however, knew a lot. She didn't want to talk about it on the telephone, so I met her for lunch.

'What's all this?' she said.

I told her about Mr Higgs and the vague theory that was beginning to crystallise in my mind. She was intrigued by the Higgs thing. 'I don't know why,' she said, 'but it rings a queer sort of bell. But you're quite wrong about Ralph.' Ralph, it appeared, was being paid by Margaret and her husband in much the same way as he had been paid by the Captain; for the same reason and with the same stipulation. 'Only for the time being,' Margaret said a little bitterly. 'When Mother dies Ralph can do what he damn well likes. But it was quite a serious business and the news of it would clearly finish her. One doesn't like to think of an old woman dying in that particular kind of misery.'

'But whatever it was, she'd probably never find out.'

'Oh yes, she would. She reads the papers. In any case, Ralph is quite capable of dropping her a little note. But at the moment I can assure you that Ralph is safe in Africa. He's not the type to take any chances with his gift horses.'

So that was that. It made me feel even worse about Mr Higgs that my simple explanation had been so easily exploded.

'Well,' I said, 'and what did he have to say today?'

'What did who say?'

'Higgs.'

'Nothing much. He's becoming a bore.'

She wasn't going to tell me any more. She wasn't going to talk about Mr Higgs because she didn't trust me. She thought

I'd put the police on him, and she didn't want that, so she said, because she had come to feel sorry for the poor crazed creature or whatever it was he happened to be. In fact, I thought to myself, my wife has become in some way fascinated by this man.

I worked at home one day, waiting for the telephone call. There was a ring at eleven-fifteen. I heard Elizabeth answer it. She said: 'No, I'm sorry; I'm afraid you've got the wrong number.' I didn't ask her about Mr Higgs. When I looked at her she seemed a long way away and her voice was measured and polite. There was some awful shaft between us and I didn't know what to do about it.

In the afternoon I took the children for a walk in the park.

'Mambi's gone to stay in the country,' Anna said. 'I'm lonely without her.'

'Well, she's coming back tonight, isn't she?'

'Daddy,' Christopher said, 'what's the matter with Mummy?'

I'm not very sure when it was that I first noticed everything was in rather a mess. I remember coming in one night and stumbling over lots of wooden toys in the hall. Quite often the cornflakes packet and the marmalade were still on the kitchen table from breakfast. Or if they weren't on the table the children had got them on to the floor and Bridget had covered most of the house with their mixed contents. Elizabeth didn't seem to notice. She sat in a dream, silent and alone, forgetting to cook the supper. The children began to do all the things they had ever wanted to do and which Elizabeth had patiently prevented, like scribbling on the walls and playing in the coal-cellar. I tried to discuss it with Elizabeth, but all she did was to smile sweetly and say she was tired.

'Why don't you see a doctor?'

She stared at me. 'A doctor?'

'Perhaps you need a tonic.' And at that point she would smile again and go to bed.

I knew that Elizabeth was still having her conversations with Mr Higgs even though she no longer mentioned them. When I asked her she used to laugh and say: 'Poor Mr Higgs was just some old fanatic.'

'Yes, but how did he – '

'Darling, you worry too much.'

I went to St Albans to see old Mrs Maugham, without very much hope. I don't know what I expected of her, since she was obviously too deaf and too senile to offer me anything at all. She lived with a woman called Miss Awpit who was employed by the old woman's children to look after her. Miss Awpit made us tea and did the interpreting.

'Mr Farrel wants to know how you are, dear,' Miss Awpit said. 'Quite well, really,' Miss Awpit said to me. 'All things being equal.'

Mrs Maugham knew who I was and all that. She asked after Elizabeth and the children. She said something to Miss Awpit and Miss Awpit said: 'She wants you to bring them to her.'

'Yes, yes,' I shouted, nodding hard. 'We shall come and see you soon. They often,' I lied, 'ask about Granny.'

'Hark at that,' shouted Miss Awpit, nudging the old lady, who snappishly told her to leave off.

I didn't quite know how to put it. I said: 'Ask her if she knows a Mr Higgs.'

Miss Awpit, imagining, I suppose, that I was making conversation, shouted: 'Mr Farrel wants to know if you know Mr Higgs.' Mrs Maugham smiled at us. 'Higgs,' Miss Awpit repeated. 'Do you know Mr Higgs at all, dear?'

'Never,' said Mrs Maugham.

'Have you ever known a Mr Higgs?' I shouted.

'Higgs?' said Mrs Maugham.

'Do you know him?' Miss Awpit asked. 'Do you know a Mr Higgs?'

'I do not,' said Mrs Maugham, suddenly in command of herself, 'know anyone of such a name. Nor would I wish to.'

'Look, Mrs Maugham,' I pursued, 'does the name mean anything at all to you?'

'I have told you, I do not know your friend. How can I be expected to know your friends, an old woman like me, stuck out here in St Albans with no one to look after me?'

'Come, come,' said Miss Awpit, 'you've got me, dear.'

But Mrs Maugham only laughed.

A week or two passed, and then one afternoon as I was sitting in the office filing my nails the telephone rang and a voice I didn't recognise said: 'Mr Farrel?'

I said 'Yes', and the voice said: 'This is Miss Awpit. You know, Mrs Maugham's Miss Awpit.'

'Of course. Good afternoon, Miss Awpit. How are you?'

'Very well, thank you. I'm ringing to tell you something about Mrs Maugham.'

'Yes?'

'Well, you know when you came here the other week you were asking about a Mr Higgs?'

'Yes, I remember.'

'Well, as you sounded rather anxious about him I just thought I'd tell you. I thought about it and then I decided. I'll ring Mr Farrel, I said, just to tell him what she said.'

'Yes, Miss Awpit?'

'I hope I'm doing the right thing.'

'What did Mrs Maugham say?'

'Well, it's funny in a way. I hope you won't think I'm being very stupid or anything.'

I had the odd feeling that Miss Awpit was going to die as she was speaking, before she could tell me. I said:

'I assure you, you are doing the right thing. What did Mrs Maugham say?'

'Well, it was at breakfast one morning. She hadn't had a good night at all. So she said, but you know what it's like with old people. I mean, quite frankly I had to get up myself in the night and I heard her sleeping as deep and sweet as you'd wish. Honestly, Mr Farrel, I often wish I had her constitution myself – '

'You were telling me about Mr Higgs.'

'I'm sorry?'

'You were telling me about Mr Higgs.'

'Well, it's nothing really. You'll probably laugh when you hear. Quite honestly I was in two minds whether or not to bother you. You see, all Mrs Maugham said was: "It's funny that man suddenly talking about Mr Higgs like that. You know, Ethel, I haven't heard Mr Higgs mentioned for almost thirty years." So I said "Yes", leading her on, you see. "And who was Mr Higgs, dear, thirty years ago?" And she said: "Oh nobody at all. He was just Elizabeth's little friend"!'

'Elizabeth's?'

'Just what I said, Mr Farrel. She got quite impatient with me. "Just someone Elizabeth used to talk to," she said, "when she was three. You know the way children invent things." '

'Like Mambi,' I said, not meaning to say it, since Miss Awpit wouldn't understand.

'Oh dear, Mr Farrel,' said Miss Awpit, 'I knew you'd laugh.'

I left the office and took a taxi all the way home. Elizabeth was in the garden. I sat beside her and I held her hands.

'Look,' I said. 'Let's have a holiday. Let's go away, just the two of us. We need a rest.'

'You're spying on me,' Elizabeth said. 'Which isn't new, I suppose. You've got so mean, darling, ever since you became jealous of poor Mr Higgs. How could you be jealous of a man like Mr Higgs?'

'Elizabeth, I know who Mr Higgs is. I can tell you – '

'There's nothing to be jealous about. All the poor creature does is to ring me up and tell me all the things he read in my diaries the time he came to paint the hall. And then he tries to comfort me about the children. He tells me not to worry about Bridget. But I can't help worrying because I know she's going to have this hard time. She's going to grow big and lumpy, poor little Bridget, and she's not going to be ever able to pass an exam, and in the end she'll go and work in a post office. But Mr Higgs – '

'Let me tell you about Mr Higgs. Let me just remind you.'

'You don't know him, darling. You've never spoken to him. Mr Higgs is very patient, you know. First of all, he did all the talking, and now, you see, he kindly allows me to. Poor Mr Higgs is an inmate of a home. He's an institutionalised person, darling. There's no need to be jealous at all.'

I said nothing. I sat there holding her two hands and looking at her. Her face was just the same; even her eyes betrayed no hint of the confusion that held her. She smiled when she spoke of Mr Higgs. She made a joke, laughing, calling him the housewife's friend.

'It was funny,' she said, 'the first time I saw Christopher as an adult, sitting in a room with that awful woman. She was leaning back in a chair, staring at him and attempting to torture him with words. And then there was Anna, half a mile away across London, in a house in a square. All the lights were on because of the party, and Anna was in that red suit, and she was laughing and saying how she hated Christopher, how she had hated him from the first moment she saw him. And when she said that, I couldn't remember what moment she meant. I couldn't quite remember where it was that Anna and Christopher had met. Well, it goes to show.' Elizabeth paused. 'Well, doesn't it?' she said. 'I mean, imagine my thinking that poor Mr Higgs was evil! The kindest, most long-suffering man that ever walked on two legs. I mean, all I had to do was to remind Mr Higgs that I'd forgotten and Mr Higgs could tell me. "They met in a garden," he could say, "at an ordinary little tea-party." And Bridget was operated on several times, and counted the words in telegrams.'

Elizabeth talked on of the children and of Mr Higgs. I rang up our doctor, and he came, and then a little later my wife was taken from the house. I sat alone with Bridget on my knee until it was time to go and fetch Christopher and Anna.

'Mummy's ill,' I said in the car. 'She's had to go away for a little.' I would tell them the story gradually, and one day perhaps we might visit her and she might still understand who we were. 'Ill?' they said. 'But Mummy's never ill.' I stopped the car by our house, thinking that only death could make the house seem so empty, and thinking too that death was easier to understand. We made tea, I remember, the children and I, not saying very much more.

Going Home

'Mulligatawny soup,' Carruthers said in the dining-car. 'Roast beef, roast potatoes, Yorkshire pudding, mixed vegetables.'

'And madam?' murmured the waiter.

Miss Fanshawe said she'd have the same. The waiter thanked her. Carruthers said:

'Miss Fanshawe'll take a medium dry sherry. Pale ale for me, please.'

The waiter paused. He glanced at Miss Fanshawe, shaping his lips.

'I'm sixteen and a half,' Carruthers said. 'Oh, and a bottle of Beaune. 1962.'

It was the highlight of every term and every holiday for Carruthers, coming like a no-man's-land between the two: the journey with Miss Fanshawe to their different homes. Not once had she officially complained, either to his mother or to the school. She wouldn't do that; it wasn't in Miss Fanshawe to complain officially. And as for him, he couldn't help himself.

'Always Beaune on a train,' he said now, 'because of all the burgundies it travels happiest.'

'Thank you, sir,' the waiter said.

'Thank *you*, old chap.'

The waiter went, moving swiftly in the empty dining-car. The train slowed and then gathered speed again. The fields it passed through were bright with sunshine; the water of a stream glittered in the distance.

'You shouldn't lie about your age,' Miss Fanshawe reproved, smiling to show she hadn't been upset by the lie. But lies like that, she explained, could get a waiter into trouble.

Carruthers, a sharp-faced boy of thirteen, laughed a familiar harsh laugh. He said he didn't like the waiter, a remark that Miss Fanshawe ignored.

'What weather!' she remarked instead. 'Just look at those weeping willows!' She hadn't ever noticed them before, she added, but Carruthers contradicted that, reminding her that she had often before remarked on those weeping willows. She smiled, with false vagueness in her face, slightly shaking her head. 'Perhaps it's just that everything looks so different this lovely summer. What will you do, Carruthers? Your mother took you to Greece last year, didn't she? It's almost a shame to leave England, I always think, when the weather's like this. So green in the long warm days –'

'Miss Fanshawe, why are you pretending nothing has happened?'

'Happened? My dear, what has happened?'

Carruthers laughed again, and looked through the window at cows resting in the shade of an oak-tree. He said, still watching the cows, craning his neck to keep them in view:

'Your mind is thinking about what has happened and all the time you're attempting to make ridiculous conversation about the long warm days. Your heart is beating fast, Miss Fanshawe; your hands are trembling. There are two little dabs of red high up on your cheeks, just beneath your spectacles. There's a pink flush all over your neck. If you were alone, Miss Fanshawe, you'd be crying your heart out.'

Miss Fanshawe, who was thirty-eight, fair-haired and untouched by beauty, said that she hadn't the foggiest idea what Carruthers was talking about. He shook his head, implying that she lied. He said:

'Why are we being served by a man whom neither of us likes when we should be served by someone else? Just look at those weeping willows, you say.'

'Don't be silly, Carruthers.'

'What has become, Miss Fanshawe, of the other waiter?'

'Now please don't start any nonsense. I'm tired and – '

'It was he who gave me a taste for pale ale, d'you remember that? In your company, Miss Fanshawe, on this train. It was he who told us that Beaune travels best. Have a cig, Miss Fanshawe?'

'No, and I wish you wouldn't either.'

'Actually Mrs Carruthers allows me the odd smoke these days. Ever since my thirteenth birthday, May the twenty-sixth. How can she stop me, she says, when day and night she's at it like a factory chimney herself?'

'Your birthday's May the twenty-sixth? I never knew. Mine's two days later.' She spoke hastily, and with an eagerness that was as false as the vague expression her face had borne a moment ago.

'Gemini, Miss Fanshawe.'

'Yes: Gemini. Queen Victoria – '

'The sign of passion. Here comes the interloper.'

The waiter placed sherry before Miss Fanshawe and beer in front of Carruthers. He murmured deferentially, inclining his head.

'We've just been saying,' Carruthers remarked, 'that you're a new one on this line.'

'Newish, sir. A month – no, tell a lie, three weeks yesterday.'

'We knew your predecessor.'

'Oh yes, sir?'

'He used to say this line was as dead as a doornail. Actually, he enjoyed not having anything to do. Remember, Miss Fanshawe?'

Miss Fanshawe shook her head. She sipped her sherry, hoping the waiter would have the sense to go away. Carruthers said:

'In all the time Miss Fanshawe and I have been travelling together there hasn't been a solitary soul besides ourselves in this dining-car.'

The waiter said it hardly surprised him. You didn't get many, he agreed, and added, smoothing the table-cloth, that it would just be a minute before the soup was ready.

'Your predecessor,' Carruthers said, 'was a most extraordinary man.'

'Oh yes, sir?'

'He had the gift of tongues. He was covered in freckles.'

'I see, sir.'

'Miss Fanshawe here had a passion for him.'

The waiter laughed. He lingered for a moment and then, since Carruthers was silent, went away.

'Now look here, Carruthers,' Miss Fanshawe began.

'Don't you think Mrs Carruthers is the most vulgar woman you've ever met?'

'I wasn't thinking of your mother. I will not have you talk like this to the waiter. Please now.'

'She wears a scent called "In Love", by Norman Hartnell. A woman of fifty, as thin as fuse wire. My God!'

'Your mother – '

'My mother doesn't concern you – oh, I agree. Still you don't want to deliver me to the female smelling of drink and tobacco smoke. I always brush my teeth in the lavatory, you know. For your sake, Miss Fanshawe.'

'Please don't engage the waiter in conversation. And please don't tell lies about the waiter who was here before. It's ridiculous the way you go on – '

'You're tired, Miss Fanshawe.'

'I'm always tired at the end of term.'

'That waiter used to say – '

'Oh, for heaven's sake, stop about that waiter!'

'I'm sorry.' He seemed to mean it, but she knew he didn't. And even when he spoke again, when his voice was softer, she knew that he was still pretending. 'What shall we talk about?' he asked, and with a weary cheerfulness she reminded him that she'd wondered what he was going to do in the holidays. He didn't reply. His head was bent. She knew that he was smiling.

'I'll walk beside her,' he said. 'In Rimini and Venice. In Zürich may be. By Lake Lugano. Or the Black Sea. New faces will greet her in an American Bar in Copenhagen. Or near the Spanish Steps – in Babbington's English Tea-Rooms. Or in Bandol or Cassis, the Ritz, the Hotel Excelsior in old Madrid. What shall we talk about, Miss Fanshawe?'

'You could tell me more. Last year in Greece – '

'I remember once we talked about guinea-pigs. I told you how I killed a guinea-pig that Mrs Carruthers gave me. Another time we talked about Rider Minor. D'you remember that?'

'Yes, but let's not – '

'McGullam was unpleasant to Rider Minor in the changing-room. McGullam and Travers went after Rider Minor with a little piece of wood.'

'You told me, Carruthers.'

He laughed.

'When I first arrived at Ashleigh Court the only person who spoke to me was Rider Minor. And of course the Sergeant-Major. The Sergeant-Major told me never to take to cigs. He described the lungs of a friend of his.'

'He was quite right.'

'Yes, he was. Cigs can give you a nasty disease.'

'I wish you wouldn't smoke.'

'I like your hat.'

'Soup, madam,' the waiter murmured. 'Sir.'

'Don't you like Miss Fanshawe's hat?' Carruthers smiled, pointing at Miss Fanshawe, and when the waiter said that the hat was very nice Carruthers asked him his name.

Miss Fanshawe dipped a spoon into her soup. The waiter offered her a roll. His name, he said, was Atkins.

'Are you wondering about us, Mr Atkins?'

'Sir?'

'Everyone has a natural curiosity, you know.'

'I see a lot of people in my work, sir.'

'Miss Fanshawe's an undermatron at Ashleigh Court Preparatory School for Boys. They use her disgracefully at the end of term – patching up clothes so that the mothers won't complain, packing trunks, sorting out laundry. From dawn till midnight Miss Fanshawe's on the trot. That's why she's tired.'

Miss Fanshawe laughed. 'Take no notice of him,' she said. She broke her roll and buttered a piece of it. She pointed at wheat ripening in a field. The harvest would be good this year, she said.

'At the end of each term,' Carruthers went on, 'she has to sit with me on this train because we travel in the same direction. I'm out of her authority really, since the term is over. Still, she has to keep an eye.'

The waiter, busy with the wine, said he understood. He raised his eyebrows at Miss Fanshawe and winked, but she did not encourage this, pretending not to notice it.

'Imagine, Mr Atkins,' Carruthers said, 'a country house in the mock Tudor style, with bits built on to it: a rackety old gymn and an art-room, and changing-rooms that smell of perspiration. There are a hundred and three boys at Ashleigh Court, in narrow iron beds with blue rugs on them, which Miss Fanshawe has to see are all kept tidy. She does other things as well: she wears a white overall and gives out medi-

cines. She pours out cocoa in the dining-hall and at eleven
o'clock every morning she hands each boy four *petit beurre*
biscuits. She isn't allowed to say Grace. It has to be a master
who says Grace: "For what we're about to receive . . ." Or the
Reverend T. L. Edwards, who owns and runs the place,
T.L.E., known to generations as a pervert. He pays boys,
actually.'

The waiter, having meticulously removed a covering of red
foil from the top of the wine-bottle, wiped the cork with a
napkin before attempting to draw it. He glanced quickly at
Miss Fanshawe to see if he could catch her eye in order to put
her at her ease with an understanding gesture, but she appeared to be wholly engaged with her soup.

'The Reverend Edwards is a law unto himself,' Carruthers
said. 'Your predecessor was intrigued by him.'

'Please take no notice of him.' She tried to sound bracing,
looking up suddenly and smiling at the waiter.

'The headmaster accompanied you on the train, did he,
sir?'

'No, no, no, no. The Reverend Edwards was never on this
train in his life. No, it was simply that your predecessor was
interested in life at Ashleigh Court. He would stand there
happily listening while we told him the details: you could say
he was fascinated.'

At this Miss Fanshawe made a noise that was somewhere
between a laugh and a denial.

'You could pour the Beaune now, Mr Atkins,' Carruthers
suggested.

The waiter did so, pausing for a moment, in doubt as to
which of the two he should offer a little of the wine to taste.
Carruthers nodded to him, indicating that it should be he. The
waiter complied and when Carruthers had given his approval
he filled both their glasses and lifted from before them their
empty soup-plates.

'I've asked you not to behave like that,' she said when the waiter had gone.

'Like what, Miss Fanshawe?'

'You know, Carruthers.'

'The waiter and I were having a general conversation. As before, Miss Fanshawe, with the other waiter. Don't you remember? Don't you remember my telling him how I took forty of Hornsby's football cards? And drank the communion wine in the Reverend's cupboard?'

'I don't believe – '

'And I'll tell you another thing. I excused myself into Rider Minor's gum-boots.'

'Please leave the waiter alone. Please let's have no scenes this time, Carruthers.'

'There weren't scenes with the other waiter. He enjoyed everything we said to him. You could see him quite clearly trying to visualise Ashleigh Court, and Mrs Carruthers in her awful clothes.'

'He visualised nothing of the sort. You gave him drink that I had to pay for. He was obliged to listen to your fantasies.'

'He enjoyed our conversation, Miss Fanshawe. Why is it that people like you and I are so unpopular?'

She didn't answer, but sighed instead. He would go on and on, she knew; and there was nothing she could do. She always meant not to protest, but when it came to the point she found it hard to sit silent, mile after mile.

'You know what I mean, Miss Fanshawe? At Ashleigh Court they say you have an awkward way of walking. And I've got no charm: I think that's why they don't much like me. But how for God's sake could any child of Mrs Carruthers have charm?'

'Please don't speak of your mother like that – '

'And yet men fancy her. Awful men arrive at week-ends, as

keen for sex as the Reverend Edwards is. "Your mother's a most elegant woman," a hard-eyed lecher remarked to me last summer, in the Palm Court of a Greek hotel.'

'Don't drink too much of that wine. The last time – '

' "You're staggering," she said the last time. I told her I had 'flu. She's beautiful, I dare say, in her thin way. D'you think she's beautiful?'

'Yes, she is.'

'She has men all over the place. Love flows like honey while you make do with waiters on a train.'

'Oh, don't be so *silly*, Carruthers.'

'She snaps her fingers and people come to comfort her with lust. A woman like that's never alone. While you – '

'Will you please stop talking about me!'

'You have a heart in your breast like anyone else, Miss Fanshawe.'

The waiter, arrived again, coughed. He leaned across the table and placed a warmed plate in front of Miss Fanshawe and a similar one in front of Carruthers. There was a silence while he offered Miss Fanshawe a silver-plated platter with slices of roast beef on it and square pieces of Yorkshire pudding. In the silence she selected what she wanted, a small portion, for her appetite on journeys with Carruthers was never great. Carruthers took the rest. The waiter offered vegetables.

'Miss Fanshawe ironed that blouse at a quarter to five this morning,' Carruthers said. 'She'd have ironed it last night if she hadn't been so tired.'

'A taste more carrots, sir?'

'I don't like carrots, Mr Atkins.'

'Peas, sir?'

'Thank you. She got up from her small bed, Mr Atkins, and her feet were chilly on the linoleum. She shivered, Mr. Atkins, as she slipped her night-dress off. She stood there naked,

thinking of another person. What became of your predecessor?'

'I don't know, sir. I never knew the man at all. All right for
you, madam?'

'Yes, thank you.'

'He used to go back to the kitchen, Mr Atkins, and tell the
cook that the couple from Ashleigh Court were on the train
again. He'd lean against the sink while the cook poked about
among his pieces of meat, trying to find us something to eat.
Your predecessor would suck at the butt of a cig and occasionally he'd lift a can of beer to his lips. When the cook
asked him what the matter was he'd say it was fascinating, a
place like Ashleigh Court with boys running about in grey
uniforms and an undermatron watching her life go by.'

'Excuse me, sir.'

The waiter went. Carruthers said:

' "She makes her own clothes," the other waiter told the
cook. "She couldn't give a dinner party the way the young
lad's mother could. She couldn't chat to this person and that,
moving about among décolleté women and outshining every
one of them." Why is she an undermatron at Ashleigh
Court Preparatory School for Boys, owned and run by
the Reverend T. L. Edwards, known to generations as a
pervert?'

Miss Fanshawe, with an effort, laughed. 'Because she's
qualified for nothing else,' she lightly said.

'I think that freckled waiter was sacked because he interfered with the passengers. "Vegetables?" he suggested, and
before he could help himself he put the dish of cauliflowers on
the table and put his arms around a woman. "All tickets
please," cried the ticket-collector and then he saw the waiter
and the woman on the floor. You can't run a railway company
like that.'

'Carruthers – '

'Was it something like that, Miss Fanshawe? D'you think?'

'Of course it wasn't.'

'Why not?'

'Because you've just made it up. The man was a perfectly ordinary waiter on this train.'

'That's not true.'

'Of course it is.'

'I love this train, Miss Fanshawe.'

'It's a perfectly ordinary – '

'Of course it isn't.'

Carruthers laughed gaily, waiting for the waiter to come back, eating in silence until it was time again for their plates to be cleared away.

'Trifle, madam?' the waiter said. 'Cheese and biscuits?'

'Just coffee, please.'

'Sit down, why don't you, Mr Atkins? Join us for a while.'

'Ah no, sir, no.'

'Miss Fanshawe and I don't have to keep up appearances on your train. D'you understand that? We've been keeping up appearances for three long months at Ashleigh Court and it's time we stopped. Shall I tell you about my mother, Mr Atkins?'

'Your mother, sir?'

'Carruthers – '

'In 1960, when I was three, my father left her for another woman: she found it hard to bear. She had a lover at the time, a Mr Tennyson, but even so she found it hard to forgive my father for taking himself off.'

'I see, sir.'

'It was my father's intention that I should accompany him to his new life with the other woman, but when it came to the point the other woman decided against that. Why should she

be burdened with my mother's child? she wanted to know:
you can see her argument, Mr Atkins.'

'I must be getting on now, sir.'

'So my father arranged to pay my mother an annual sum, in
return for which she agreed to give me house room. I go with
her when she goes on holiday to a smart resort. My father's a
thing of the past. What d'you think of all that, Mr Atkins?
Can you visualise Mrs Carruthers at a resort? She's not at all
like Miss Fanshawe.'

'I'm sure she's not –'

'Not at all.'

'Please let go my sleeve, sir.'

'We want you to sit down.'

'It's not my place, sir, to sit down with the passengers in
the dining-car.'

'We want to ask you if you think it's fair that Mrs Carruthers should round up all the men she wants while Miss
Fanshawe has only the furtive memory of a waiter on a train, a
man who came to a sticky end, God knows.'

'Stop it!' cried Miss Fanshawe. 'Stop it! Stop it! Let go his
jacket and let him go away –'

'I have things to do, sir.'

'He smelt of fried eggs, a smell that still comes back to her
at night.'

'You're damaging my jacket. I must ask you to release me
at once.'

'Are you married, Mr Atkins?'

'Carruthers!' Her face was crimson and her neck blotched
with a flushing that Carruthers had seen before. 'Carruthers,
for heaven's sake behave yourself!'

'The Reverend Edwards isn't married, as you might guess,
Mr Atkins.'

The waiter tried to pull his sleeve out of Carruthers'
grasp, panting a little from embarrassment and from the

effort. 'Let go my jacket!' he shouted. 'Will you let me go!'

Carruthers laughed, but did not release his grasp. There was a sound of ripping as the jacket tore.

'Miss Fanshawe'll stitch it for you,' Carruthers said at once, and added more sharply when the waiter raised a hand to strike him: 'Don't do that, please. Don't threaten a passenger, Mr Atkins.'

'You've ruined this jacket. You bloody little – '

'Don't use language in front of the lady.' He spoke quietly, and to a stranger entering the dining-car at that moment it might have seemed that the waiter was in the wrong, that the torn sleeve of his jacket was the just result of some attempted insolence on his part.

'You're mad,' the waiter shouted at Carruthers, his face red and sweating in his anger. 'That child's a raving lunatic,' he shouted as noisily at Miss Fanshawe.

Carruthers was humming a hymn. 'Lord, dismiss us,' he softly sang, 'with Thy blessing.'

'Put any expenses on my bill,' whispered Miss Fanshawe. 'I'm very sorry.'

'Ashleigh Court'll pay,' Carruthers said, not smiling now, his face all of a sudden as sombre as the faces of the other two.

No one spoke again in the dining-car. The waiter brought coffee, and later presented a bill.

The train stopped at a small station. Three people got out as Miss Fanshawe and Carruthers moved down the corridor to their compartment. They walked in silence, Miss Fanshawe in front of Carruthers, he drawing his right hand along the glass of the windows. There'd been an elderly man in their compartment when they'd left it: to Miss Fanshawe's relief he was no longer there. Carruthers slid the door across. She found her book and opened it at once.

'I'm sorry,' he said when she'd read a page.

She turned the page, not looking up, not speaking.

'I'm sorry I tormented you,' he said after another pause.

She still did not look up, but spoke while moving her eyes along a line of print. 'You're always sorry,' she said.

Her face and neck were still hot. Her fingers tightly held the paper-backed volume. She felt taut and rigid, as though the unpleasantness in the dining-car had coiled some part of her up. On other journeys she'd experienced a similar feeling, though never as unnervingly as she experienced it now. He had never before torn a waiter's clothing.

'Miss Fanshawe?'

'I want to read.'

'I'm not going back to Ashleigh Court.'

She went on reading and then, when he'd repeated the statement, she slowly raised her head. She looked at him and thought, as she always did when she looked at him, that he was in need of care. There was a barrenness in his sharp face; his eyes reflected the tang of a bitter truth.

'I took the Reverend Edwards' cigarette-lighter. He's told me he won't have me back.'

'That isn't true, Carruthers – '

'At half-past eleven yesterday morning I walked into the Reverend's study and lifted it from his desk. Unfortunately he met me on the way out. Ashleigh Court, he said, was no place for a thief.'

'But why? Why did you do such a silly thing?'

'I don't know. I don't know why I do a lot of things. I don't know why I pretend you were in love with a waiter. This is the last horrid journey for you, Miss Fanshawe.'

'So you won't be coming back – '

'The first time I met you I was crying in a dormitory. D'you remember that? Do you, Miss Fanshawe?'

'Yes, I remember.'

' "Are you missing your mummy?" you asked me, and I said no. I was crying because I'd thought I'd like Ashleigh Court. I'd thought it would be heaven, a place without Mrs Carruthers. I didn't say that; not then.'

'No.'

'You brought me to your room and gave me liquorice all-sorts. You made me blow my nose. You told me not to cry because the other boys would laugh at me. And yet I went on crying.'

In the fields men were making hay. Children in one field waved at the passing train. The last horrid journey, she thought; she would never see the sharp face again, nor the bitterness reflected in the eyes. He'd wept, as others occasionally had to; she'd been, for a moment, a mother to him. His own mother didn't like him, he'd later said – on a journey – because his features reminded her of his father's features.

'I don't know why I'm so unpleasant, Miss Fanshawe. The Reverend stared at me last night and said he had a feeling in his bones that I'd end up badly. He said I was a useless sort of person, a boy he couldn't ever rely on. I'd let him down, he said, thieving and lying like a common criminal. "I'm chalking you up as a failure for Ashleigh," he said. "I never had much faith in you, Carruthers." '

'He's a most revolting man.' She said it without meaning to, and yet the words came easily from her. She said it because it didn't matter any more, because he wasn't going to return to Ashleigh Court to repeat her words.

'You were kind to me that first day,' Carruthers said. 'I liked that holy picture in your room. You told me to look at it, I remember. Your white overall made a noise when you walked.'

She wanted to say that once she had told lies too, that at St Monica's School for Girls she'd said the King, the late George VI, had spoken to her when she stood in the crowd. She wanted to say that she'd stolen two rubbers from Elsie Grantham and poured ink all over the face of a clock, and had never been found out.

She closed her eyes, longing to speak, longing above all things in the world to fill the compartment with the words that had begun, since he'd told her, to pound in her brain. All he'd ever done on the train was to speak a kind of truth about his mother and the school, to speak in their no-man's-land, as now and then he'd called it. Tormenting her was incidental; she knew it was. Tormenting her was just by chance, a thing that happened.

His face was like a flint. No love had ever smoothed his face, and while she looked at it she felt, unbearably now, the urge to speak as he had spoken, so many times. He smiled at her. 'Yes,' he said. 'The Reverend's a most revolting man.'

'I'm thirty-eight,' she said and saw him nod as though, precisely, he'd guessed her age a long time ago. 'Tonight we'll sit together in the bungalow by the sea where my parents live and they'll ask me about the term at Ashleigh. "Begin at the beginning, Beryl," my mother'll say and my father'll set his deaf-aid. "The first day? What happened the first day, Beryl?" And I shall tell them. "Speak up," they'll say, and in a louder voice I'll tell them about the new boys, and the new members of staff. Tomorrow night I'll tell some more, and on and on until the holidays and the term are over. "Wherever are you going?" my mother'll say when I want to go out for a walk. "Funny time," she'll say, "to go for a walk." No matter what time it is.'

He turned his head away, gazing through the window as earlier she had gazed through the window of the dining-car, in awkwardness.

'I didn't fall in love with a freckled waiter,' he heard her say, 'but God knows the freckled waiter would have done.'

He looked at her again. 'I didn't mean, Miss Fanshawe – '

'If he had suddenly murmured while offering me the vegetables I'd have closed my eyes with joy. To be desired, to be
desired in any way at all . . .'

'Miss Fanshawe – '

'Born beneath Gemini, the sign of passion, you said. Yet
who wants to know about passion in the heart of an ugly
undermatron? Different for your mother, Carruthers: your
mother might weep and tear away her hair, and others would
weep in pity because of all her beauty. D'you see, Carruthers?
D'you understand me?'

'No, Miss Fanshawe. No, I don't think I do. I'm not
as – '

'There was a time one Christmas, after a party in the staff-
room, when a man who taught algebra took me up to a loft,
the place where the Wolf Cubs meet. We lay down on an old
tent, and then suddenly this man was sick. That was in 1954.
I didn't tell them that in the bungalow: I've never told them
the truth. I'll not say tonight, eating cooked ham and salad,
that the boy I travelled with created a scene in the dining-car,
or that I was obliged to pay for damage to a waiter's
clothes.'

'Shall we read now, Miss Fanshawe?'

'How can we read, for God's sake, when we have other
things to say? What was it like, d'you think, on all the
journeys to see you so unhappy? Yes, you'll probably go to the
bad. He's right: you have the look of a boy who'll end like
that. The unhappy often do.'

'Unhappy, Miss Fanshawe? Do I seem unhappy?'

'Oh, for God's sake, tell the truth! The truth's been there
between us on all our journeys. We've looked at one another
and seen it, over and over again.'

'Miss Fanshawe, I don't understand you. I promise you, I
don't understand – '

'How could I ever say in that bungalow that the algebra

teacher laid me down on a tent and then was sick? Yet I can say it now to you, a thing I've never told another soul.'

The door slid open and a woman wearing a blue hat, a smiling, red-faced woman, asked if the vacant seats were taken. In a voice that amazed Carruthers further Miss Fanshawe told her to go away.

'Well, really!' said the woman.

'Leave us in peace, for God's sake!' shrieked Miss Fanshawe, and the woman, her smile all gone, backed into the corridor. Miss Fanshawe rose and shut the door again.

'It's different in that bungalow by the sea,' she then quite quietly remarked, as though no red-faced woman had backed away astonished. 'Not like an American Bar in Copenhagen or the Hotel Excelsior in Madrid. Along the walls the coloured geese stretch out their necks, the brass is polished and in its place. Inch by inch oppression fills the air. On the chintz covers in the sitting-room there's a pattern of small wild roses, the stair-carpet's full of fading lupins. *To W. J. Fanshawe on the occasion of his retirement*, says the plaque on the clock on the sitting-room mantelpiece, *from his friends in the Prudential*. The clock has a gold-coloured face and four black pillars of ersatz material: it hasn't chimed since 1958. At night, not far away, the sea tumbles about, seeming too real to be true. The seagulls shriek when I walk on the beach, and when I look at them I think they're crying out with happiness.'

He began to speak, only to speak her name, for there was nothing else he could think of to say. He changed his mind and said nothing at all.

'Who would take me from it now? Who, Carruthers? What freckled waiter or teacher of algebra? What assistant in a shop, what bank-clerk, postman, salesman of cosmetics? They see a figure walking in the wind, discs of thick glass on her eyes, breasts as flat as paper. Her movement's awkward, they say, and when she's close enough they raise their hats and turn away: they mean no harm.'

'I see,' he said.

'In the bungalow I'm frightened of both of them: all my life I've been afraid of them. When I was small and wasn't pretty they made the best of things, and longed that I should be clever instead. "Read to us, Beryl," my father would say, rubbing his hands together when he came in from his office. And I would try to read. "Spell *merchant*," my father would urge as though his life depended upon it, and the letters would become jumbled in my mind. Can you see it, Carruthers, a child with glasses and an awkward way of walking and two angry figures, like vultures, unforgiving? They'd exchange a glance, turning their eyes away from me as though in shame. "Not bright," they'd think. "Not bright, to make up for the other." '

'How horrid, Miss Fanshawe.'

'No, no. After all, was it nice for them that their single child should be a gawky creature who blushed when people spoke? How could they help themselves, any more than your mother can?'

'Still, my mother – '

' "Going to the pictures?" he said the last time I was home. "What on earth are you doing that for?" And then she got the newspaper which gave the programme that was showing. "*Tarzan and the Apemen*", she read out. "My dear, at your age!" I wanted to sit in the dark for an hour or two, not having to talk about the term at Ashleigh Court. But how could I say that to them? I felt the redness coming in my face. "For children surely," my father said, "a film like that." And then he laughed. "Beryl's made a mistake," my mother explained, and she laughed too.'

'And did you go, Miss Fanshawe?'

'Go?'

'To *Tarzan and the Apemen*?'

'No, I didn't go. I don't possess courage like that: as soon as I enter the door of the bungalow I can feel their disappointment all round me and I'm terrified all over again. I've thought of not going back but I haven't even the courage for that: they've sucked everything out of me. D'you understand?'

'Well – '

'Why is God so cruel that we leave the ugly school and travel together to a greater ugliness when we could travel to something nice?'

'Nice, Miss Fanshawe? *Nice*?'

'You know what I mean, Carruthers.'

He shook his head. Again he turned it away from her, looking at the window, wretchedly now.

'Of course you do,' her voice said, 'if you think about it.'

'I really – '

'Funny our birthdays being close together!' Her mood was gayer suddenly. He turned to look at her and saw she was smiling. He smiled also.

'I've dreamed this train went on for ever,' she said, 'on and on until at last you stopped engaging passengers and waiters in fantastic conversation. "I'm better now," you said, and then you went to sleep. And when you woke I gave you liquorice allsorts. "I understand," I said: "it doesn't matter." '

'I know I've been very bad to you, Miss Fanshawe. I'm sorry – '

'I've dreamed of us together in my parents' bungalow, of my parents dead and buried and your thin mother gone too, and Ashleigh Court a thing of the nightmare past. I've seen us walking over the beaches together, you growing up, me cooking for you and mending your clothes and knitting you pullovers. I've brought you fresh brown eggs and made you apple dumplings. I've watched you smile over crispy chops.'

'Miss Fanshawe – '

'I'm telling you about a dream in which ordinary things are marvellous. Tea tastes nicer and the green of the grass is a fresher green than you've ever noticed before, and the air is rosy, and happiness runs about. I would take you to a cinema on a Saturday afternoon and we would buy chips on the way home and no one would mind. We'd sit by the fire and say whatever we liked to one another. And you would no longer steal things or tell lies, because you'd have no need to. Nor would you mock an unpretty undermatron.'

'Miss Fanshawe, I – I'm feeling tired. I think I'd like to read.'

'Why should they have a child and then destroy it? Why should your mother not love you because your face is like your father's face?'

'My mother – '

'Your mother's a disgrace,' she cried in sudden, new emotion. 'What life is it for a child to drag around hotels and lovers, a piece of extra luggage, alone, unloved?'

'It's not too bad. I get quite used to it – '

'Why can He not strike them dead?' she whispered. 'Why can't He make it possible? By some small miracle, surely to God?'

He wasn't looking at her. He heard her weeping and listened to the sound, not knowing what to do.

'You're a sorrowful mess, Carruthers,' she whispered. 'Yet you need not be.'

'Please. Please, Miss Fanshawe – '

'You'd be a different kind of person and so would I. You'd have my love, I'd care about the damage that's been done to you. You wouldn't come to a bad end: I'd see to that.'

He didn't want to turn his head again. He didn't want to see her, but in spite of that he found himself looking at her.

She, too, was gazing at him, tears streaming on her cheeks. He spoke slowly and with as much firmness as he could gather together.

'What you're saying doesn't make any sense, Miss Fanshawe.'

'The waiter said that you were mad. Am I crazy too? Can people go mad like that, for a little while, on a train? Out of loneliness and locked-up love? Or desperation?'

'I'm sure it has nothing to do with madness, Miss Fanshawe – '

'The sand blows on to my face, and sometimes into my eyes. In my bedroom I shake it from my sandals. I murmur in the sitting-room. "Really, Beryl," my mother says, and my father sucks his breath in. On Sunday mornings we walk to church, all three of us. I go again, on my own, to Evensong: I find that nice. And yet I'm glad when it's time to go back to Ashleigh Court. Are you ever glad, Carruthers?'

'Sometimes I have been. But not always. Not always at all. I – '

' "Let's go for a stroll," the algebra teacher said. His clothes were stained with beer. "Let's go up there," he said. "It's nice up there." And in the pitch dark we climbed to the loft where the Wolf Cubs meet. He lit his cigarette-lighter and spread the tent out. I don't mind what happens, I thought. Anything is better than nothing happening all my life. And then the man was sick.'

'You told me that, Miss Fanshawe.'

' "You're getting fat," my mother might have said. "Look at Beryl, Dad, getting fat." And I would try to laugh. "A drunk has made me pregnant," I might have whispered in the bungalow, suddenly finding the courage for it. And they would look at me and see that I was happy, and I would kneel by my bed and pour my thanks out to God, every night of my life, while waiting for my child.' She paused and gave a little laugh. 'They are waiting for us, those people, Carruthers.'

'Yes.'

'The clock on the mantelpiece still will not chime. "Cocoa," my mother'll say at half-past nine. And when they die it'll be too late.'

He could feel the train slowing, and sighed within him, a gesture of thanksgiving. In a moment he would walk away from her: he would never see her again. It didn't matter what had taken place, because he wouldn't ever see her again. It didn't matter, all she had said, or all he had earlier said himself.

He felt sick in his stomach after the beer and the wine and the images she'd created of a life with her in a seaside bungalow. The food she'd raved about would be appalling; she'd never let him smoke. And yet, in the compartment now, while they were still alone, he was unable to prevent himself from feeling sorry for her. She was right when she spoke of her craziness: she wasn't quite sane beneath the surface, she was all twisted up and unwell.

'I'd better go and brush my teeth,' he said. He rose and lifted his overnight case from the rack.

'Don't go,' she whispered.

His hand, within the suitcase, had already grasped a blue sponge-bag. He released it and closed the case. He stood, not wishing to sit down again. She didn't speak. She wasn't looking at him now.

'Will you be all right, Miss Fanshawe?' he said at last, and repeated the question when she didn't reply. 'Miss Fanshawe?'

'I'm sorry you're not coming back to Ashleigh, Carruthers. I hope you have a pleasant holiday abroad.'

'Miss Fanshawe, will you – '

'I'll stay in England, as I always do.'

'We'll be there in a moment,' he said.

'I hope you won't go to the bad, Carruthers.'

They passed by houses now; the backs of houses, suburban gardens. Posters advertised beer and cigarettes and furniture. *Geo. Small. Seeds*, one said.

'I hope not, too,' he said.

'Your mother's on the platform. Where she always stands.'

'Good-bye, Miss Fanshawe.'

'Good-bye, Carruthers. Good-bye.'

Porters stood waiting. Mail-bags were on a trolley. A voice called out, speaking of the train they were on.

She didn't look at him. She wouldn't lift her head: he knew the tears were pouring on her cheeks now, more than before, and he wanted to say, again, that he was sorry. He shivered standing in the doorway, looking at her, and then he closed the door and went away.

She saw his mother greet him, smiling, in red as always she was. They went together to collect his luggage from the van, out of her sight, and when the train pulled away from the station she saw them once again, the mother speaking and Carruthers just as he always was, laughing his harsh laugh.

An Evening
with John Joe Dempsey

In Keogh's one evening Mr Lynch talked about the Piccadilly tarts, and John Joe Dempsey on his fifteenth birthday closed his eyes and travelled into a world he did not know. 'Big and little,' said Mr Lynch, 'winking their eyes at you and enticing you up to them. Wetting their lips,' said Mr Lynch, 'with the ends of their tongues.'

John Joe Dempsey had walked through the small town that darkening autumn evening, from the far end of North Street where he and his mother lived, past the cement building that was the Coliseum Cinema, past Kelly's Atlantic Hotel and a number of shops that were now closed for the day. 'Go to Keogh's like a good boy,' his mother had requested, for as well as refreshments and stimulants Keogh's public house sold a variety of groceries: it was for a pound of rashers that Mrs Dempsey had sent her son.

'Who is there?' Mr Lynch had called out from the licensed area of the premises, hearing John Joe rapping with a coin to draw attention to his presence. A wooden partition with panes of glass in the top half of it rose to a height of eight feet between the grocery and the bar. 'I'm here for rashers,' John Joe explained through the pebbly glass. 'Isn't it a stormy evening, Mr Lynch? I'm fifteen today, Mr Lynch.'

There was a silence before a door in the partition opened and Mr Lynch appeared. 'Fifteen?' he said. 'Step in here, boy, and have a bottle of stout.'

John Joe protested that he was too young to drink a bottle

of stout and then said that his mother required the rashers immediately. 'Mrs Keogh's gone out to Confession,' Mr Lynch said. 'I'm in charge till her ladyship returns.'

John Joe, knowing that Mr Lynch would not be prepared to set the bacon machine in action, stepped into the bar to await the return of Mrs Keogh, and Mr Lynch darted behind the counter for two bottles of stout. Having opened and poured them, he began about the Piccadilly tarts.

'You've got to an age,' Mr Lynch said, 'when you would have to be advised. Did you ever think in terms of emigration to Britain?'

'I did not, Mr Lynch.'

'I would say you were right to leave it alone, John Joe. Is that the first bottle of stout you ever had?'

'It is, Mr Lynch.'

'A bottle of stout is an acquired taste. You have to have had a dozen bottles or maybe more before you do get an urge for it. With the other matter it's different.'

Mr Lynch, now a large, fresh-faced man of fifty-five who was never seen without a brown hat on his head, had fought for the British Army during the Second World War, which was why one day in 1947 he had found himself, with companions, in Piccadilly Circus. As he listened, John Joe recalled that he'd heard boys at the Christian Brothers' referring to some special story that Mr Lynch confidentially told to those whom he believed would benefit from it. He had heard boys sniggering over this story, but he had never sought to discover its content, not knowing it had to do with Piccadilly tarts.

'There was a fellow by the name of Baker,' said Mr Lynch, 'who'd been telling us that he knew the ropes. Baker was a London man. He knew the places, he was saying, where he could find the glory girls, but when it came to the point of the matter, John Joe, we hardly needed a guide.'

Because, explained Mr Lynch, the tarts were everywhere. They stood in the doorways of shops showing off the stature of their legs. Some would speak to you, Mr Lynch said, addressing you fondly and stating their availability. Some had their bosoms cocked out so that maybe they'd strike a passing soldier and entice him away from his companions. 'I'm telling you this, John Joe, on account of your daddy being dead. Are you fancying that stout?'

John Joe nodded his head. Thirteen years ago his father had fallen to his death from a scaffold, having been by trade a builder. John Joe could not remember him, although he knew what he had looked like from a photograph that was always on view on the kitchen dresser. He had often wondered what it would be like to have that bulky man about the house, and more often still he listened to his mother talking about him. But John Joe didn't think about his father now, in spite of Mr Lynch's reference to him: keen to hear more about the women of Piccadilly, he asked what had happened when Mr Lynch and his companions finished examining them in the doorways.

'I saw terrible things in Belgium,' replied Mr Lynch meditatively. 'I saw a Belgian woman held down on the floor while four men satisfied themselves on her. No woman could be the same after that. Combat brings out the brute in a man.'

'Isn't it shocking what they'd do, Mr Lynch? Wouldn't it make you sick?'

'If your daddy was alive today, he would be telling you a thing or two in order to prepare you for your manhood and the temptations in another country. Your mother wouldn't know how to tackle a matter like that, nor would Father Ryan, nor the Christian Brothers. Your daddy might have sat you down in this bar and given you your first bottle of stout. He might have told you about the facts of life.'

'Did one of the glory girls entice yourself, Mr Lynch?'

'Listen to me, John Joe.' Mr Lynch regarded his companion through small blue eyes, both of which were slightly bloodshot. He lit a cigarette and drew on it before continuing. Then he said: 'Baker had the soldiers worked up with his talk of the glory girls taking off their togs. He used to describe the motion of their haunches. He used to lie there at night in the dug-out describing the private areas of the women's bodies. When the time came we went out with Baker and Baker went up to the third one he saw and said could the six of us make arrangements with her. He was keen to strike a bargain because we had only limited means on account of having remained in a public house for four hours. Myself included, we were in an intoxicated condition.'

'What happened, Mr Lynch?'

'I would not have agreed to an arrangement like that if it hadn't been for drink. I was a virgin boy, John Joe. Like yourself.'

'I'm that way, certainly, Mr Lynch.'

'We marched in behind the glory girl, down a side-street. "Bedad, you're fine men," she said. We had bottles of beer in our pockets. "We'll drink that first," she said, "before we get down to business." '

John Joe laughed. He lifted the glass of stout to his lips and took a mouthful in a nonchalant manner, as though he'd been drinking stout for half a lifetime and couldn't do without it.

'Aren't you the hard man, Mr Lynch!' he said.

'You've got the wrong end of the stick,' replied Mr Lynch sharply. 'What happened was, I had a vision on the street. Amn't I saying to you those girls are no good to any man? I had a vision of the Virgin when we were walking along.'

'How d'you mean, Mr Lynch?'

'There was a little statue of the Holy Mother in my bedroom at home, a little special one my mother gave me at the occasion of my First Communion. It came into my mind, John Joe, when the six of us were with the glory girl. As soon as the glory girl said we'd drink the beer before we got down to business I saw the statue of the Holy Mother, as clear as if it was in front of me.'

John Joe, who had been anticipating an account of the soldiers' pleasuring, displayed disappointment. Mr Lynch shook his head at him.

'I was telling you a moral story,' he said reprovingly. 'The facts of life is one thing, John Joe, but keep away from dirty women.'

John Joe was a slight youth, pale of visage, as his father had been, and with large, awkward hands that bulged in his trouser pockets. He had no friends at the Christian Brothers' School he attended, being regarded there, because of his private nature and lack of interest in either scholastic or sporting matters, as something of an oddity – an opinion that was strengthened by his association with an old, simple-minded dwarf called Quigley, with whom he was regularly to be seen collecting minnows in a jam-jar or walking along the country roads. In class at the Christian Brothers' John Joe would drift into a meditative state and could not easily be reached. 'Where've you gone, boy?' Brother Leahy would whisper, standing above him. His fingers would reach out for a twist of John Joe's scalp, and John Joe would rise from the ground with the Brother's thumb and forefinger tightening the short hairs of his neck, yet seeming not to feel the pain. It was only when the other hand of Brother Leahy gripped one of his ears that he would return to the classroom with a cry of anguish, and the boys and Brother Leahy would laugh. 'What'll we make of you?' Brother Leahy would murmur, returning to the blackboard while John Joe rubbed his head and his ear.

'There is many a time in the years afterwards,' said Mr Lynch ponderously, 'when I have gone through in my mind that moment in my life. I was tempted in bad company: I was two minutes off damnation.'

'I see what you mean, Mr Lynch.'

'When I came back to West Cork my mother asked me was I all right. Well, I was, I said. "I had a bad dream about you," my mother said. "I had a dream one night your legs were on fire." She looked at my legs, John Joe, and to tell you the truth of it she made me slip down my britches. "There's no harm there," she said. 'Twas only afterwards I worked it out: she had that dream in the very minute I was standing on the street seeing the vision in my brain. What my mother dreamed, John Joe, was that I was licked by the flames of Hell. She was warned that time, and from her dream she sent out a message that I was to receive a visit from the little statue. I'm an older man now, John Joe, but that's an account I tell to every boy in this town that hasn't got a father. That little story is an introduction to life and manhood. Did you enjoy the stout?'

'The stout's great stuff, Mr Lynch.'

'No drink you can take, John Joe, will injure you the way a dirty woman would. You might go to twenty million Confessions and you wouldn't relieve your heart and soul of a dirty woman. I didn't marry myself, out of shame for the memory of listening to Baker making that bargain. Will we have another bottle?'

John Joe, wishing to hear in further detail the bargain that Baker had made, said he could do with another drop. Mr Lynch directed him to a crate behind the counter. 'You're acquiring the taste,' he said.

John Joe opened and poured the bottles. Mr Lynch offered him a cigarette, which he accepted. In the Coliseum Cinema he had seen Piccadilly Circus, and in one particular film there had been Piccadilly tarts, just as Mr Lynch described, loitering in doorways provocatively. As always, coming out of the Coliseum, it had been a little strange to find himself again among small shops that sold clothes and hardware and meat, among vegetable shops and tiny confectioners' and tobacconists' and public houses. For a few minutes after the Coliseum's programme was over the three streets of the town were busy with people going home, walking or riding on bicycles, or driving cars to distant farms, or going towards the chip-shop. When he was alone, John Joe usually leaned against the window of a shop to watch the activity before returning home himself; when his mother accompanied him to the pictures they naturally went home at once, his mother chatting on about the film they'd seen.

'The simple thing is, John Joe, keep a certain type of thought out of your mind.'

'Thought, Mr Lynch?'

'Of a certain order.'

'Ah, yes. Ah, definitely, Mr Lynch. A young fellow has no time for that class of thing.'

'Live a healthy life.'

'That's what I'm saying, Mr Lynch.'

'If I hadn't had a certain type of thought I wouldn't have found myself on the street that night. It was Baker who called them the glory girls. It's a peculiar way of referring to the sort they are.'

'Excuse me, Mr Lynch, but what kind of an age would they be?'

'They were all ages, boy. There were nippers and a few more of them had wrinkles on the flesh of their faces. There were some who must have weighed fourteen stone and others you could put in your pocket.'

'And was the one Baker made the bargain with a big one or a little one?'

'She was medium-sized, boy.'

'And had she black hair, Mr Lynch?'

'As black as your boot. She had a hat on her head that was a disgrace to the nation, and black gloves on her hands. She was carrying a little umbrella.'

'And, Mr Lynch, when your comrades met up with you again, did they tell you a thing at all?'

Mr Lynch lifted the glass to his lips. He filled his mouth with stout and savoured the liquid before allowing it to pass into his stomach. He turned his small eyes on the youth and regarded him in silence.

'You have pimples on your chin,' said Mr Lynch in the end. 'I hope you're living a clean life, now.'

'A healthy life, Mr Lynch.'

'It is a question your daddy would ask you. You know what I mean? There's some lads can't leave it alone.'

'They go mad in the end, Mr Lynch.'

'There was fellows in the British Army that couldn't leave it alone.'

'They're a heathen crowd, Mr Lynch. Isn't there terrible reports in the British papers?'

'The body is God-given. There's no need to abuse it.'

'I've never done that thing, Mr Lynch.'

'I couldn't repeat,' said Mr Lynch, 'what the glory girl said when I walked away.'

John Joe, whose classroom meditations led him towards the naked bodies of women whom he had seen only clothed and whose conversations with the town's idiot, Quigley, were of an obscene nature, said it was understandable that Mr Lynch could not repeat what the girl had said to him. A girl like that, he added, wasn't fit to be encountered by a decent man.

'Go behind the counter,' said Mr Lynch, 'and lift out two more bottles.'

John Joe walked to the crate of stout bottles. 'I looked in at a window one time,' Quigley had said to him, 'and I saw Mrs Nugent resisting her husband. Nugent took no notice of her at all; he had the clothes from her body like you'd shell a pod of peas.'

'I don't think Baker lived,' said Mr Lynch. 'He'd be dead of disease.'

'I feel sick to think of Baker, Mr Lynch.'

'He was like an animal.'

All the women of the town – and most especially Mrs Taggart, the wife of a postman – John Joe had kept company with in his imagination. Mrs Taggart was a well-built woman, a foot taller than himself, a woman with whom he had seen himself walking in the fields on the Ballydehob road. She had found him alone and had said that she was crossing the fields to where her husband had fallen into a bog-hole, and would he be able to come with her? She had a heavy, chunky face and a wide neck on which the fat lay in encircling folds, like a fleshy necklace. Her hair was grey and black, done up in hairpins. 'I was only codding you,' she said when they reached the side of a secluded hillock. 'You're a good-looking fellow, Dempsey.' On the side of the hillock, beneath a tree, Mrs Taggart commenced to rid herself of her outer garments, remarking that it was hot. 'Slip out of that little jersey,' she urged. 'Wouldn't it bake you today?' Sitting beside him in her underclothes, Mrs Taggart asked him if he liked sunbathing. She drew her petticoat up so that the sun might reach the tops of her legs. She asked him to put his hand on one of her legs so that he could feel the muscles; she was a strong woman, she said, and added that the strongest muscles she possessed were the muscles of her stomach. 'Wait till I show you,' said Mrs Taggart.

On other occasions he found himself placed differently with Mrs Taggart: once, his mother had sent him round to her house to inquire if she had any eggs for sale and after she had put a dozen eggs in a basket Mrs Taggart asked him if he'd take a look at a thorn in the back of her leg. Another time he was passing her house and he heard her crying out for help. When he went inside he discovered that she had jammed the door of the bathroom and couldn't get out. He managed to release the door and when he entered the bathroom he discovered that Mrs Taggart was standing up in the bath, seeming to have forgotten that she hadn't her clothes on.

Mrs Keefe, the wife of a railway official, another statuesque woman, featured as regularly in John Joe's imagination, as did a Mrs O'Brien, a Mrs Summers, and a Mrs Power. Mrs Power kept a bread-shop, and a very pleasant way of passing the time when Brother Leahy was talking was to walk into Mrs Power's shop and hear her saying that she'd have to slip into the bakery for a small pan loaf and would he like to accompany her? Mrs Power wore a green overall with a belt that was tied in a knot at the front. In the bakery, while they were chatting, she would attempt to untie the belt but always found it difficult. 'Can you aid me?' Mrs Power would ask and John Joe would endeavour to loose the knot that lay tight against Mrs Power's stout stomach. 'Where've you gone, boy?' Brother Leahy's voice would whisper over and over again like a familiar incantation and John Joe would suddenly shout, realising he was in pain.

'It was the end of the war,' said Mr Lynch. 'The following morning myself and a gang of the other lads got a train up to Liverpool, and then we crossed back to Dublin. There was a priest on the train and I spoke to him about the whole thing. Every man was made like that, he said to me, only I was lucky to be rescued in the nick of time. If I'd have taken his name I'd have sent him the information about my mother's dream. I think that would have interested him, John Joe. Wouldn't you think so?'

'Ah, it would of course.'

'Isn't it a great story, John Joe?'

'It is, Mr Lynch.'

'Don't forget it ever, boy. No man is clear of temptations. You don't have to go to Britain to get temptations.'

'I understand you, Mr Lynch.'

Quigley had said that one night he looked through a window and saw the Protestant clergyman, the Reverend Johnson, lying on the floor with his wife. There was another time, he said, that he observed Hickey the chemist being coaxed from an arm-chair by certain activities on the part of Mrs Hickey. Quigley had climbed up on the roof of a shed and had seen Mrs Swanton being helped out of her stockings by Swanton, the builder and decorator. Quigley's voice might continue for an hour and a half, for there was hardly a man and his wife in the town whom he didn't claim to have observed in intimate circumstances. John Joe did not ever ask how, when there was no convenient shed to climb on to, the dwarf managed to make his way to so many exposed upstairs windows. Such a question would have been wholly irrelevant.

At Mass, when John Joe saw the calves of women's legs stuck out from the kneeling position, he experienced an excitement that later bred new fantasies within him. 'That Mrs Dwyer,' he would say to the old dwarf, and the dwarf would reply that one night in February he had observed Mrs Dwyer preparing herself for the return of her husband from a County Council meeting in Cork. From the powdered body of Mrs Dwyer, as described by Quigley, John Joe would move to an image that included himself. He saw himself pushing open the hall-door of the Dwyers' house, having been sent to the house with a message from his mother, and hearing Mrs Dwyer's voice calling out, asking him to come upstairs. He stood on a landing and Mrs Dwyer came to him with a red coat wrapped round her to cover herself up. He could smell the powder on her body; the coat kept slipping from her shoulders. 'I have some magazines for your mother,' she said. 'They're inside the bedroom.' He went and sat on the bed while she collected a pile of magazines. She sat beside him then, drawing his attention to a story here and there that might be of particular interest to his mother. Her knee was pressed against his, and in a moment she put her arm round his shoulders and said he was a good-looking lad. The red coat fell back on to the bed when Mrs Dwyer took one of John Joe's large hands and placed it on her stomach. She then suggested, the evening being hot, that he should take off his jersey and his shirt.

Mrs Keogh, the owner of the public house, had featured also in John Joe's imagination and in the conversation of the old dwarf. Quigley had seen her, he said, a week before her husband died, hitting her husband with a length of wire because he would not oblige her with his attentions. 'Come down to the cellar,' said Mrs Keogh while Brother Leahy scribbled on the blackboard. 'Come down to the cellar, John Joe, and help me with a barrel.' He descended the cellar steps in front of her and when he looked back he saw her legs under her dark mourning skirt. 'I'm lost these days,' she said, 'since Mr Keogh went on.' They moved the barrel together and then Mrs Keogh said it was hot work and it would be better if they took off their jerseys. 'Haven't you the lovely arms!' she said as they rolled the barrel from one corner of the cellar to another. 'Will we lie down here for a rest?'

'We'll chance another bottle,' suggested Mr Lynch. 'Is it going down you all right?'

'My mother'll be waiting for the rashers, Mr Lynch.'

'No rasher can be cut, boy, till Mrs Keogh returns. You could slice your hand off on an old machine like that.'

'We'll have one more so.'

At the Christian Brothers', jokes were passed about that concerned grisly developments in the beds of freshly wedded couples, or centred around heroes who carried by chance strings of sausages in their pockets and committed unfortunate errors when it came to cutting one off for the pan. Such yarns, succeeding generally, failed with John Joe, for they seemed to him to be lacking in quality.

'How's your mammy?' Mr Lynch asked, watching John Joe pouring the stout.

'Ah, she's all right. I'm only worried she's waiting on the rashers – '

'There's honour due to a mother.'

John Joe nodded. He held the glass at an angle to receive dark foaming liquid, as Mr Lynch had shown him. Mr Lynch's mother, now seventy-nine, was still alive. They lived together in a house which Mr Lynch left every morning in order to work in the office of a meal business and which he left every evening in order to drink bottles of stout in Keogh's. The bachelor state of Mr Lynch was one which John Joe wondered if he himself would one day share. Certainly, he saw little attraction in the notion of marriage, apart from the immediate physical advantage. Yet Mr Lynch's life did not seem enviable either. Often on Sunday afternoons he observed the meal clerk walking slowly with his mother on his arm, seeming as lost in gloom as the married men who walked beside women pushing prams. Quigley, a bachelor also, was a happier man than Mr Lynch. He lived in what amounted to a shed at the bottom of his niece's garden. Food was carried to him, but there were few, with the exception of John Joe, who lingered in his company. On Sundays, a day which John Joe, like Mr Lynch, spent with his mother, Quigley walked alone.

'When'll you be leaving the Brothers?' Mr Lynch asked.

'In June.'

'And you'll be looking out for employment, John Joe?'

'I was thinking I'd go into the sawmills.'

Mr Lynch nodded approvingly. 'There's a good future in the sawmills,' he said. 'Is the job fixed up?'

'Not yet, Mr Lynch. They might give me a trial.'

Mr Lynch nodded again, and for a moment the two sat in silence. John Joe could see from the thoughtful way Mr Lynch was regarding his stout that there was something on his mind. Hoping to hear more about the Piccadilly tarts, John Joe patiently waited.

'If your daddy was alive,' said Mr Lynch eventually, 'he might mention this to you, boy.'

He drank more stout and wiped the foam from his lips with the back of his hand. 'I often see you out with Quigley. Is it a good thing to be spending your hours with a performer like that? Quigley's away in the head.'

'You'd be sorry for the poor creature, Mr Lynch.'

Mr Lynch said there was no need to feel sorry for Quigley, since that was the way Quigley was made. He lit another cigarette. He said:

'Maybe they would say to themselves up at the sawmills that you were the same way as Quigley. If he keeps company with Quigley, they might say, aren't they two of a kind?'

'Ah, I don't think they'd bother themselves, Mr Lynch. Sure, if you do the work well what would they have to complain of?'

'Has the manager up there seen you out with Quigley and the jam-jars?'

'I don't know, Mr Lynch.'

'Everything I'm saying to you is for your own good in the future. Do you understand that? If I were in your shoes I'd let Quigley look after himself.'

For years his mother had been saying the same to him. Brother Leahy had drawn him aside one day and had pointed out that an elderly dwarf wasn't a suitable companion for a young lad, especially since the dwarf was not sane. 'I see you took no notice of me,' Brother Leahy said six months later. 'Tell me this, young fellow-me-lad, what kind of a conversation do you have with old Quigley?' They talked, John Joe said, about trees and the flowers in the hedgerows. He liked to listen to Quigley, he said, because Quigley had acquired a knowledge of such matters. 'Don't tell me lies,' snapped Brother Leahy, and did not say anything else.

Mrs Keogh returned from Confession. She came breathlessly into the bar, with pink cheeks, her ungloved hands the colour of meat. She was a woman of advanced middle age, a rotund woman who approached the proportions that John Joe most admired. She wore spectacles and had grey hair that was now a bit windswept. Her hat had blown off on the street, she said: she'd nearly gone mad trying to catch it. 'Glory be to God,' she cried when she saw John Joe. 'What's that fellow doing with a bottle of stout?'

'We had a man-to-man talk,' explained Mr Lynch. 'I started him off on the pleasures of the bottle.'

'Are you mad?' shouted Mrs Keogh with a loud laugh. 'He's under age.'

'I came for rashers,' said John Joe. 'A pound of green rashers, Mrs Keogh. The middle cut.'

'You're a shocking man,' said Mrs Keogh to Mr Lynch. She threw off her coat and hat. 'Will you pour me a bottle,' she asked, 'while I attend to this lad? Finish up that now, Mr Dempsey.'

She laughed again. She went away and they heard from the grocery the sound of the bacon machine.

John Joe finished his stout and stood up.

'Good-night, Mr Lynch.'

'Remember about Quigley like a good fellow. When the day will come that you'll want to find a girl to marry, she might be saying you were the same type as Quigley. D'you understand me, John Joe?'

'I do, Mr Lynch.'

He passed through the door in the partition and watched

Mrs Keogh slicing the bacon. He imagined her, as Quigley had said he'd seen her, belabouring her late husband with a length of wire. He imagined her as he had seen her himself, taking off her jersey because it was hot in the cellar, and then unzipping her green tweed skirt.

'I've sliced it thin,' she said. 'It tastes better thin, I think.'

'It does surely, Mrs Keogh.'

'Are you better after your stout? Don't go telling your mammy now.' Mrs Keogh laughed again, revealing long, crowded teeth. She weighed the bacon and wrapped it, munching a small piece of lean. 'If there's parsley in your mammy's garden,' she advised, 'chew a bit to get the smell of the stout away, in case she'd be cross with Mr Lynch. Or a teaspoon of tea-leaves.'

'There's no parsley, Mrs Keogh.'

'Wait till I get you the tea then.'

She opened a packet of tea and poured some on to the palm of his hand. She told him to chew it slowly and thoroughly and to let the leaves get into all the crevices of his mouth. She fastened the packet again, saying that no one would miss the little she'd taken from it. 'Four and two for the rashers,' she said.

He paid the money, with his mouth full of dry tea-leaves. He imagined Mrs Keogh leaning on her elbows on the counter and asking him if he had a kiss for her at all, calling him Mr Dempsey. He imagined her face stuck out towards his and her mouth open, displaying the big teeth, and her tongue damping her lips as the tongues of the Piccadilly tarts did, according to Mr Lynch. With the dryness in his own mouth and a gathering uneasiness in his stomach, his lips would go out to hers and he would taste her saliva.

'Good-night so, Mrs Keogh.'

'Good-night, Mr Dempsey. Tell your mother I was asking for her.'

He left the public house. The wind which had dislodged Mrs Keogh's hat felt fresh and cold on his face. The pink wash on a house across the street seemed pinker than it had seemed before, the ground moved beneath his feet, the street lighting seemed brighter. Youths and girls stood outside the illuminated windows of the small sweet-shops, waiting for the Coliseum to open. Four farmers left Regan's public house and mounted four bicycles and rode away, talking loudly. *Your Murphy Dealer* announced a large coloured sign in the window of a radio shop. Two boys that he had known at school came out of a shop eating biscuits from a paper bag. 'How're you, John Joe?' one of them said. 'How's Quigley these days?' They had left the school now: one of them worked in Kilmartin's the hardware's, the other in the Courthouse. They were wearing blue serge suits; their hair had been combed with care, and greased to remain tidy. They would go to the Coliseum, John Joe guessed, and sit behind two girls, giggling and whispering during the programme. Afterwards they would follow the girls for a little while, pretending to have no interest in them; they would buy chips in the chip-shop before they went home.

Thursday, Friday, Saturday, announced the sign outside the Coliseum: *The Rains Came.* As John Joe read them, the heavy black letters shifted, moving about on green paper that flapped in the wind, fixed with drawing-pins to an unpainted board. Mr Daly, the owner of the grey Coliseum, arrived on his bicycle and unlocked his property. *Sunday Only: Spencer Tracy in Boom Town.* In spite of the sickness in his stomach and the unpleasant taste of tea-leaves in his mouth, John Joe felt happy and was aware of an inclination to loiter for a long time outside the cinema instead of returning to his mother.

'It's great tonight, John Joe,' Mr Daly said. 'Are you coming in?'

John Joe shook his head. 'I have to bring rashers home to my mother,' he said. He saw Mrs Daly approaching with a torch, for the small cinema was a family business. Every night and twice on Sundays, Mr Daly sold the tickets while his wife showed the customers to their seats. 'I looked in a window one time,' Quigley had said, 'and she was trying to put on her underclothes. Daly was standing in his socks.'

A man and a girl came out of a sweet-shop next to the cinema, the girl with a box of Urney chocolates in her hand. She was thanking the man for them, saying they were lovely. 'It's a great show tonight, John Joe,' Mrs Daly said, repeating the statement of her husband, repeating what she and he said every day of their lives. John Joe wagged his head at her. It looked a great show definitely, he said. He imagined her putting on her underclothes. He imagined her one night, unable because of a cold to show the customers to their seats, remaining at home in bed while her husband managed as best he could. 'I made a bit of bread for Mrs Daly,' his mother said. 'Will you carry it down to her, John Joe?' He rang the bell and waited until she came to the door with a coat over her night-dress. He handed her the bread wrapped in creased brown paper and she asked him to step into the hall out of the wind. 'Will you take a bottle, John Joe?' Mrs Daly said. He followed her into the kitchen, where she poured them each a glass of stout. 'Isn't it shocking hot in here?' she said. She took off her coat and sat at the kitchen table in her night-dress. 'You're a fine young fellow,' she said, touching his hand with her fingers.

John Joe walked on, past Riordan's the draper's and Kelly's Atlantic Hotel. A number of men were idling outside the entrance to the bar, smoking cigarettes, one of them leaning on a bicycle. 'There's a dance in Clonakilty,' a tall man said. 'Will we drive over to that?' The others took no notice of this suggestion. They were talking about the price of turkeys.

'How're you, John Joe?' shouted a red-haired youth who worked in the sawmills. 'Quigley was looking for you.'

'I was up in Keogh's for my mother.'

'You're a decent man,' said the youth from the sawmills, going into the bar of Kelly's Hotel.

At the far end of North Street, near the small house where he lived with his mother, he saw Quigley waiting for him. Once he had gone to the Coliseum with Quigley, telling his mother he was going with Kinsella, the boy who occupied the desk next to his at the Christian Brothers'. The occasion, the first and only time that Quigley had visited the Coliseum, had not been a success. Quigley hadn't understood what was happening and had become frightened. He'd begun to mutter and kick the seats in front of him. 'Take him off out of here,' Mr Daly had whispered, flashing his wife's torch. 'He'll bring the house down.' They had left the cinema after only a few minutes and had gone instead to the chip-shop.

'I looked in a window last night,' said Quigley now, hurrying to his friend's side, 'and, God, I saw a great thing.'

'I was drinking stout with Mr Lynch in Keogh's,' said John Joe. He might tell Quigley about the glory girls that Mr Lynch had advised him against, and about Baker who had struck a bargain with one of them, but it wouldn't be any use because Quigley never listened. No one held a conversation with Quigley: Quigley just talked.

'It was one o'clock in the morning,' said Quigley. His voice continued while John Joe opened the door of his mother's house and closed it behind him. Quigley would wait for him in the street and later on they'd perhaps go down to the chip-shop together.

'John Joe, where've you been?' demanded his mother,

coming into the narrow hall from the kitchen. Her face was red from sitting too close to the range, her eyes had anger in them. 'What kept you, John Joe?'

'Mrs Keogh was at Confession.'

'What's that on your teeth?'

'What?'

'You've got dirt on your teeth.'

'I'll brush them then.'

He handed her the rashers. They went together to the kitchen, which was a small, low room with a flagged floor and a dresser that reached to the ceiling. On this, among plates and dishes, was the framed photograph of John Joe's father.

'Were you out with Quigley?' she asked, not believing that Mrs Keogh had kept him waiting for more than an hour.

He shook his head, brushing his teeth at the sink. His back was to her, and he imagined her distrustfully regarding him, her dark eyes gleaming with a kind of jealousy, her small wiry body poised as if to spring on any lie he should utter. Often he felt when he spoke to her that for her the words came physically from his lips, that they were things she could examine after he'd ejected them, in order to assess their truth.

'I talked to Mr Lynch,' he said. 'He was looking after the shop.'

'Is his mother well?'

'He didn't say.'

'He's very good to her.'

She unwrapped the bacon and dropped four rashers on to a pan that was warming on the range. John Joe sat down at the kitchen table. The feeling of euphoria that had possessed him outside the Coliseum was with him no longer; the floor was steady beneath his chair.

'They're good rashers,' his mother said.

'Mrs Keogh cut them thin.'

'They're best thin. They have a nicer taste.'

'Mrs Keogh said that.'

'What did Mr Lynch say to you? Didn't he mention the old mother?'

'He was talking about the war he was in.'

'It nearly broke her heart when he went to join it.'

'It was funny all right.'

'We were a neutral country.'

Mr Lynch would be still sitting in the bar of Keogh's. Every night of his life he sat there with his hat on his head, drinking bottles of stout. Other men would come into the bar and he would discuss matters with them and with Mrs Keogh. He would be drunk at the end of the evening. John Joe wondered if he chewed tea so that the smell of the stout would not be detected by his mother when he returned to her. He would return and tell her some lies about where he had been. He had joined the British Army in order to get away from her for a time, only she'd reached out to him from a dream.

'Lay the table, John Joe.'

He put a knife and a fork for each of them on the table, and found butter and salt and pepper. His mother cut four pieces of griddle bread and placed them to fry on the pan. 'I looked in a window one time,' said the voice of Quigley, 'and Mrs Sullivan was caressing Sullivan's legs.'

'We're hours late with the tea,' his mother said. 'Are you starving, pet?'

'Ah, I am, definitely.'

'I have nice fresh eggs for you.'

It was difficult for her sometimes to make ends meet. He knew it was, yet neither of them had ever said anything. When he went to work in the sawmills it would naturally be easier, with a sum each week to add to the pension.

She fried the eggs, two for him and one for herself. He watched her basting them in her expert way, intent upon what she was doing. Her anger was gone, now that he was safely in the kitchen, waiting for the food she cooked. Mr Lynch would have had his tea earlier in the evening, before he went down to Keogh's. 'I'm going out for a long walk,' he probably said to his mother, every evening after he'd wiped the egg from around his mouth.

'Did he tell you an experience he had in the war?' his mother asked, placing the plate of rashers, eggs and fried bread in front of him. She poured boiling water into a brown enamel tea-pot and left it on the range to draw.

'He told me about a time they were attacked by the Germans,' John Joe said. 'Mr Lynch was nearly killed.'

'She thought he'd never come back.'

'Oh, he came back all right.'

'He's very good to her now.'

When Brother Leahy twisted the short hairs on his neck and asked him what he'd been dreaming about he usually said he'd been working something out in his mind, like a long division sum. Once he said he'd been trying to translate a sentence into Irish, and another time he'd said he'd been solving a puzzle that had appeared in the *Sunday Independent*. Recalling Brother Leahy's face, he ate the fried food. His mother repeated that the eggs were fresh. She poured him a cup of tea.

'Have you homework to do?'

He shook his head, silently registering that lie, knowing that there was homework to be done, but wishing instead to accompany Quigley to the chip-shop.

'Then we can listen to the wireless,' she said.

'I thought maybe I'd go out for a walk.'

Again the anger appeared in her eyes. Her mouth tightened, she laid down her knife and fork.

'I thought you'd stop in, John Joe,' she said, 'on your birthday.'

'Ah, well now – '

'I have a little surprise for you.'

She was telling him lies, he thought, just as he had told her
lies. She began to eat again, and he could see in her face a
reflection of the busyness that had developed in her mind.
What could she find to produce as a surprise? She had given
him that morning a green shirt that she knew he'd like because
he liked the colour. There was a cake that she'd made, some of
which they'd have when they'd eaten what was in front of
them now. He knew about this birthday cake because he had
watched her decorating it with hundreds and thousands: she
couldn't suddenly say it was a surprise.

'When I've washed the dishes,' she said, 'we'll listen to the
wireless and we'll look at that little thing I have.'

'All right,' he said.

He buttered bread and put a little sugar on the butter,
which was a mixture he liked. She brought the cake to the
table and cut them each a slice. She said she thought the
margarine you got nowadays was not as good as margarine in
the past. She turned the wireless on. A woman was singing.

'Try the cake now,' she said. 'You're growing up, John
Joe.'

'Fifteen.'

'I know, pet.'

Only Quigley told the truth, he thought. Only Quigley was
honest and straightforward and said what was in his mind.
Other people told Quigley to keep that kind of talk to himself
because they knew it was the truth, because they knew they
wanted to think the thoughts that Quigley thought. 'I looked
in a window,' Quigley had said to him when he was nine years
old, the first time he had spoken to him, 'I saw a man and
woman without their clothes on.' Brother Leahy would wish
to imagine as Quigley imagined, and as John Joe imagined
too. And what did Mr Lynch think about when he walked in

gloom with his mother on a Sunday? Did he dream of the medium-sized glory girl he had turned away from because his mother had sent him a Virgin Mary from her dreams? Mr Lynch was not an honest man. It was a lie when he said that shame had kept him from marrying. It was his mother who prevented that, with her dreams of legs on fire and her First Communion statues. Mr Lynch had chosen the easiest course: bachelors might be gloomy on occasion, but they were untroubled men in some respects, just as men who kept away from the glory girls were.

'Isn't it nice cake?'

'Yes,' he said.

'This time next year you'll be in the sawmills.'

'I will.'

'It's good there's work for you.'

'Yes.'

They ate the two pieces of cake and then she cleared away the dishes and put them in the sink. He sat on a chair by the range. The men who'd been loitering outside Kelly's Hotel might have driven over to Clonakilty by now, he thought. They'd be dancing with girls and later they'd go back to their wives and say they'd been somewhere else, playing cards together in Kelly's maybe. Within the grey cement of the Coliseum the girl who'd brought the box of chocolates would be eating them, and the man who was with her would be wanting to put his hands on her.

Why couldn't he say to his mother that he'd drunk three bottles of stout in Keogh's? Why couldn't he say he could see the naked body of Mrs Taggart? Why hadn't he said to Mr Lynch that he should tell the truth about what was in his mind, like Quigley told the truth? Mr Lynch spent his life returning to the scenes that obsessed him, to the Belgian woman on the ground and the tarts of Piccadilly Circus. Yet he spoke of them only to fatherless boys, because it was the only excuse for mentioning them that he'd been able to think up.

'I have this for you,' she said.

She held towards him an old fountain-pen that had belonged to his father, a pen he had seen before. She had taken it from a drawer of the dresser, where it was always kept.

'I thought you could have it on your fifteenth birthday,' she said.

He took it from her, a black and white pen that hadn't been filled with ink for thirteen years. In the drawer of the dresser there was a pipe of his father's, and a tie-pin and a bunch of keys and a pair of bicycle clips. She had washed and dried the dishes, he guessed, racking her mind to think of something she might offer him as the surprise she'd invented. The pen was the most suitable thing; she could hardly offer him the bicycle clips.

'Wait till I get you the ink,' she said, 'and you can try it out.' From the wireless came the voice of a man advertising household products. 'Bird's Custard,' urged the voice gently, 'and Bird's Jelly De Luxe.'

He filled the pen from the bottle of ink she handed him. He sat down at the kitchen table again and tried the nib out on the piece of brown paper that Mrs Keogh had wrapped round the rashers and which his mother had neatly folded away for further use.

'Isn't it great it works still?' she said. 'It must be a good pen.'

It's hot in here, he wrote. *Wouldn't you take off your jersey?*

'That's a funny thing to write,' his mother said.

'It came into my head.'

They didn't like him being with Quigley because they knew what Quigley talked about when he spoke the truth. They were jealous because there was no pretence between Quigley and himself. Even though it was only Quigley who talked, there was an understanding between them: being with Quigley was like being alone.

'I want you to promise me a thing,' she said, 'now that you're fifteen.'

He put the cap on the pen and bundled up the paper that had contained the rashers. He opened the top of the range and dropped the paper into it. She would ask him to promise not to hang about with the town's idiot any more. He was a big boy now, he was big enough to own his father's fountain-pen and it wasn't right that he should be going out getting minnows in a jam-jar with an elderly affected creature. It would go against his chances in the sawmills.

He listened to her saying what he had anticipated she would say. She went on talking, telling him about his father and the goodness there had been in his father before he fell from the scaffold. She took from the dresser the framed photograph that was so familiar to him and she put it into his hands, telling him to look closely at it. It would have made no difference, he thought, if his father had lived. His father would have been like the others; if ever he'd have dared to mention the nakedness of Mrs Taggart his father would have beaten him with a belt.

'I am asking you for his sake,' she said, 'as much as for my own and for yours, John Joe.'

He didn't understand what she meant by that, and he didn't inquire. He would say what she wished to hear him say, and he would keep his promise to her because it would be the easiest thing to do. Quigley wasn't hard to push away, you could tell him to get away like you'd tell a dog. It was funny that they should think that it would make much difference to him now, at this stage, not having Quigley to listen to.

'All right,' he said.

'You're a good boy, John Joe. Do you like the pen?'

'It's a lovely pen.'

'You might write better with that one.'

She turned up the volume of the wireless and together they sat by the range, listening to the music. To live in a shed like Quigley did would not be too bad: to have his food carried down through a garden by a niece, to go about the town in that special way, alone with his thoughts. Quigley did not have to pretend to the niece who fed him. He didn't have to say he'd been for a walk when he'd been drinking in Keogh's or that he'd been playing cards with men when he'd been dancing in Clonakilty. Quigley didn't have to chew tea and keep quiet. Quigley talked; he said the words he wanted to say. Quigley was lucky being how he was.

'I will go to bed now,' he said eventually.

They said good-night to one another, and he climbed the stairs to his room. She would rouse him in good time, she called after him. 'Have a good sleep,' she said.

He closed the door of his room and looked with affection at his bed, for in the end there was only that. It was a bed that, sagging, held him in its centre and wrapped him warmly. There was ornamental brass-work at the head but not at the foot, and on the web of interlocking wire the hair mattress was thin. John Joe shed his clothes, shedding also the small town and his mother and Mr Lynch and the fact that he, on his fifteenth birthday, had drunk his first stout and had chewed tea. He entered his iron bed and the face of Mr Lynch passed from his mind and the voices of boys telling stories about freshly married couples faded away also. No one said to him now that he must not keep company with a crazed dwarf. In his iron bed, staring into the darkness, he made of the town what he wished to make of it, knowing that he would not be drawn away from his dreams by the tormenting fingers of a Christian Brother. In his iron bed he heard again only the voice of the town's idiot and then that voice, too, was there no more. He travelled alone, visiting in his way the women of the town, adored and adoring, more alive in his bed than ever he was at the Christian Brothers' School, or in the grey Coliseum, or in the chip-shop, or Keogh's public house, or his mother's kitchen, more alive than ever he would be at the sawmills. In his bed he entered a paradise: it was grand being alone.

The Mark-2 Wife

Standing alone at the Lowhrs' party, Anna Mackintosh thought about her husband Edward, establishing him clearly for this purpose in her mind's eye. He was a thin man, forty-one years of age, with fair hair that was often untidy. In the seventeen years they'd been married he had changed very little: he was still nervous with other people, and smiled in the same abashed way, and his face was still almost boyish. She believed she had failed him because he had wished for children and she had not been able to supply any. She had, over the years, developed a nervous condition about this fact and in the end, quite some time ago now, she had consulted a psychiatrist, a Dr Abbatt, at Edward's pleading.

In the Lowhrs' rich drawing-room, its walls and ceiling gleaming with a metallic surface of ersatz gold, Anna listened to dance music coming from a tape-recorder and continued to think about her husband. In a moment he would be at the party too, since they had agreed to meet there, although by now it was three-quarters of an hour later than the time he had stipulated. The Lowhrs were people he knew in a business way, and he had said he thought it wise that he and Anna should attend this gathering of theirs. She had never met them before, which made it more difficult for her, having to wait about, not knowing a soul in the room. When she thought about it she felt hard done by, for although Edward was kind to her and always had been, it was far from considerate to be as late as this. Because of her nervous condition she felt afraid and had developed a sickness in her stomach. She looked at her watch and sighed.

People arrived, some of them kissing the Lowhrs, others nodding and smiling. Two dark-skinned maids carried trays of drinks among the guests, offering them graciously and murmuring thanks when a glass was accepted. 'I'll be there by half-past nine,' Edward had said that morning. 'If you don't turn up till ten you won't have to be alone at all.' He had kissed her after that, and had left the house. I'll wear the blue, she thought, for she liked the colour better than any other: it suggested serenity to her, and the idea of serenity, especially as a quality in herself, was something she valued. She had said as much to Dr Abbatt, who had agreed that serenity was something that should be important in her life.

An elderly couple, tall twig-like creatures of seventy-five, a General Ritchie and his wife, observed the lone state of Anna Mackintosh and reacted in different ways. 'That woman seems out of things,' said Mrs Ritchie. 'We should go and talk to her.'

But the General gave it as his opinion that there was something the matter with this woman who was on her own. 'Now, don't let's get involved,' he rather tetchily begged. 'In any case she doesn't look in the mood for chat.'

His wife shook her head. 'Our name is Ritchie,' she said to Anna, and Anna, who had been looking at the whisky in her glass, lifted her head and saw a thin old woman who was as straight as a needle, and behind her a man who was thin also but who stooped a bit and seemed to be cross. 'He's an old soldier,' said Mrs Ritchie. 'A general that was.'

Strands of white hair trailed across the pale dome of the old man's head. He had sharp eyes, like a terrier's, and a grey moustache. 'It's not a party I care to be at,' he muttered, holding out a bony hand. 'My wife's the one for this.'

Anna said who she was and added that her husband was late and that she didn't know the Lowhrs.

'We thought it might be something like that,' said Mrs Ritchie. 'We don't know anyone either, but at least we have one another to talk to.' The Lowhrs, she added, were an awfully nice, generous couple.

'We met them on a train in Switzerland,' the General murmured quietly.

Anna glanced across the crowded room at the people they spoke of. The Lowhrs were wholly different in appearance from the Ritchies. They were small and excessively fat, and they both wore glasses and smiled a lot. Like two balls, she thought.

'My husband knows them in a business way,' she said. She looked again at her watch: the time was half-past ten. There was a silence, and then Mrs Ritchie said:

'They invited us to two other parties in the past. It's very kind, for we don't give parties ourselves any more. We live a quiet sort of life now.' She went on talking, saying among other things that it was pleasant to see the younger set at play. When she stopped, the General added:

'The Lowhrs feel sorry for us, actually.'

'They're very kind,' his wife repeated.

Anna had been aware of a feeling of uneasiness the moment she'd entered the golden room, and had Edward been with her she'd have wanted to say that they should turn round and go away again. The uneasiness had increased whenever she'd noted the time, and for some reason these old people for whom the Lowhrs were sorry had added to it even more. She would certainly talk this over with Dr Abbatt, she decided, and then, quite absurdly, she felt an urge to telephone Dr Abbatt and tell him at once about the feeling she had. She closed her eyes, thinking that she would keep them like that for only the slightest moment so that the Ritchies wouldn't notice and think it odd. While they were still closed she heard Mrs Ritchie say:

'Are you all right, Mrs Mackintosh?'

She opened her eyes and saw that General Ritchie and his wife were examining her face with interest. She imagined them wondering about her, a woman of forty whose husband was an hour late. They'd be thinking, she thought, that the absent husband didn't have much of a feeling for his wife to be as careless as that. And yet, they'd probably think, he must have had a feeling for her once since he had married her in the first place.

'It's just,' said Mrs Ritchie, 'that I had the notion you were going to faint.'

The voice of Petula Clark came powerfully from the tape-recorder. At one end of the room people were beginning to dance in a casual way, some still holding their glasses in their hands.

'The heat could have affected you,' said the General, bending forward so that his words would reach her.

Anna shook her head. She tried to smile, but the smile failed to materialise. She said:

'I never faint, actually.'

She could feel a part of herself attempting to bar from her mind the entry of unwelcome thoughts. Hastily she said, unable to think of anything better:

'My husband's really frightfully late.'

'You know,' said General Ritchie, 'it seems to me we met your husband here.' He turned to his wife. 'A fair-haired man – he said his name was Mackintosh. Is your husband fair, Mrs Mackintosh?'

'Of course,' cried Mrs Ritchie. 'Awfully nice.'

Anna said that Edward was fair. Mrs Ritchie smiled at her husband and handed him her empty glass. He reached out for Anna's. She said:

'Whisky, please. By itself.'

'He's probably held up in bloody traffic,' said the General before moving off.

'Yes, probably that,' Mrs Ritchie said. 'I do remember him well, you know.'

'Edward did come here before. I had a cold.'

'Completely charming. We said so afterwards.'

One of the dark-skinned maids paused with a tray of drinks. Mrs Ritchie explained that her husband was fetching some. 'Thank you, madam,' said the dark-skinned maid, and the General returned.

'It isn't the traffic,' Anna said rather suddenly and loudly. 'Edward's not held up like that at all.'

The Ritchies sipped their drinks. They can sense I'm going to be a nuisance, Anna thought. 'I'm afraid it'll be boring,' he had said. 'We'll slip away at eleven and have dinner in Charlotte Street.' She heard him saying it now, quite distinctly. She saw him smiling at her.

'I get nervous about things,' she said to the Ritchies. 'I worry unnecessarily. I try not to.'

Mrs Ritchie inclined her head in a sympathetic manner; the General coughed. There was a silence and then Mrs Ritchie spoke about episodes in their past. Anna looked at her watch and saw that it was five to eleven. 'Oh God,' she said.

The Ritchies asked her again if she was all right. She began to say she was but she faltered before the sentence was complete, and in that moment she gave up the struggle. What was the point, she thought, of exhausting oneself being polite and making idle conversation when all the time one was in a frightful state?

'He's going to be married again,' she said quietly and evenly. 'His Mark-2 wife.'

She felt better at once. The sickness left her stomach; she drank a little whisky and found its harsh taste a comfort.

'Oh, I'm terribly sorry,' said Mrs Ritchie.

Anna had often dreamed of the girl. She had seen her, dressed all in purple, with slim hips and a purple bow in her black hair. She had seen the two of them together in a speed-boat, the beautiful young creature laughing her head off like a figure in an advertisement. She had talked for many hours to Dr Abbatt about her, and Dr Abbatt had made the point that the girl was simply an obsession. 'It's just a little nonsense,' he had said to her kindly, more than once. Anna knew in her calmer moments that it was just a little nonsense, for Edward was always kind and had never ceased to say he loved her. But in bad moments she argued against that conclusion, remind-ing herself that other kind men who said they loved their wives often made off with something new. Her own marriage being childless would make the whole operation simpler.

'I hadn't thought it would happen at a party,' Anna said to the Ritchies. 'Edward has always been decent and con-siderate. I imagined he would tell me quietly at home, and comfort me. I imagined he would be decent to the end.'

'You and your husband are not yet separated then?' Mrs Ritchie inquired.

'This is the way it is happening,' Anna repeated. 'D'you understand? Edward is delayed by his Mark-2 wife because she insists on delaying him. She's demanding that he should make his decision and afterwards that he and she should come to tell me, so that I won't have to wait any more. You under-stand,' she repeated, looking closely from one face to the other, 'that this isn't Edward's doing?'

'But, Mrs Mackintosh – '

'I have a woman's intuition about it. I have felt my woman's intuition at work since the moment I entered this room. I know precisely what's going to happen.'

Often, ever since the obsession had begun, she had won-dered if she had any rights at all. Had she rights in the matter, she had asked herself, since she was running to fat and could supply no children? The girl would repeatedly give birth and everyone would be happy, for birth was a happy business. She had suggested to Dr Abbatt that she probably hadn't any rights, and for once he had spoken to her sternly. She said it now to the Ritchies, because it didn't seem to matter any more what words were spoken. On other occasions, when she was at home, Edward had been late and she had sat and waited for him, pretending it was a natural thing for him to be late. And when he arrived her fears had seemed absurd.

'You understand?' she said to the Ritchies.

The Ritchies nodded their thin heads, the General embarrassed, his wife concerned. They waited for Anna to speak. She said:

'The Lowhrs will feel sorry for me, as they do for you. "This poor woman," they'll cry, "left all in the lurch at our party! What a ghastly thing!" I should go home, you know, but I haven't even the courage for that.'

'Could we help at all?' asked Mrs Ritchie.

'You've been married all this time and not come asunder. Have you had children, Mrs Ritchie?'

Mrs Ritchie replied that she had had two boys and a girl. They were well grown up by now, she explained, and among them had provided her and the General with a dozen grandchildren.

'What did you think of my husband?'

'Charming, Mrs Mackintosh, as I said.'

'Not the sort of man who'd mess a thing like this up? You thought the opposite, I'm sure: that with bad news to break he'd choose the moment elegantly. Once he would have.'

'I don't understand,' protested Mrs Ritchie gently, and the General lent his support to that with a gesture.

'Look at me,' said Anna. 'I've worn well enough. Neither I nor Edward would deny it. A few lines and flushes, fatter and coarser. No one can escape all that. Did you never feel like a change, General?'

'A change?'

'I have to be rational. I have to say that it's no reflection on me. D'you understand that?'

'Of course it's no reflection.'

'It's like gadgets in shops. You buy a gadget and you develop an affection for it, having decided on it in the first place because you thought it was attractive. But all of a sudden there are newer and better gadgets in the shops. More up-to-date models.' She paused. She found a handkerchief and blew her nose. She said:

'You must excuse me: I am not myself tonight.'

'You mustn't get upset. Please don't,' Mrs Ritchie said.

Anna drank all the whisky in her glass and lifted another glass from a passing tray. 'There are too many people in this room,' she complained. 'There's not enough ventilation. It's ideal for tragedy.'

Mrs Ritchie shook her head. She put her hand on Anna's arm. 'Would you like us to go home with you and see you safely in?'

'I have to stay here.'

'Mrs Mackintosh, your husband would never act like that.'

'People in love are cruel. They think of themselves: why should they bother to honour the feelings of a discarded wife?'

'Oh, come now,' said Mrs Ritchie.

At that moment a bald man came up to Anna and took her glass from her hand and led her, without a word, on to the dancing area. As he danced with her, she thought that something else might have happened. Edward was not with anyone, she said to herself: Edward was dead. A telephone had rung in the Lowhrs' house and a voice had said that, en route to their party, a man had dropped dead on the pavement. A maid had taken the message and, not quite understanding it, had done nothing about it.

'I think we should definitely go home now,' General Ritchie said to his wife. 'We could be back for *A Book at Bedtime*.'

'We cannot leave her as easily as that. Just look at the poor creature.'

'That woman is utterly no concern of ours.'

'Just look at her.'

The General sighed and swore and did as he was bidden.

'My husband was meant to turn up,' Anna said to the bald man. 'I've just thought he may have died.' She laughed to indicate that she did not really believe this, in case the man became upset. But the man seemed not to be interested. She could feel his lips playing with a strand of her hair. Death, she thought, she could have accepted.

Anna could see the Ritchies watching her. Their faces were grave, but it came to her suddenly that the gravity was artificial. What, after all, was she to them that they should bother? She was a wretched woman at a party, a woman in a state, who was making an unnecessary fuss because her husband was about to give her her marching orders. Had the Ritchies been mocking her, she wondered, he quite directly, she in some special, subtle way of her own?

'Do you know those people I was talking to?' she said to her partner, but with a portion of her hair still in his mouth he made no effort at reply. Passing near to her, she noticed the thick, square fingers of Mr Lowhr embedded in the flesh of his wife's shoulder. The couple danced by, seeing her and smiling, and it seemed to Anna that their smiles were as empty as the Ritchies' sympathy.

'My husband is leaving me for a younger woman,' she said to the bald man, a statement that caused him to shrug. He had

pressed himself close to her, his knees on her thighs, forcing
her legs this way and that. His hands were low on her body
now, advancing on her buttocks. He was eating her hair.

'I'm sorry,' Anna said. 'I'd rather you didn't do that.'

He released her where they stood and smiled agreeably:
she could see pieces of her hair on his teeth. He walked away,
and she turned and went in the opposite direction.

'We're really most concerned,' said Mrs Ritchie. She and
her husband were standing where Anna had left them, as
though waiting for her. General Ritchie held out her glass to
her.

'Why should you be concerned? That bald man ate my
hair. That's what people do to used-up women like me. They
eat your hair and force their bodies on you. You know, General.'

'Certainly, I don't. Not at all.'

'That man knew all about me. D'you think he'd have taken
his liberties if he hadn't? A man like that can guess.'

'Nonsense,' said Mrs Ritchie firmly. She stared hard at
Anna, endeavouring to impress upon her the errors in her
logic.

'If you want to know, that man's a drunk,' said the General.
'He was far gone when he arrived here and he's more so
now.'

'Why are you saying that?' Anna cried shrilly. 'Why are
you telling me lies and mocking me?'

'Lies?' demanded the General, snapping the word out.
'Lies?'

'My dear, we're not mocking you at all,' murmured Mrs
Ritchie.

'You and those Lowhrs and everyone else, God knows. The
big event at this party is that Edward Mackintosh will reject
his wife for another.'

'Oh now, Mrs Mackintosh – '

'Second marriages are often happier, you know. No reason why they shouldn't be.'

'We would like to help if we could,' Mrs Ritchie said.

'Help? In God's name, how can I be helped? How can two elderly strangers help me when my husband gives me up? What kind of help? Would you give me money – an income, say? Or offer me some other husband? Would you come to visit me and talk to me so that I shouldn't be lonely? Or strike down my husband, General, to show your disapproval? Would you scratch out the little girl's eyes for me, Mrs Ritchie? Would you slap her brazen face?'

'We simply thought we might help in some way,' Mrs Ritchie said. 'Just because we're old and pretty useless doesn't mean we can't make an effort.'

'We are all God's creatures, you are saying. We should offer aid to one another at all opportunities, when marriages get broken and decent husbands are made cruel. Hold my hands then, and let us wait for Edward and his Mark-2 wife. Let's all three speak together and tell them what we think.'

She held out her hands, but the Ritchies did not take them.

'We don't mean to mock you, as you seem to think,' the General said. 'I must insist on that, madam.'

'You're mocking me with your talk about helping. The world is not like that. You like to listen to me for my entertainment value: I'm a good bit of gossip for you. I'm a woman going on about her husband and then getting insulted by a man and seeing the Lowhrs smiling over it. Tell your little grandchildren that some time.'

Mrs Ritchie said that the Lowhrs, she was sure, had not smiled at any predicament that Anna had found herself in, and the General impatiently repeated that the man was drunk.

'The Lowhrs smiled,' Anna said, 'and you have mocked me too. Though perhaps you don't even know it.'

As she pushed a passage through the people, she felt the sweat running on her face and her body. There was a fog of smoke in the room by now, and the voices of the people, struggling to be heard above the music, were louder than before. The man she had danced with was sitting in a corner with his shoes off, and a woman in a crimson dress was trying to persuade him to put them on again. At the door of the room she found Mr Lowhr. 'Shall we dance?' he said.

She shook her head, feeling calmer all of a sudden. Mr Lowhr suggested a drink.

'May I telephone?' she said. 'Quietly somewhere?'

'Upstairs,' said Mr Lowhr, smiling immensely at her. 'Up two flights, the door ahead of you: a tiny guest-room. Take a glass with you.'

She nodded, saying she'd like a little whisky.

'Let me give you a tip,' Mr Lowhr said as he poured her some from a nearby bottle. 'Always buy Haig whisky. It's distilled by a special method.'

'You're never going so soon?' said Mrs Lowhr, appearing at her husband's side.

'Just to telephone,' said Mr Lowhr. He held out his hand with the glass of whisky in it. Anna took it, and as she did so she caught a glimpse of the Ritchies watching her from the other end of the room. Her calmness vanished. The Lowhrs, she noticed, were looking at her too, and smiling. She wanted to ask them why they were smiling, but she knew if she did that they'd simply make some polite reply. Instead she said:

'You shouldn't expose your guests to men who eat hair. Even unimportant guests.'

She turned her back on them and passed from the room. She crossed the hall, sensing that she was being watched. 'Mrs Mackintosh,' Mr Lowhr called after her.

His plumpness filled the doorway. He hovered, seeming uncertain about pursuing her. His face was bewildered and apparently upset.

'Has something disagreeable happened?' he said in a low voice across the distance between them.

'You saw. You and your wife thought fit to laugh, Mr Lowhr.'

'I do assure you, Mrs Mackintosh, I've no idea what you're talking about.'

'It's fascinating, I suppose. Your friends the Ritchies find it fascinating too.'

'Look here, Mrs Mackintosh – '

'Oh, don't blame them. They've nothing left but to watch and mock, at an age like that. The point is, there's a lot of hypocrisy going on tonight.' She nodded at Mr Lowhr to emphasise that last remark, and then went swiftly upstairs.

'I imagine the woman's gone off home,' the General said. 'I dare say her husband's drinking in a pub.'

'I worried once,' replied Mrs Ritchie, speaking quietly, for she didn't wish the confidence to be heard by others. 'That female, Mrs Flynn.'

The General roared with laughter. 'Trixie Flynn,' he shouted. 'Good God, she was a free-for-all!'

'Oh, do be quiet.'

'Dear girl, you didn't ever think – '

'I didn't know what to think, if you want to know.'

Greatly amused, the General seized what he hoped would be his final drink. He placed it behind a green plant on a table. 'Shall we dance one dance,' he said, 'just to amuse them? And then when I've had that drink to revive me we can thankfully make our way.'

But he found himself talking to nobody, for when he had

turned from his wife to secrete his drink she had moved away. He followed her to where she was questioning Mrs Lowhr.

'Some little tiff,' Mrs Lowhr was saying as he approached.

'Hardly a tiff,' corrected Mrs Ritchie. 'The woman's terribly upset.' She turned to her husband, obliging him to speak.

'Upset,' he said.

'Oh, there now,' cried Mrs Lowhr, taking each of the Ritchies by an arm. 'Why don't you take the floor and forget it?'

They both of them recognised from her tone that she was thinking that the elderly exaggerated things and didn't always understand the ways of marriage in the modern world. The General especially resented the insinuation. He said:

'Has the woman gone away?'

'She's upstairs telephoning. Some silly chap upset her apparently, during a dance. That's all it is, you know.'

'You've got the wrong end of the stick entirely,' said the General angrily, 'and you're trying to say we have. The woman believes her husband may arrive here with the girl he's chosen as his second wife.'

'But that's ridiculous!' cried Mrs Lowhr with a tinkling laugh.

'It is what the woman thinks,' said the General loudly, 'whether it's ridiculous or not.' More quietly, Mrs Ritchie added:

'She thinks she has a powerful intuition when all it is is a disease.'

'I'm cross with this Mrs Mackintosh for upsetting you two dear people!' cried Mrs Lowhr with a shrillness that matched her roundness and her glasses. 'I really and truly am.'

A big man came up as she spoke and lifted her into his arms, preparatory to dancing with her. 'What could anyone do?' she called back at the Ritchies as the man rotated her away. 'What can you do for a nervy woman like that?'

There was dark wallpaper on the walls of the room: black and brown with little smears of muted yellow. The curtains matched it; so did the bedspread on the low single bed, and the covering on the padded headboard. The carpet ran from wall to wall and was black and thick. There was a narrow wardrobe with a door of padded black leather and brass studs and an ornamental brass handle. The dressing table and the stool in front of it reflected this general motif in different ways. Two shelves, part of the bed, attached to it on either side of the pillows, served as bedside tables: on each there was a lamp and a book, and on one of them a white telephone.

As Anna closed and locked the door, she felt that in a dream she had been in a dark room in a house where there was a party, waiting for Edward to bring her terrible news. She drank a little whisky and moved towards the telephone. She dialled a number and when a voice answered her call she said:

'Dr Abbatt? It's Anna Mackintosh.'

His voice, as always, was so soft she could hardly hear it. 'Ah, Mrs Mackintosh,' he said.

'I want to talk to you.'

'Of course, Mrs Mackintosh, of course. Tell me now.'

'I'm at a party given by people called Lowhr. Edward was to be here but he didn't turn up. I was all alone and then two old people like scarecrows talked to me. They said their name was Ritchie. And a man ate my hair when we were dancing. The Lowhrs smiled at that.'

'I see. Yes?'

'I'm in a room at the top of the house. I've locked the door.'

'Tell me about the room, Mrs Mackintosh.'

'There's black leather on the wardrobe and the dressing table. Curtains and things match. Dr Abbatt?'

'Yes?'

'The Ritchies are people who injure other people, I think. Intentionally or unintentionally, it never matters.'

'They are strangers to you, these Ritchies?'

'They atempted to mock me. People know at this party, Dr Abbatt; they sense what's going to happen because of how I look.'

Watching for her to come downstairs, the Ritchies stood in the hall and talked to one another.

'I'm sorry,' said Mrs Ritchie. 'I know it would be nicer to go home.'

'What can we do, old sticks like us? We know not a thing about such women. It's quite absurd.'

'The woman's on my mind, dear. And on yours too. You know it.'

'I think she'll be more on our minds if we come across her again. She'll turn nasty, I'll tell you that.'

'Yes, but it would please me to wait a little.'

'To be insulted,' said the General.

'Oh, do stop being so cross, dear.'

'The woman's a stranger to us. She should regulate her life and have done with it. She has no right to bother people.'

'She is a human being in great distress. No, don't say anything, please, if it isn't pleasant.'

The General went into a sulk, and at the end of it he said grudgingly:

'Trixie Flynn was nothing.'

'Oh, I know. Trixie Flynn is dead and done for years ago. I didn't worry like this woman if that's what's on your mind.'

'It wasn't,' lied the General. 'The woman worries ridiculously.'

'I think, you know, we may yet be of use to her: I have a feeling about that.'

'For God's sake, leave the feelings to her. We've had enough of that for one day.'

'As I said to her, we're not entirely useless. No one ever can be.'

'You feel you're being attacked again, Mrs Mackintosh. Are you calm? You haven't been drinking too much?'

'A little.'

'I see.'

'I am being replaced by a younger person.'

'You say you're in a bedroom. Is it possible for you to lie on the bed and talk to me at the same time? Would it be comfortable?'

Anna placed the receiver on the bed and settled herself. She picked it up again and said:

'If he died, there would be a funeral and I'd never forget his kindness to me. I can't do that if he has another wife.'

'We have actually been over this ground,' said Dr Abbatt more softly than ever. 'But we can of course go over it again.'

'Any time, you said.'

'Of course.'

'What has happened is perfectly simple. Edward is with the girl. He is about to arrive here to tell me to clear off. She's insisting on that. It's not Edward, you know.'

'Mrs Mackintosh, I'm going to speak firmly now. We've agreed between us that there's no young girl in your husband's life. You have an obsession, Mrs Mackintosh, about

the fact that you have never had children and that men sometimes marry twice – '

'There's such a thing as the Mark-2 wife,' Anna cried.
'You know there is. A girl of nineteen who'll delightedly give
birth to Edward's sons.'

'No, no – '

'I had imagined Edward telling me. I had imagined him
pushing back his hair and lighting a cigarette in his untidy
way. "I'm terribly sorry," he would say, and leave me nothing
to add to that. Instead it's like this: a nightmare.'

'It is not a nightmare, Mrs Mackintosh.'

'This party is a nightmare. People are vultures here.'

'Mrs Mackintosh, I must tell you that I believe you're
seeing the people at this party in a most exaggerated
light.'

'A man – '

'A man nibbled your hair. Worse things can happen. This
is not a nightmare, Mrs Mackintosh. Your husband has been
delayed. Husbands are always being delayed. D'you see? You
and I and your husband are all together trying to rid you of
this perfectly normal obsession you've developed. We mustn't
complicate matters, now must we?'

'I didn't run away, Dr Abbatt. I said to myself I mustn't
run away from this party. I must wait and face whatever was to
happen. You told me to face things.'

'I didn't tell you, my dear. We agreed between us. We
talked it out, the difficulty about facing things, and we saw the
wisdom of it. Now I want you to go back to the party and wait
for your husband.'

'He's more than two hours late.'

'My dear Mrs Mackintosh, an hour or so is absolutely
nothing these days. Now listen to me please.'

She listened to the soft voice as it reminded her of all that
between them they had agreed. Dr Abbatt went over the

ground, from the time she had first consulted him to the
present moment. He charted her obsession until it seemed
once again, as he said, a perfectly normal thing for a woman of
forty to have.

After she had said good-bye, Anna sat on the bed feeling
very calm. She had read the message behind Dr Abbatt's
words: that it was ridiculous, her perpetually going on in this
lunatic manner. She had come to a party and in no time at all
she'd been behaving in a way that was, she supposed, mildly
crazy. It always happened, she knew, and it would as long as
the trouble remained: in her mind, when she began to worry,
everything became jumbled and unreal, turning her into an
impossible person. How could Edward, for heaven's sake, be
expected to live with her fears and her suppositions? Edward
would crack as others would, tormented by an impossible
person. He'd become an alcoholic or he'd have some love
affair with a woman just as old as she was, and the
irony of that would be too great. She knew, as she sat there,
that she couldn't help herself and that as long as she
lived with Edward she wouldn't be able to do any better.
'I have lost touch with reality,' she said. 'I shall let
him go, as a bird is released. In my state how can I have
rights?'

She left the room and slowly descended the stairs. There
were framed prints of old motor-cars on the wall and she
paused now and again to examine one, emphasising to herself her own continued calmness. She was thinking that she'd
get herself a job. She might even tell Edward that Dr Abbatt
had suggested that their marriage should end since she wasn't
able to live with her thoughts any more. She'd insist on a
divorce at once. She didn't mind the thought of it now, because of course it would be different: she was doing what she
guessed Dr Abbatt had been willing her to do for quite a long
time really: she was taking matters into her own hands, she

was acting positively – rejecting, not being rejected herself. Her marriage was ending cleanly and correctly.

She found her coat and thanked the dark-skinned maid who held it for her. Edward was probably at the party by now, but in the new circumstances that was neither here nor there. She'd go home in a taxi and pack a suitcase and then telephone for another taxi. She'd leave a note for Edward and go to a hotel, without telling him where.

'Good-night,' she said to the maid. She stepped towards the hall-door as the maid opened it for her, and as she did so she felt a hand touch her shoulder. 'No, Edward,' she said. 'I must go now.' But when she turned she saw that the hand belonged to Mrs Ritchie. Behind her, looking tired, stood the General. For a moment there was a silence. Then Anna, speaking to both of them, said:

'I'm extremely sorry. Please forgive me.'

'We were worried about you,' said Mrs Ritchie. 'Will you be all right, my dear?'

'The fear is worse than the reality, Mrs Ritchie. I can no longer live with the fear.'

'We understand.'

'It's strange,' Anna said, passing through the doorway and standing at the top of the steps that led to the street. 'Strange, coming to a party like this, given by people I didn't know and meeting you and being so rude. Please don't tell me if my husband is here or not. It doesn't concern me now. I'm quite calm.'

The Ritchies watched her descend the steps and call out to a passing taxi-cab. They watched the taxi drive away.

'Calm!' said General Ritchie.

'She's still in a state, poor thing,' agreed his wife. 'I do feel sorry.'

They stood on the steps of the Lowhrs' house, thinking about the brief glance they had had of another person's life, bewildered by it and saddened, for they themselves, though often edgy on the surface, had had a happy marriage.

'At least she's standing on her own feet now,' Mrs Ritchie said. 'I think it'll save her.'

A taxi drew up at the house and the Ritchies watched it, thinking for a moment that Anna Mackintosh, weak in her resolve, had returned in search of her husband. But it was a man who emerged and ran up the steps in a manner which suggested that, like the man who had earlier misbehaved on the dance-floor, he was not entirely sober. He passed the Ritchies and entered the house. 'That is Edward Mackintosh,' said Mrs Ritchie.

The girl who was paying the taxi-driver paused in what she was doing to see where her companion had dashed away to and observed two thin figures staring at her from the lighted doorway, murmuring to one another.

'Cruel,' said the General. 'The woman said so: we must give her that.'

'He's a kind man,' replied Mrs Ritchie. 'He'll listen to us.'

'To us, for heaven's sake?'

'We have a thing to do, as I said we might have.'

'The woman has gone. I'm not saying I'm not sorry for her – '

'And who shall ask for mercy for the woman, since she cannot ask herself? There is a little to be saved, you know: she has made a gesture, poor thing. It must be honoured.'

'My dear, we don't know these people; we met the woman quite in passing.'

The girl came up the steps, settling her purse into its right place in her handbag. She smiled at the Ritchies, and they thought that the smile had a hint of triumph about it, as though it was her first smile since the victory that Anna Mackintosh had said some girl was winning that night.

'Even if he'd listen,' muttered the General when the girl had passed by, 'I doubt that she would.'

'It's just that a little time should be allowed to go by,' his wife reminded him. 'That's all that's required. Until the woman's found her feet again and feels she has a voice in her own life.'

'We're interfering,' said the General, and his wife said nothing. They looked at one another, remembering vividly the dread in Anna Mackintosh's face and the confusion that all her conversation had revealed.

The General shook his head. 'We are hardly the happiest choice,' he said, in a gentler mood at last, 'but I dare say we must try.'

He closed the door of the house and they paused for a moment in the hall, talking again of the woman who had told them her troubles. They drew a little strength from that, and felt armed to face once more the Lowhrs' noisy party. Together they moved towards it and through it, in search of a man they had met once before on a similar occasion. 'We are sorry for interfering,' they would quietly say; and making it seem as natural as they could, they would ask him to honour, above all else and in spite of love, the gesture of a woman who no longer interested him.

'A tall order,' protested the General, pausing in his forward motion, doubtful again.

'When the wrong people do things,' replied his wife, 'it sometimes works.' She pulled him on until they stood before Edward Mackintosh and the girl he'd chosen as his Mark-2 wife. They smiled at Edward Mackintosh and shook hands with him, and then there was a silence before the General said that it was odd, in a way, what they had to request.

The Grass Widows

The headmaster of a great English public school visited every
summer a village in County Galway for the sake of the fishing
in a number of nearby rivers. For more than forty years this
stern, successful man had brought his wife to the Slieve
Gashal Hotel, a place, so he said, he had come to love. A
smiling man called Mr Doyle had been for all the headmaster's experience of the hotel its obliging proprietor: Mr
Doyle had related stories to the headmaster late at night in the
hotel bar, after the headmaster's wife had retired to bed; they
had discussed together the fruitfulness of the local rivers, although in truth Mr Doyle had never held a rod in his life.
'You feel another person,' the headmaster had told generations of his pupils, 'among blue mountains, in the quiet little
hotel.' On walks through the school grounds with a senior boy
on either side of him he had spoken of the soft peace of the
riverside and of the unrivalled glory of being alone with one's
mind. He talked to his boys of Mr Doyle and his unassuming
ways, and of the little village that was a one-horse place and
none the worse for that, and of the good plain food that came
from the Slieve Gashal's kitchen.

To Jackson Major the headmaster enthused during all the
year that Jackson Major was head boy of the famous school,
and Jackson Major did not ever forget the paradise that
then had formed in his mind. 'I know a place,' he said
to his fiancée long after he had left the school, 'that's perfect for our honeymoon.' He told her about the heathery

hills that the headmaster had recalled for him, and the lakes and rivers and the one-horse little village in which, near a bridge, stood the ivy-covered bulk of the Slieve Gashal Hotel. 'Lovely, darling,' murmured the bride-to-be of Jackson Major, thinking at the time of a clock in the shape of a human hand that someone had given them and which would naturally have to be changed for something else. She'd been hoping that he would suggest Majorca for their honeymoon, but if he wished to go to this other place she didn't intend to make a fuss. 'Idyllic for a honeymoon,' the headmaster had once remarked to Jackson Major, and Jackson Major had not forgotten. *Steady but unimaginative* were words that had been written of him on a school report.

The headmaster, a square, bald man with a head that might have been carved from oak, a man who wore rimless spectacles and whose name was Angusthorpe, discovered when he arrived at the Slieve Gashal Hotel in the summer of 1968 that in the intervening year a tragedy had occurred. It had become the custom of Mr Angusthorpe to book his fortnight's holiday by saying simply to Mr Doyle: 'Till next year then,' an anticipation that Mr Doyle would translate into commercial terms, reserving the same room for the headmaster and his wife in twelve months' time. No letters changed hands during the year, no confirmation of the booking was ever necessary: Mr Angusthorpe and his wife arrived each summer after the trials of the school term, knowing that their room would be waiting for them, with sweet-peas in a vase in the window, and Mr Doyle full of welcome in the hall. 'He died in Woolworth's in Galway,' said Mr Doyle's son in the summer of 1968. 'He was buying a shirt at the time.'

Afterwards, Mr Angusthorpe said to his wife that when Mr Doyle's son spoke those words he knew that nothing was ever going to be the same again. Mr Doyle's son, known locally as Scut Doyle, went on speaking while the headmaster and his

small wife, grey-haired, and bespectacled also, stood in the
hall. He told them that he had inherited the Slieve Gashal and
that for all his adult life he had been employed in the accounts
department of a paper-mill in Dublin. 'I thought at first I'd
sell the place up,' he informed the Angusthorpes, 'and then I
thought maybe I'd attempt to make a go of it. "Will we have a
shot at it?" I said to the wife, and, God bless her, she said why
wouldn't I?' While he spoke, the subject of his last remarks
appeared behind him in the hall, a woman whose appearance
did not at all impress Mr Angusthorpe. She was pale-faced
and fat and, so Mr Angusthorpe afterwards suggested to his
wife, sullen. She stood silently by her husband, whose appearance did not impress Mr Angusthorpe either, since the
new proprietor of the Slieve Gashal, a man with shaking
hands and cocky black moustache, did not appear to have
shaved himself that day. 'One or other of them, if not both,'
said Mr Angusthorpe afterwards, 'smelt of drink.'

The Angusthorpes were led to their room by a girl whose
age Mr Angusthorpe estimated to be thirteen. 'What's
become of Joseph?' he asked her as they mounted the stairs,
referring to an old porter who had always in the past been
spick and span in a uniform, but the child seemed not to
understand the question, for she offered it no reply. In the
room there were no sweet-peas, and although they had entered by a door that was familiar to them, the room itself was
greatly altered: it was, to begin with, only half the size it had
been before. 'Great heavens!' exclaimed Mr Angusthorpe,
striking a wall with his fist and finding it to be a partition. 'He
had the carpenters in,' the child said.

Mr Angusthorpe, in a natural fury, descended the stairs
and shouted in the hall. 'Mr Doyle!' he called out in his
peremptory headmaster's voice. 'Mr Doyle! Mr Doyle!'

Doyle emerged from the back regions of the hotel, with a
cigarette in his mouth. There were feathers on his clothes,

and he held in his right hand a half-plucked chicken. In explanation he said that he had been giving his wife a hand. She was not herself, he confided to Mr Angusthorpe, on account of it being her bad time of the month.

'Our room,' protested Mr Angusthorpe. 'We can't possibly sleep in a tiny space like that. You've cut the room in half, Mr Doyle.'

Doyle nodded. All the bedrooms in the hotel, he told Mr Angusthorpe, had been divided, since they were uneconomical otherwise. He had spent four hundred and ten pounds having new doorways made and putting on new wallpaper. He began to go into the details of this expense, plucking feathers from the chicken as he stood there. Mr Angusthorpe coldly remarked that he had not booked a room in which you couldn't swing a cat.

'Excuse me, sir,' interrupted Doyle. 'You booked a room a year ago: you did not reserve a specific room. D'you know what I mean, Mr Angusthorpe? I have no note that you specified with my father to have the exact room again.'

'It was an understood thing between us –'

'My father unfortunately died.'

Mr Angusthorpe regarded the man, disliking him intensely. It occurred to him that he had never in his life carried on a conversation with a hotel proprietor who held in his right hand a half-plucked chicken and whose clothes had feathers on them. His inclination was to turn on his heel and march with his wife from the unsatisfactory hotel, telling, if need be, this unprepossessing individual to go to hell. Mr Angusthorpe thought of doing that, but then he wondered where he and his wife could go. Hotels in the area were notoriously full at this time of year, in the middle of the fishing season.

'I must get on with this for the dinner,' said Doyle, 'or the wife will be having me guts for garters.' He winked at Mr Angusthorpe, flicking a quantity of cigarette ash from the pale flesh of the chicken. He left Mr Angusthorpe standing there.

The child had remained with Mrs Angusthorpe while the headmaster had sought an explanation downstairs. She had stood silently by the door until Mrs Angusthorpe, fearing a violent reaction on the part of her husband if he discovered the child present when he returned, suggested that she should go away. But the child had taken no notice of that and Mrs Angusthorpe, being unable to think of anything else to say, had asked her at what time of year old Mr Doyle had died. 'The funeral was ten miles long, missus,' replied the child. 'Me father wasn't sober till the Monday.' Mr Angusthorpe, returning, asked the child sharply why she was lingering and the child explained that she was waiting to be tipped. Mr Angusthorpe gave her a threepenny-piece.

In the partitioned room, which now had a pink wallpaper on the walls and an elaborate frieze from which flowers of different colours cascaded down the four corners, the Angusthorpes surveyed their predicament. Mr Angusthorpe told his wife the details of his interview with Doyle, and when he had talked for twenty minutes he came more definitely to the conclusion that the best thing they could do would be to remain for the moment. The rivers could hardly have altered, he was thinking, and that the hotel was now more than inadequate was a consequence that would affect his wife more than it would affect him. In the past she had been wont to spend her days going for a brief walk in the morning and returning to the pleasant little dining-room for a solitary lunch, and then sleeping or reading until it was time for a cup of tea, after which she would again take a brief walk. She was usually sitting by the fire in the lounge when he returned from his day's excursion. Perhaps all that would be less attractive now, Mr Angusthorpe thought, but there was little he could do about it and it was naturally only fair that they should at least remain for a day or two.

That night the dinner was well below the standard of the dinners they had in the past enjoyed in the Slieve Gashal. Mrs Angusthorpe was unable to consume her soup because there were quite large pieces of bone and gristle in it. The headmaster laughed over his prawn cocktail because, he said, it tasted of absolutely nothing at all. He had recovered from his initial shock and was now determined that the hotel must be regarded as a joke. He eyed his wife's plate of untouched soup, saying it was better to make the best of things. Chicken and potatoes and mashed turnip were placed before them by a nervous woman in the uniform of a waitress. Turnip made Mrs Angusthorpe sick in the stomach, even the sight of it: at another time in their life her husband might have remembered and ordered the vegetable from the table, but what he was more intent upon now was discovering if the Slieve Gashal still possessed a passable hock, which surprisingly it did. After a few glasses, he said:

'We'll not come next year, of course. While I'm out with the rod, my dear, you might scout around for another hotel.'

They never brought their car with them, the headmaster's theory being that the car was something they wished to escape from. Often she had thought it might be nice to have a car at the Slieve Gashal so that she could drive around the countryside during the day, but she saw his argument and had never pressed her view. Now, it seemed, he was suggesting that she should scout about for another hotel on foot.

'No, no,' he said. 'There is an excellent bus service in Ireland.' He spoke with a trace of sarcasm, as though she should have known that no matter what else he expected of her, he did not expect her to tramp about the roads looking for another hotel. He gave a little laugh, leaving the matter vaguely with her, his eyes like the eyes of a fish behind his rimless spectacles. Boys had feared him and disliked him too, some even had hated him; yet others had been full of a respect that seemed at times like adoration. As she struggled with her watery turnips she could sense that his mind was quite made up: he intended to remain for the full fortnight in the changed hotel because the lure of the riverside possessed him too strongly to consider an alternative.

'I might find a place we could move to,' she said. 'I mean, in a day or so.'

'They'll all be full, my dear.' He laughed without humour in his laugh, not amused by anything. 'We must simply grin and bear it. The chicken,' he added, 'might well have been worse.'

'Excuse me,' Mrs Angusthorpe said, and quickly rose from the table and left the dining-room. From a tape-recorder somewhere dance music began to play.

'Is the wife all right?' Doyle asked Mr Angusthorpe, coming up and sitting down in the chair she had vacated. He had read in a hotelier's journal that tourists enjoyed a friendly atmosphere and the personal attention of the proprietor.

'We've had a long day,' responded the headmaster genially enough.

'Ah well, of course you have.'

The dining-room was full, indicating that business was still brisk in the hotel. Mr Angusthorpe had noted a familiar face or two and had made dignified salutations. These people would surely have walked out if the hotel was impossible in all respects.

'At her time of the month,' Doyle was saying, 'the wife gets as fatigued as an old horse. Like your own one, she's gone up to her bed already.'

'My wife – '

'Ah, I wasn't suggesting Mrs Angusthorpe was that way at all. They have fatigue in common tonight, sir, that's all I meant.'

Doyle appeared to be drunk. There was a bleariness about his eyes that suggested inebriation to Mr Angusthorpe and his shaking hands might well be taken as a sign of repeated over-indulgence.

'She wakes up at two a.m. as lively as a bird,' said Doyle. 'She's keen for a hug and a pat –'

'Quite so,' interrupted Mr Angusthorpe quickly. He looked unpleasantly at his unwelcome companion. He allowed his full opinion of the man to pervade his glance.

'Well, I'll be seeing you,' said Doyle, rising and seeming to be undismayed. 'I'll tell the wife you were asking for her,' he added with a billowing laugh, before moving on to another table.

Shortly after that, Mr Angusthorpe left the dining-room, having resolved that he would not relate this conversation to his wife. He would avoid Doyle in the future, he promised himself, and when by chance they did meet he would make it clear that he did not care to hear his comments on any subject. It was a pity that the old man had died and that all this nastiness had grown up in his place, but there was nothing whatsoever that might be done about it and at least the weather looked good. He entered the bar and dropped into conversation with a man he had met several times before, a solicitor from Dublin, a bachelor called Gorman.

'I was caught the same way,' Mr Gorman said, 'only everywhere else is full. It's the end of the Slieve Gashal, you know: the food's inedible.'

He went on to relate a series of dishes that had already been served during his stay, the most memorable of which appeared to be a rabbit stew that had had a smell of ammonia. 'There's margarine every time instead of butter, and some queer type of marmalade in the morning: it has a taste of tin to it. The same mashed turnip,' said Gorman, 'is the only vegetable he offers.'

The headmaster changed the subject, asking how the rivers were. The fishing was better than ever he'd known it, Mr Gorman reported, and he retailed experiences to prove the claim. 'Isn't it all that matters in the long run?' suggested Mr Gorman, and Mr Angusthorpe readily agreed that it was. He would refrain from repeating to his wife the information about the marmalade that tasted of tin, or the absence of variation where vegetables were concerned. He left the bar at nine o'clock, determined to slip quietly into bed without disturbing her.

In the middle of that night, at midnight precisely, the Angusthorpes were awakened simultaneously by a noise from the room beyond the new partition.

'Put a pillow down, darling,' a male voice was saying as clearly as if its possessor stood in the room beside the Angusthorpes' bed.

'Couldn't we wait until another time?' a woman pleaded in reply. 'I don't see what good a pillow will do.'

'It'll lift you up a bit,' the man explained. 'It said in the book to put a pillow down if there was difficulty.'

'I don't see – '

'It'll make entry easier,' said the man. 'It's a well-known thing.'

Mrs Angusthorpe switched on her bedside light and saw that her husband was pretending to be asleep. 'I'm going to rap on the wall,' she whispered. 'It's disgusting, listening to this.'

'I think I'm going down,' said the man.

'My God,' whispered Mr Angusthorpe, opening his eyes. 'It's Jackson Major.'

At breakfast, Mrs Angusthorpe ate margarine on her toast

and the marmalade that had a taste of tin. She did not say anything. She watched her husband cutting into a fried egg on a plate that bore the marks of the waitress's two thumbs. Eventually he placed his knife and fork together on the plate and left them there.

For hours they had lain awake, listening to the conversation beyond the inadequate partition. The newly wed wife of Jackson Major had wept and said that Jackson had better divorce her at once. She had designated the hotel they were in as a frightful place, fit only for Irish tinkers. 'That filthy meal!' the wife of Jackson Major had cried emotionally. 'That awful drunk man!' And Jackson Major had apologised and had mentioned Mr Angusthorpe by name, wondering what on earth his old headmaster could ever have seen in such an establishment. 'Let's try again,' he had suggested, and the Angusthorpes had listened to a repetition of Mrs Jackson's unhappy tears. 'How can you rap on the wall?' Mr Angusthorpe had angrily whispered. 'How can we even admit that conversation can be heard? Jackson was head boy.'

'In the circumstances,' said Mrs Angusthorpe at breakfast, breaking the long silence, 'it would be better to leave.'

He knew it would be. He knew that on top of everything else the unfortunate fact that Jackson Major was in the room beyond the partition and would sooner or later discover that the partition was far from soundproof could be exceedingly embarrassing in view of what had taken place during the night. There was, as well, the fact that he had enthused so eloquently to Jackson Major about the hotel that Jackson Major had clearly, on his word alone, brought his bride there. He had even said, he recalled, that the Slieve Gashal would be ideal for a honeymoon. Mr Angusthorpe considered all that yet could not forget his forty years' experience of the surrounding rivers, or the information of Mr Gorman that the rivers this year were better than ever.

'We could whisper,' he suggested in what was itself a whisper. 'We could whisper in our room so that they wouldn't know you can hear.'

'Whisper?' she said. She shook her head.

She remembered days in the rain, walking about the one-horse village with nothing whatsoever to do except to walk about, or lie on her bed reading detective stories. She remembered listening to his reports of his day and feeling sleepy listening to them. She remembered thinking, once or twice, that it had never occurred to him that what was just a change and a rest for her could not at all be compared to the excitements he derived from his days on the river-bank, alone with his mind. He was a great, successful man, big and square and commanding, with the cold eyes of the fish he sought in mountain rivers. He had made a firm impression on generations of boys, and on parents and governors, and often on a more general public, yet he had never been able to give her children. She had needed children because she was, compared with him, an unimportant kind of person.

She thought of him in Chapel, gesturing at six hundred boys from the pulpit, in his surplice and red academic hood, releasing words from his throat that were as cold as ice and cleverly made sense. She thought of a time he had expelled two boys, when he had sat with her in their drawing-room waiting for a bell to ring. When the chiming had ceased he had risen and gone without a word from the room, his oaken face pale with suppressed emotion. She knew he saw in the crime of the two boys a failure on his part, yet he never mentioned it to her. He had expelled the boys in public, castigating them with bitterness in his tone, hating them and hating himself, yet rising above his shame at having failed with them: dignity was his greatest ally.

She sat with him once a week at the high table in the dining-hall, surrounded by his prefects, who politely chatted to her. She remembered Jackson Major, a tall boy with short black hair who would endlessly discuss with her husband a web of school affairs. 'The best head boy I remember,' her husband's voice said again, coming back to her over a number of years: 'I made no mistake with Jackson.' Jackson Major had set a half-mile record that remained unbroken to this day. There had been a complaint from some child's mother, she recalled, who claimed that her son had been, by Jackson Major, too severely caned. *We must not forget,* her husband had written to that mother, *that your son almost caused another boy to lose an eye. It was for that carelessness that he was punished. He bears no resentment: boys seldom do.*

Yet now this revered, feared, and clever man was suggesting that they should whisper for a fortnight in their bedroom, so that the couple next door might not feel embarrassment, so that he himself might remain in a particularly uncomfortable hotel in order to fish. It seemed to Mrs Angusthorpe that there were limits to the role he had laid down for her and which for all her married life she had ungrudgingly accepted. She hadn't minded being bored for this fortnight every year, but now he was asking more than that she could continue to feel bored; he was asking her to endure food that made her sick, and to conduct absurd conversations in their bedroom.

'No,' she said, 'we could not whisper.'

'I meant it only for kindness. Kindness to them, you see – '

'You have compensations here. I have none, you know.'

He looked sharply at her, as at an erring new boy who had not yet learnt the ways of school.

'I think we should leave at once,' she said. 'After breakfast.'

That suggestion, he pointed out to her, was nonsensical.
They had booked a room in the hotel: they were obliged to
pay for it. He was exhausted, he added, after a particularly
trying term.

'It's what I'd like,' she said.

He spread margarine on his toast and added to it some of
the marmalade. 'We must not be selfish,' he said, suggesting
that both of them were on the point of being selfish and that
together they must prevent themselves.

'I'd be happier,' she began, but he swiftly interrupted her,
reminding her that his holiday had been spoilt enough already
and that he for his part was intent on making the best of
things. 'Let's simply enjoy what we can,' he said, 'without
making a fuss about it.'

At that moment Jackson Major and his wife, a pretty,
pale-haired girl called Daphne, entered the dining-room.
They stood at the door, endeavouring to catch the eye of a
waitress, not sure about where to sit. Mrs Jackson indicated a
table that was occupied by two men, reminding her husband
that they had sat at it last night for dinner. Jackson Major
looked towards it and looked impatiently away, seeming annoyed with his wife for bothering to draw his attention to
a table at which they clearly could not sit. It was then, while
still annoyed, that he noticed the Angusthorpes.

Mrs Angusthorpe saw him murmuring to his wife. He led
the way to their table, and Mrs Angusthorpe observed that his
wife moved less eagerly than he.

'How marvellous, sir,' Jackson Major said, shaking his
headmaster by the hand. Except for a neat moustache, he had
changed hardly at all, Mrs Angusthorpe noticed; a little fatter
in the face, perhaps, and the small pimples that had marked
his chin as a schoolboy had now cleared up completely. He
introduced his wife to the headmaster, and then he turned to
Mrs Angusthorpe and asked her how she was. Forgetfully, he

omitted to introduce his wife to her, but she, in spite of that, smiled and nodded at his wife.

'I'm afraid it's gone down awfully, Jackson,' Mr Angusthorpe said. 'The hotel's changed hands, you know. We weren't aware ourselves.'

'It seems quite comfortable, sir,' Jackson Major said, sitting down and indicating that his wife should do the same.

'The food was nice before,' said Mrs Angusthorpe. 'It's really awful now.'

'Oh, I wouldn't say awful, dear,' Mr Angusthorpe corrected her. 'One becomes used to a hotel,' he explained to Jackson Major. 'Any change is rather noticeable.'

'We had a perfectly ghastly dinner,' Daphne Jackson said.

'Still,' said Mr Angusthorpe, as though she had not spoken, 'we'll not return another year. My wife is going to scout around for a better place. You've brought your rod, Jackson?'

'Well, yes, I did. I thought that maybe if Daphne felt tired I might once or twice try out your famous rivers, sir.'

Mrs Angusthorpe saw Mrs Jackson glance in surprise at her new husband, and she deduced that Mrs Jackson hadn't been aware that a fishing-rod had comprised part of her husband's luggage.

'Capital,' cried Mr Angusthorpe, while the waitress took the Jacksons' order for breakfast. 'You could scout round together,' he said, addressing the two women at once, 'while I show Jackson what's what.'

'It's most kind of you, sir,' Jackson Major said, 'but I think, you know – '

'Capital,' cried Mr Angusthorpe again, his eyes swivelling from face to face, forbidding defiance. He laughed his humourless laugh and he poured himself more tea. 'I told you, dear,' he said to Mrs Angusthorpe. 'There's always a silver lining.'

In the hall of the Slieve Gashal Doyle took a metal stand from beneath the reception desk and busied himself arranging picture postcards on it. His wife had bought the stand in Galway, getting it at a reduced price because it was broken. He was at the moment offended with his wife because of her attitude when he had entered the hotel kitchen an hour ago with a number of ribs of beef. 'Did you drop that meat?' she had said in a hard voice, looking up from the table where she was making bread. 'Is that dirt on the suet?' He had replied that he'd been obliged to cross the village street hurriedly, to avoid a man on a bicycle. 'You dropped the meat on the road,' she accused. 'D'you want to poison the bloody lot of them?' Feeling hard done by, he had left the kitchen.

While he continued to work with the postcards, Mr Angusthorpe and Jackson Major passed before him with their fishing-rods. 'We'll be frying tonight,' he observed jollily, wagging his head at their two rods. They did not reply: weren't they the queer-looking eejits, he thought, with their sporty clothes and the two tweed hats covered with artificial flies. 'I'll bring it up, sir,' Jackson Major was saying, 'at the Old Boys' Dinner in the autumn.' It was ridiculous, Doyle reflected, going to all that trouble to catch a few fish when all you had to do was to go out at night and shine a torch into the water. 'Would you be interested in postcards, gentlemen?' he inquired, but so absorbed were Mr Angusthorpe and Jackson Major in their conversation that again neither of them made a reply.

Some time later, Daphne Jackson descended the stairs of the hotel. Doyle watched her, admiring her slender legs and the flowered dress she was wearing. A light blue cardigan

hung casually from her shoulders, its sleeves not occupied by
her arms. Wouldn't it be great, he thought, to be married to a
young body like that? He imagined her in a bedroom, taking
off her cardigan and then her dress. She stood in her underclothes; swiftly she lifted them from her body.

'Would you be interested in postcards at all?' inquired
Doyle. 'I have the local views here.'

Daphne smiled at him. Without much interest, she examined the cards on the stand, and then she moved towards the
entrance door.

'There's a lovely dinner we have for you today,' said Doyle.
'Ribs of beef that I'm just after handing over to the wife. As
tender as an infant.'

He held the door open for her, talking all the time, since he
knew they liked to be talked to. He asked her if she was going
for a walk and told her that a walk would give her a healthy
appetite. The day would keep good, he promised; he had
read it in the paper.

'Thank you,' she said.

She walked through a sunny morning that did little to raise
her spirits. Outside the hotel there was a large expanse of
green grass, bounded on one side by the short village street.
She crossed an area of the grass and then passed the butcher's
shop in which earlier Doyle had purchased the ribs of beef.
She glanced in and the butcher smiled and waved at her, as
though he knew her well. She smiled shyly back. Outside a
small public house a man was mending a bicycle, which was
upturned on the pavement: a child pushing a pram spoke to
the man and he spoke to her. Farther on, past a row of cot-
tages, a woman pumped water into a bucket from a green
pump at the road's edge, and beyond it, coming towards her
slowly, she recognised the figure of Mrs Angusthorpe.

'So we are grass widows,' said Mrs Angusthorpe when she
had arrived at a point at which it was suitable to speak.

'Yes.'

'I'm afraid it's our fault, for being here. My husband's, I mean, and mine.'

'My husband could have declined to go fishing.'

The words were sour. They were sour and icy, Mrs Angusthorpe thought, matching her own mood. On her brief walk she had that morning disliked her husband more than ever she had disliked him before, and there was venom in her now. Once upon a time he might at least have heard her desires with what could even have been taken for understanding. He would not have acted upon her desires, since it was not in his nature to do so, but he would not have been guilty, either, of announcing in so obviously false a way that they should enjoy what they could and not make a fuss. There had been a semblance of chivalry in the attitude from which, at the beginning of their marriage, he had briefly regarded her; but forty-seven years had efficiently disposed of that garnish of politeness. A week or so ago a boy at the school had been casual with her, but the headmaster, hearing her report of the matter, had denied that what she stated could ever have occurred: he had moulded the boy in question, he pointed out, he had taken a special interest in the boy because he recognised in him qualities that were admirable: she was touchy, the headmaster said, increasingly touchy these days. She remembered in the first year of their marriage a way he had of patiently leaning back in his chair, puffing at the pipe he affected in those days and listening to her, seeming actually to weigh her arguments against his own. It was a long time now since he had weighed an argument of hers, or even devoted a moment of passing consideration to it. It was a long time since he could possibly have been concerned as to whether or not she found the food in a hotel unpalatable. She was angry when she thought of it this morning, not because she was unused to these circumstances of her life but because, quite suddenly, she had seen her state of resignation as an insult to the woman she once, too long ago, had been.

'I would really like to talk to you,' Mrs Angusthorpe said, to Daphne Jackson's surprise. 'It might be worth your while to stroll back to that hotel with me.'

On her short, angry walk she had realised, too, that once she had greatly disliked Jackson Major because he reminded her in some ways of her husband. A priggish youth, she had recalled, a tedious bore of a boy who had shown her husband a ridiculous respect while also fearing and resembling him. On her walk she had remembered the day he had broken the half-mile record, standing in the sports field in his running clothes, deprecating his effort because he knew his headmaster would wish him to act like that. What good was winning a half-mile race if he upset his wife the first time he found himself in a bedroom with her?

'I remember your husband as a boy,' said Mrs Angusthorpe. 'He set an athletic record which has not yet been broken.'

'Yes, he told me.'

'He had trouble with his chin. Pimples that wouldn't go away. I see all that's been overcome.'

'Well, yes – '

'And trouble also because he beat a boy too hard. The mother wrote, enclosing the opinion of a doctor.'

Daphne frowned. She ceased to walk. She stared at Mrs Angusthorpe.

'Oh yes,' said Mrs Angusthorpe.

They passed the butcher's shop, from the doorway of which the butcher now addressed them. The weather was good, the butcher said: it was a suitable time for a holiday. Mrs Angusthorpe smiled at him and bowed. Daphne, frowning still, passed on.

'You're right,' Mrs Angusthorpe said next, 'when you say

that your husband could have declined to go fishing.'

'I think he felt – '

'Odd, I thought, to have a fishing-rod with him in the first place. Odd on a honeymoon.'

They entered the hotel. Doyle came forward to meet them. 'Ah, so you've palled up?' he said. 'Isn't that grand?'

'We could have sherry,' Mrs Angusthorpe suggested, 'in the bar.'

'Of course you could,' said Doyle. 'Won't your two husbands be pegging away at the old fish for the entire day?'

'They promised to be back for lunch,' Daphne said quickly, her voice seeming to herself to be unduly weak. She cleared her throat and remarked to Doyle that the village was pretty. She didn't really wish to sit in the hotel bar drinking sherry with the wife of her husband's headmaster. It was all ridiculous, she thought, on a honeymoon.

'Go down into the bar,' said Doyle, 'and I'll be down myself in a minute.'

Mrs Angusthorpe seized with the fingers of her left hand the flowered material of Daphne's dress. 'The bar's down here,' she said, leading the way without releasing her hold.

They sat at a table on which there were a number of absorbent mats which advertised brands of beer. Doyle brought them two glasses of sherry, which Mrs Angusthorpe ordered him to put down to her husband's account. 'Shout out when you're in need of a refill,' he invited. 'I'll be up in the hall.'

'The partition between our bedrooms is far from soundproof,' said Mrs Angusthorpe when Doyle had gone. 'We were awakened in the night.'

'Awakened?'

'As if you were in the room beside us, we heard a conversation.'

'My God!'

'Yes.'

Blood rushed to Daphne Jackson's face. She was aware of an unpleasant sensation in her stomach. She turned her head away. Mrs Angusthorpe said:

'People don't speak out. All my married life, for instance, I haven't spoken out. My dear, you're far too good for Jackson Major.'

It seemed to Daphne, who had been Daphne Jackson for less than twenty-four hours, that the wife of her husband's headmaster was insane. She gulped at the glass of sherry before her, unable to prevent herself from vividly recalling the awfulness of the night before in the small bedroom. He had come at her as she was taking off her blouse. His right hand had shot beneath her underclothes, pressing at her and gripping her. All during their inedible dinner he had been urging her to drink whisky and wine, and drinking quantities of both himself. In bed he had suddenly become calmer, remembering instructions read in a book.

'Pack a suitcase,' said Mrs Angusthorpe, 'and go.'

The words belonged to a nightmare and Daphne was aware of wishing that she was asleep and dreaming. The memory of tension on her wedding day, and of guests standing around in sunshine in a London garden, and then the flight by plane, were elements that confused her mind as she listened to this small woman. The tension had been with her as she walked towards the altar and had been with her, too, in her parents' garden. Nor had it eased when she escaped with her husband on a Viscount: it might even have increased on the flight and on the train to Galway, and then in the hired car that had carried her to the small village. It had certainly increased while she attempted to eat stringy chicken at a late hour in the dining-room, while her husband smiled at her and talked about intoxicants. The reason he had talked so much about whisky and wine, she now concluded, was because he'd been aware of the tension that was coiled within her.

'You have made a mistake,' came the voice of Mrs Angusthorpe, 'but even now it is not too late to rectify it. Do not accept it, reject your error, Mrs Jackson.'

Doyle came into the bar and brought to them, without their demanding it, more sherry in two new glasses. Daphne heard him remarking that the brand of sherry was very popular in these parts. It was Spanish sherry, he said, since he would stock nothing else. He talked about Spain and Spaniards, saying that at the time of the Spanish Armada Spanish sailors had been wrecked around the nearby coast.

'I love my husband,' Daphne said when Doyle had gone again.

She had met her husband in the Hurlingham Club. He had partnered her in tennis and they had danced together at a charity dance. She'd listened while he talked one evening, telling her that the one thing he regretted was that he hadn't played golf as a child. Golf was a game, he'd said, that must be started when young if one was ever to achieve championship distinction. With tennis that wasn't quite so important, but it was, of course, as well to start tennis early also. She had thought he was rather nice. There was something about his distant manner that attracted her; there was a touch of arrogance in the way he didn't look at her when he spoke. She'd make him look at her, she vowed.

'My dear,' said Mrs Angusthorpe, 'I've seen the seamy side of Jackson Major. The more I think of him the more I can recall. He forced his way up that school, snatching at chances that weren't his to take, putting himself first, like he did in the half-mile race. There was cruelty in Jackson Major's eye, and ruthlessness and dullness. Like my husband, he has no sense of humour.'

'Mrs Angusthorpe, I really can't listen to all this. I was married yesterday to a man I'm in love with. It'll be all right – '

'Why will it be all right?'

'Because,' snapped Daphne Jackson with sudden spirit, 'I shall ask my husband as soon as he returns to take me at once from this horrible hotel. My marriage does not at all concern you, Mrs Angusthorpe.'

'They are talking now on a riverside, whispering maybe so as not to disturb their prey. They are murmuring about the past, of achievements on the sports field and marches undertaken by a cadet force. While you and I are having a different kind of talk.'

'What our husbands are saying to one another, Mrs Angusthorpe, may well make more sense.'

'What they are not saying is that two women in the bar of this hotel are unhappy. They have forgotten about the two women: they are more relaxed and contented than ever they are with us.'

Mrs Angusthorpe, beady-eyed as she spoke, saw the effect of her words reflected in the uneasy face of the woman beside her. She felt herself carried away by this small triumph, she experienced a headiness that was blissful. She saw in her mind another scene, imagining herself, over lunch, telling her husband about the simple thing that had happened. She would watch him sitting there in all his dignity: she would wait until he was about to pass a forkful of food to his mouth and then she would say: 'Jackson Major's wife has left him already.' And she would smile at him.

'You walked across the dining-room at breakfast,' said Mrs Angusthorpe. 'An instinct warned me then that you'd made an error.'

'I haven't made an error. I've told you, Mrs Angusthorpe –'

'Time will erode the polish of politeness. One day soon you'll see amusement in his eyes when you offer an opinion.'

'Please stop, Mrs Angusthorpe. I must go away if you continue like this – '

' "This man's a bore," you'll suddenly say to yourself, and look at him amazed.'

'Mrs Angusthorpe – '

'Amazed that you could ever have let it happen.'

'Oh God, please stop,' cried Daphne, tears coming suddenly from her eyes, her hands rushing to her cheeks.

'Don't be a silly girl,' whispered Mrs Angusthorpe, grasping the arm of her companion and tightening her fingers on it until Daphne felt pain. She thought as she felt it that Mrs Angusthorpe was a poisonous woman. She struggled to keep back further tears, she tried to wrench her arm away.

'I'll tell the man Doyle to order you a car,' said Mrs Angusthorpe. 'It'll take you into Galway. I'll lend you money, Mrs Jackson. By one o'clock tonight you could be sitting in your bed at home, eating from a tray that your mother brought you. A divorce will come through and one day you'll meet a man who'll love you with a tenderness.'

'My husband loves me, Mrs Angusthorpe – '

'Your husband should marry a woman who's keen on horses or golf, a woman who might take a whip to him, being ten years older than himself. My dear, you're like me: you're a delicate person.'

'Please let go my arm. You've no right to talk to me like this – '

'He is my husband's creature, my husband moulded him. The best head boy he'd ever known, he said to me.'

Daphne, calmer now, did not say anything. She felt the pressure on her arm being removed. She stared ahead of her, at a round mat on the table that advertised Celebration Ale. Without wishing to and perhaps, she thought, because she was so upset, she saw herself suddenly as Mrs Angusthorpe had suggested, sitting up in her own bedroom with a tray of food on her knees and her mother standing beside her, saying it was all right. 'I suddenly realised,' she heard herself saying. 'He took me to this awful hotel, where his old headmaster was. He gave me wine and whisky, and then in bed I thought I might be sick.' Her mother replied to her, telling her that it wasn't a disgrace, and her father came in later and told her not to worry. It was better not to be unhappy, her father said: it was better to have courage now.

'Let me tell Doyle to order a car at once.' Mrs Angusthorpe was on her feet, eagerness in her eyes and voice. Her cheeks were flushed from sherry and excitement.

'You're quite outrageous,' said Daphne Jackson.

She left the bar and in the hall Doyle again desired her as she passed. He spoke to her, telling her he'd already ordered a few more bottles of that sherry so that she and Mrs Angusthorpe could sip a little as often as they liked. It was sherry, he repeated, that was very popular in the locality. She nodded and mounted the stairs, not hearing much of what he said, feeling that as she pushed one leg in front of another her whole body would open and tears would gush from everywhere. Why did she have to put up with talk like that on the first morning of her honeymoon? Why had he casually gone out fishing with his old headmaster? Why had he brought her to this terrible place and then made her drink so that the tension would leave her body? She sobbed on the stairs, causing Doyle to frown and feel concerned for her.

'Are you all right?' Jackson Major asked, standing in the doorway of their room, looking to where she sat, by the window. He closed the door and went to her. 'You've been all right?' he said.

She nodded, smiling a little. She spoke in a low voice: she

said she thought it possible that conversations might be heard through the partition wall. She pointed to the wall she spoke of. 'It's only a partition,' she said.

He touched it and agreed, but gave it as his opinion that little could be heard through it since they themselves had not heard the people on the other side of it. Partitions nowadays, he pronounced, were constructed always of soundproof material.

'Let's have a drink before lunch,' she said.

In the hour that had elapsed since she had left Mrs Angusthorpe in the bar she had changed her stockings and her dress. She had washed her face in cold water and had put lipstick and powder on it. She had brushed her suède shoes with a rubber brush.

'All right,' he said. 'We'll have a little drink.'

He kissed her. On the way downstairs he told her about the morning's fishing and the conversations he had had with his old headmaster. Not asking her what she'd like, he ordered both of them gin and tonic in the bar.

'I know her better than you do, sir,' Doyle said, bringing her a glass of sherry, but Jackson Major didn't appear to realise what had happened, being still engrossed in the retailing of the conversations he had had with his old headmaster.

'I want to leave this hotel,' she said. 'At once, darling, after lunch.'

'Daphne – '

'I do.'

She didn't say that Mrs Angusthorpe had urged her to leave him, nor that the Angusthorpes had lain awake during the night, hearing what there was to hear. She simply said she didn't at all like the idea of spending her honeymoon in a hotel which also contained his late headmaster and the headmaster's wife. 'They remember you as a boy,' she said. 'For some reason it makes me edgy. And anyway it's such a nasty hotel.'

She leaned back after that speech, glad that she'd been able to make it as she'd planned to make it. They would move on after lunch, paying whatever money must necessarily be paid. They would find a pleasant room in a pleasant hotel and the tension inside her would gradually relax. In the Hurlingham Club she had made this tall man look at her when he spoke to her, she had made him regard her and find her attractive, as she found him. They had said to one another that they had fallen in love, he had asked her to marry him, and she had happily agreed: there was nothing the matter.

'My dear, it would be quite impossible,' he said.

'Impossible?'

'At this time of year, in the middle of the season? Hotel rooms are gold dust, my dear. Angusthorpe was saying as much. His wife's a good sort, you know – '

'I want to leave here.'

He laughed good-humouredly. He gestured with his hands, suggesting his helplessness.

'I cannot stay here,' she said.

'You're tired, Daphne.'

'I cannot stay here for a fortnight with the Angusthorpes. She's a woman who goes on all the time; there's something the matter with her. While you go fishing – '

'Darling, I had to go this morning. I felt it polite to go. If you like, I'll not go out again at all.'

'I've told you what I'd like.'

'Oh, for God's sake!' He turned away from her. She said:

'I thought you would say yes at once.'

'How the hell can I say yes when we've booked a room for the next fortnight and we're duty-bound to pay for it? Do you really think we can just walk up to that man and say we don't like his hotel and the people he has staying here?'

'We could make some excuse. We could pretend – '

'Pretend? Pretend, Daphne?'

'Some illness. We could say my mother's ill,' she hurriedly said. 'Or some aunt who doesn't even exist. We could hire a car and drive around the coast – '

'Daphne – '

'Why not?'

'For a start, I haven't my driving licence with me.'

'I have.'

'I doubt it, Daphne.'

She thought, and then she agreed that she hadn't. 'We could go to Dublin,' she said with a fresh burst of urgency. 'Dublin's a lovely place, people say. We could stay in Dublin and – '

'My dear, this is a tourist country. Millions of tourists come here every summer. Do you really believe we'd find decent accommodation in Dublin in the middle of the season?'

'It wouldn't have to be decent. Some little clean hotel – '

'Added to which, Daphne, I must honestly tell you that I have no wish to go gallivanting on my honeymoon. Nor do I care for the notion of telling lies about the illness of people who are not ill, or do not even exist.'

'I'll tell the lies. I'll talk to Mr Doyle directly after lunch. I'll talk to him now.' She stood up. He shook his head, reaching for the hand that was nearer to him.

'What's the matter?' he asked.

Slowly she sat down again.

'Oh, darling,' she said.

'We must be sensible, Daphne. We can't just go gallivanting off – '

'Why do you keep on about gallivanting? What's it matter whether we're gallivanting or not so long as we're enjoying ourselves?'

'Daphne – '

'I'm asking you to do something to please me.'

Jackson Major, about to reply, changed his mind. He smiled at his bride. After a pause, he said:

'If you really want to, Daphne – '

'Well, I do. I think perhaps it'll be awkward here with the Angusthorpes. And it's not what we expected.'

'It's just a question,' said Jackson Major, 'of what we could possibly do. I've asked for my mail to be forwarded here and, as I say, I really believe it would be a case of out of the frying-pan into nothing at all. It might prove horribly difficult.'

She closed her eyes and sat for a moment in silence. Then she opened them and, being unable to think of anything else to say, she said:

'I'm sorry.'

He sighed, shrugging his shoulders slightly. He took her hand again. 'You do see, darling?' Before she could reply he added: 'I'm sorry I was angry with you. I didn't mean to be: I'm very sorry.'

He kissed her on the cheek that was near to him. He took her hand. 'Now tell me,' he said, 'about everything that's worrying you.'

She repeated, without more detail, what she had said already, but this time the sentences she spoke did not sound like complaints. He listened to her, sitting back and not interrupting, and then they conversed about all she had said. He agreed that it was a pity about the hotel and explained to her that what had happened, apparently, was that the old proprietor had died during the previous year. It was unfortunate too, he quite agreed, that the Angusthorpes should be here at the same time as they were because it would, of course, have been so much nicer to have been on their own. If she was worried about the partition in their room he would ask that their room should be changed for another one. He hadn't known when she'd mentioned the partition before that it was the Angusthorpes who were on the other side of it. It would be better, really, not to be in the next room to the Angusthorpes since Angusthorpe had once been his headmaster, and he was certain that Doyle would understand a thing like that and agree to change them over, even if it meant greasing Doyle's palm. 'I imagine he'd fall in with anything,' said Jackson Major, 'for a bob or two.'

They finished their drinks and she followed him to the dining-room. There were no thoughts in her mind: no voice, neither her own nor Mrs Angusthorpe's, spoke. For a reason she could not understand and didn't want to bother to understand, the tension within her had snapped and was no longer there. The desire she had felt for tears when she'd walked away from Mrs Angusthorpe was far from her now; she felt a weariness, as though an ordeal was over and she had survived it. She didn't know why she felt like that. All she knew was that he had listened to her: he had been patient and understanding, allowing her to say all that was in her mind and then being reassuring. It was not his fault that the hotel had turned out so unfortunately. Nor was it his fault that a bullying old man had sought him out as a fishing companion. He couldn't help it if his desire for her brought out a clumsiness in him. He was a man, she thought: he was not the same as she was: she must meet him half-way. He had said he was sorry for being angry with her.

In the hall they met the Angusthorpes on their way to the dining-room also.

'I'm sorry if I upset you,' Mrs Angusthorpe said to her, touching her arm to hold her back for a moment. 'I'm afraid my temper ran away with me.'

The two men went ahead, involved in a new conversation. 'We might try that little tributary this afternoon,' the headmaster was suggesting.

'I sat there afterwards, seeing how horrid it must have been for you,' Mrs Angusthorpe said. 'I was only angry at the prospect of an unpleasant fortnight. I took it out on you.'

'Don't worry about it.'

'One should keep one's anger to oneself. I feel embarrassed now,' said Mrs Angusthorpe. 'I'm not the sort of person – '

'Please don't worry,' murmured Daphne, trying hard to keep the tiredness that possessed her out of her voice. She could sleep, she was thinking, for a week.

'I don't know why I talked like that.'

'You were angry – '

'Yes,' said Mrs Angusthorpe.

She stood still, not looking at Daphne and seeming not to wish to enter the dining-room. Some people went by, talking and laughing. Mr Gorman, the solicitor from Dublin, addressed her, but she did not acknowledge his greeting.

'I think we must go in now, Mrs Angusthorpe,' Daphne said.

In her weariness she smiled at Mrs Angusthorpe, suddenly sorry for her because she had so wretched a marriage that it caused her to become emotional with strangers.

'It was just,' said Mrs Angusthorpe, pausing uncertainly in the middle of her sentence and then continuing, 'I felt that perhaps I should say something. I felt, Mrs Jackson – '

'Let's just forget it,' interrupted Daphne, sensing with alarm that Mrs Angusthorpe was about to begin all over again, in spite of her protestations.

'What?'

'I think we must forget it all.'

Daphne smiled again, to reasure the woman who'd been outrageous because her temper had run away with her. She wanted to tell her that just now in the bar she herself had had a small outburst and that in the end she had seen the absurdity of certain suggestions she had made. She wanted to say that her husband had asked her what the matter was and then had said he was sorry. She wanted to explain, presumptuously perhaps, that there must be give and take in marriage, that a bed of roses was something that couldn't be shared. She wanted to say that the tension she'd felt was no longer there, but she couldn't find the energy for saying it.

'Forget it?' said Mrs Angusthorpe. 'Yes, I suppose so. There are things that shouldn't be talked about.'

'It's not that really,' objected Daphne softly. 'It's just that I think you jumped to a lot of wrong conclusions.'

'I had an instinct,' began Mrs Angusthorpe with all her previous eagerness and urgency. 'I saw you at breakfast time, an innocent girl. I couldn't help remembering.'

'It's different for us,' said Daphne, feeling embarrassed to have to converse again in this intimate vein. 'At heart my husband's patient with me. And understanding too: he listens to me.'

'Of course,' agreed Mrs Angusthorpe, slowly nodding her head and moving at last towards the dining-room.

A Choice of Butchers

The upper landing of our house had brown linoleum on it and outside each of the bedroom doors there was a small black mat. From this square landing with its three mats and its window overlooking the backyard there rose a flight of uncarpeted steps that led to the attic room where Bridget, who was our maid, slept. The stairs that descended to the lower landing, where the bathroom and lavatory were and where my mother and father slept, were carpeted with a pattern of red flowers which continued downwards to a hall that also had brown linoleum on its floor. There was a hall-stand in the hall and beside it a high green plant in a brass pot, and a figure of the Holy Mother on a table, all by itself. The walls of the landings, and of the hall and the staircase, were papered gloomily in an oatmeal shade that had no pattern, only a pebbly roughness that was fashionable in my childhood in our West Cork town. On this hung two brown pictures, one of oxen dragging a plough over rough ground at sunrise, the other of a farmer leading a working horse towards a farmyard at the end of the day. It was against a background of the oatmeal shade and the oxen in the dawn that I, through the rails of the banisters on the upper landing, saw my father kissing Bridget at the end of one summer holiday.

I had come from my room on that warm September evening to watch for Henry Dukelow, who came up every night to say good-night to me. I had knelt down by the banisters, with my face against them, pressing hard so that I might be marked, so that Mr Dukelow would laugh when he saw me. 'God, you're tip-top,' my father said in a whisper that travelled easily up to me, and then he put his arms around her shoulders and roughly hugged her, with his lips pressed on to her lips.

I was seven years of age, the afterthought of the family, as my father called me. My brothers and sisters were all grown up, but I didn't feel then, not yet, that my parents had given so much to them that there wasn't a lot left to give me. Once upon a time they had all been a family like any other family: the children in turn had left home, and then, when my mother should have been resting and my father finding life less demanding, I had arrived. I did not ever doubt my parents' concern for me, but for the six months that he was in our house I felt that Mr Dukelow loved me as much as they did. 'Say good-night to him for me,' I often heard my mother calling out to him as he mounted the stairs to tell me my night-time story, and I grew up thinking of my mother as a tired person because that was what she was. Her hair was going grey and her face bore a fatigued look: Mr Dukelow said she probably didn't sleep well. There were a lot of people who didn't sleep well, he told me, sitting on my bed one night when I was seven, and I remember he went on talking about that until I must have fallen asleep myself.

Mr Dukelow, who occupied the room next to mine, taught me to play marbles on the rough surface of our backyard. He made me an aeroplane out of heavy pieces of wood he found lying about and he explained to me that although a star could fall through the sky it would never land on the earth. He told me stories about Columbus and Vasco da Gama, and about the great emperors of Europe and the Battle of the Yellow Ford. He had a good memory for what had interested him at school, but he had forgotten as easily the rest: he had been a poor scholar, he said. He told me the plots of films he'd seen and of a play called *Paddy the Next Best Thing*. He spoke very quietly and he always answered my questions: a small man, as thin as a willow, bony and pale-faced and supposed to be delicate, different from my father. He was fifty-seven; my father was fifty-nine.

In the middle of the night that my father kissed Bridget Mr Dukelow came to my room again. He switched the light on and stood there in grey-striped pyjamas that were badly torn.

'I could hear you crying,' he said. 'What's the trouble with you?'

He wore spectacles with fine wire rims, and all his face seemed to have gone into his nose, which was thin and tapering. His greased hair was black, his hands were like a skeleton's. The first night Mr Dukelow arrived in our house my father brought him into the kitchen, where my mother was reading the *Irish Press* at the table and Bridget was darning one of her black stockings. 'I've employed this man,' my father said, and as he stepped to one side of the doorway the bent figure of Mr Dukelow appeared suddenly and silently, and my father gestured in the manner of a ringmaster introducing a circus act. Mr Dukelow was carrying a cardboard suitcase that had too many clothes in it. I remember seeing the flannel material of a shirt protruding, for the case was not fastened as it was meant to be.

'What are you crying for?' he asked me on that later occasion. 'What's up with you?'

'Go away, Mr Dukelow.'

A frown appeared on his white forehead. He went away, leaving the light on, and he returned within a minute carrying a packet of cigarettes and a cigarette-lighter I'd bought in Woolworth's in Cork and given him the Christmas before. He always smoked Craven A, claiming that they were manufactured from a superior kind of tobacco. He lit one and sat on my bed. He talked, as often he did, about the moment of his arrival at our house and how he had paused for a moment outside it.

Looking at our house from the street, you saw the brown hall-door, its paintwork grained to make it seem like mahogany. There was a brass knocker and a letter-box that every morning except Sunday were cleaned with Brasso by Bridget. To the right of the hall door, and dwarfing it, were the windows of my father's butcher shop, with its sides of mutton hanging from hooks, tripe on a white enamel dish, and beef and sausages and mince and suet.

Afterwards, when he became my friend, Mr Dukelow said that he had stood on the street outside the shop, having just got off the Bantry bus. With his suitcase weighing him down, he had gazed at the windows, wondering about the shop and the house, and about my father. He had not come all the way from Bantry but from a house in the hills somewhere, where he had been employed as some kind of manservant. He had walked to a crossroads and had stood there waiting for the bus: there had been dust on his shoes that night when first he came into our kitchen. 'I looked at the meat in the window,' he told me afterwards, 'and I thought I'd rather go away again.' But my father, expecting him, had come out of the shop and had told him to come on in. My father was a big man; beside Mr Dukelow he looked like a giant.

Mr Dukelow sat on my bed, smoking his Craven A. He began to talk about the advertisement my father had placed in the *Cork Examiner* for an assistant. He repeated the words my father had employed in the advertisement and he said he'd been nervous even to look at them. 'I had no qualifications,' Mr Dukelow said. 'I was afraid.'

That night, six months before, there'd been that kind of fear in his face. 'Sit down, Mr Dukelow,' my mother had said. 'Have you had your tea?' He shook hands with my mother and myself and with Bridget, making a great thing of it, covering up his shyness. He said he'd had tea, although he confessed to me afterwards that he hadn't. 'You'll take a cup, anyway,' my mother offered, 'and a piece of fruit-cake I made?' Bridget took a kettle from the range and poured boiling water into a teapot to warm it. 'Errah, maybe he wants something stronger,' my father said, giving a great gusty laugh. 'Will we go down to Keogh's, Henry?' But my mother insisted that, first of all, before strong drink was taken, before even Mr Dukelow was led to his room, he should have a cup of tea and a slice of fruit-cake. 'He's hardly inside the door,' she said chidingly to my father, 'before you're lifting him out again.' My father, who laughed easily, laughed again. 'Doesn't he have to get to know the people of the town?' he demanded. 'It's a great little town,' he informed Mr Dukelow. 'There's tip-top business here.' My father had only seven fingers and one thumb: being a clumsy man, he had lost the others at different moments, when engaged in his trade. When he had no fingers left he would retire, he used to say, and he would laugh in his roaring way, and add that the sight of a butcher with no fingers would be more than customers could tolerate.

'I often think back,' said Mr Dukelow, 'to the kindness of your mother that first time.'

'He kissed Bridget in the hall,' I said. 'He said she was looking great.'

'Ah, no.'

'I saw him through the banisters.'

'Is it a nightmare you had? Will I get your mammy up?'

I said it wasn't a nightmare I had had: I said I didn't want my mother. My mother was sleeping beside him in their bed and she didn't know that he'd been kissing the maid.

'She'd go away,' I said. 'My mother would go away.'

'Ah no, no.'

'He was kissing Bridget.'

Once, saying good-night to me, Mr Dukelow had unexpectedly given me a kiss, but it was a kiss that wasn't at all like the kiss I had observed in the hall. Mr Dukelow had kissed me because my mother was too tired to climb the stairs; he had kissed me in case I felt neglected. Another time, just as unexpectedly, he had taken a florin from his waistcoat pocket and had put it under my pillow, telling me to buy sweets with it. 'Where d'you get that from?' my father had demanded the next day, and when I told him he hit the side of his leg with his fist, becoming angry in a way that puzzled me. Afterwards I heard him shouting at my mother that Henry Dukelow had given me a two-bob bit and had she anything to say to that? My father was sometimes so peculiar in his behaviour that I couldn't make him out. My mother's quietness was always more noticeable when he was present; I loved her for her quietness.

'He had a few jars in tonight.'

'Was he drunk, Mr Dukelow?'

'I think he was.'

'My mother –'

'Will I tell you a story?'

'No, no.'

I imagined Bridget, as I had been imagining her while I lay awake, thinking to herself that she'd give my mother her marching orders. I imagined, suddenly, my mother doing Bridget's work in the kitchen and Bridget standing at the door watching her. She was a plump girl, red-cheeked, with black curly hair. She had fat arms and legs, and she wasn't as tall as my mother. She must have been about twenty-five at the time; Mr Dukelow had told me that my mother was fifty-one. Bridget used to bring me the green glass balls that fishermen use for floating their nets, because she lived by the sea and often found them washed up on the strand. She didn't tell me stories like Mr Dukelow did, but sometimes she'd read to me out of one of the romances she borrowed from a library that the nuns ran. All the books had brown paper covers on them to keep them from getting dirty, with the titles written in ink on the front. I couldn't remember a time that Bridget hadn't been in the house, with those brown-covered volumes, cycling back from her Sunday afternoon off with fish and vegetables in a basket. I had always liked her, but she was different from my mother: I was fonder of my mother.

'If my mother died,' I said, 'he would be married to Bridget. She didn't mind it when he kissed her.'

Mr Dukelow shook his head. She might have been taken unawares, he pointed out: she might have minded it and not been able to protest owing to surprise. Maybe she'd protested, he suggested, after I'd run back to bed.

'She's going out with the porter in the Munster and Leinster Bank,' he said. 'She's keen on that fellow.'

'My father's got more money.'

'Don't worry about your father now. A little thing like that can happen and that's the end of it. Your father's a decent man.'

It was typical of Mr Dukelow to say that my father was a decent man, even though he knew my father didn't like him. In the shop Mr Dukelow outclassed him: after he'd recovered from his initial nervousness, he'd become neater with the meat than my father was, and it was impossible to imagine Mr Dukelow banging through his thin fingers with the cleaver, or letting a knife slip into his flesh. My father said Mr Dukelow had a lot to learn, but it was my father really who had a lot to learn, since he hadn't been able to learn properly in the first place. Once, a woman called Mrs Tighe had returned a piece of meat to the shop, complaining that it had a smell. 'Will you watch that, Henry?' my father expostulated after Mrs Tighe had left the shop, but Mrs Tighe hadn't said it was Mr Dukelow who had sold her the meat. I was there myself at the time and I knew from the expression on Mr Dukelow's face that it was my father who had sold the bad meat to Mrs Tighe. 'Any stuff like that,' my father said to him, 'mince up in the machine.' I could see Mr Dukelow deciding that he intended to do no such thing: it would go against his sensitivity to mince up odorous meat, not because of the dishonesty of the action but because he had become a more prideful butcher than my father, even though he was only an assistant. Mr Dukelow would throw such a piece of meat away, hiding it beneath offal so that my father couldn't accuse him of wasting anything.

In my bedroom, which had a yellow distemper on the walls and a chest of drawers painted white, with a cupboard and wash-stand to match, Mr Dukelow told me not to worry. There was a little crucifix on the wall above my bed, placed there by my mother, and there was a sacred picture opposite the bed so that I could see the face of Our Lady from where I lay. 'Say a prayer,' urged Mr Dukelow, indicating with a thin hand the two reminders of my Faith. 'I would address St Agnes on a question like that.'

Slowly he selected and lit another cigarette. 'Your father's a decent man,' he repeated, and then he must have gone away because when I woke up the light had been switched off. It was half-past seven and the first thing I thought was that the day was the last day of the summer holidays. Then I remembered my father kissing Bridget and Mr Dukelow talking to me in the night.

We all had our breakfast together in the kitchen, my mother at one end of the table, my father at the other, Bridget next to me, and Mr Dukelow opposite us. We always sat like that, for all meals, but what I hadn't paid any attention to before was that Bridget was next to my father.

'Two dozen chops,' he said, sitting there with blood on his hands. 'Did I tell you that, Henry? To go over to Mrs Ashe in the hotel.'

'I'll cut them so,' promised Mr Dukelow in his quiet way.

My father laughed. 'Errah, man, haven't I cut them myself?' He laughed again. He watched while Bridget knelt down to open the iron door of the oven. 'There's nothing like cutting chops,' he said, 'to give you an appetite for your breakfast, Bridget.'

My eyes were on a piece of fried bread on my plate. I didn't lift them, but I could feel Mr Dukelow looking at me. He knew I felt jealous because my father had addressed Bridget instead of my mother. I was jealous on my mother's behalf, because she couldn't be jealous herself, because she didn't know. Mr Dukelow sensed everything, as though there was an extra dimension to him. The chops for Mrs Ashe would have been more elegantly cut if he had cut them himself; they'd have been more cleverly cut, with less waste and in half the time.

'Ah, that's great,' said my father as Bridget placed a plate of rashers and sausages in front of him. She sat down quietly beside me. Neither she nor my mother had said anything since I'd entered the kitchen.

'Is there no potato cakes?' my father demanded, and my mother said she'd be making fresh ones today.

'The last ones were lumpy.'

'A little,' agreed my mother. 'There were a few little lumps.'

He held his knife and fork awkwardly because of the injuries to his hands. Often he put too much on his fork and pieces of bacon would fall off. Mr Dukelow, when he was eating, had a certain style.

'Well, mister-me-buck,' said my father, addressing me, 'it's the final day of your holidays.'

'Yes.'

'When I was the age you are I had to do work in my holidays. I was delivering meat at six and a half years.'

'Yes.'

'Don't the times change, Bridget?'

Bridget said that times did change. My father asked Mr Dukelow if he had worked during the holidays as a child and Mr Dukelow replied that he had worked in the fields in the summer-time, weeding, harvesting potatoes, and making hay.

'They have an easy time of it these days,' my father pronounced. He had addressed all of us except my mother. He pushed his cup towards Bridget and she passed it to my mother for more tea.

'An easy time of it,' repeated my father.

I could see him eyeing Mr Dukelow's hands as if he was thinking to himself that they didn't look as if they would be much use for harvesting potatoes. And I thought to myself that my father was wrong in this estimation: Mr Dukelow would collect the potatoes speedily, having dug them himself in a methodical way; he would toss them into sacks with a flick of the wrist, a craftsman even in that.

The postman, called Mr Dicey, who was small and inquisitive and had squinting eyes, came into the kitchen from the yard. When he had a letter for the household he delivered it in this manner, while we sat at breakfast. He would stand while the letter was opened, drinking a cup of tea.

'That's a fine morning,' said Mr Dicey. 'We'll have a fine day of it.'

'Unless it rains.' My father laughed until he was red in the face, and then abruptly ceased because no one was laughing with him. 'How're you, Dicey?' he more calmly inquired.

'I have an ache in my back,' replied Mr Dicey, handing my mother a letter.

Mr Dukelow nodded at him, greeting him in that way. Sometimes Mr Dukelow was so quiet in the kitchen that my father asked him if there was something awry with him.

'I was saying to the bucko here,' said my father, 'that when I was his age I used to deliver meat from the shop. Haven't times changed, Dicey?'

'They have not remained the same,' agreed Mr Dicey. 'You could not expect it.'

Bridget handed him a cup of tea. He stirred sugar into it, remarking to Bridget that he'd seen her out last night. It was said that Mr Dicey's curiosity was so great that he often steamed open a letter and delivered it a day late. He was interested in everyone in the town and was keen to know of fresh developments in people's lives.

'You didn't see me at all,' he said to Bridget. He paused, drinking his tea. 'You were engaged at the same time,' he said, 'with another person.'

'Oh, Bridie has her admirers all right,' said my father.

'From the Munster and Leinster Bank.' Mr Dicey laughed. 'There's a letter from your daughter,' he said to my mother. 'I know her little round-shaped writing.'

My mother, concerned with the letter, nodded.

'Bridie could claim the best,' said my father.

I looked at him and saw that he was glancing down the length of the table at my mother.

'Bridie could claim the best,' he repeated in a notably loud voice. 'Wouldn't you say that, Dicey? Isn't she a great-looking girl?'

'She is, of course,' said Mr Dicey. 'Why shouldn't she be?'

'It's a wonder she never claimed Henry Dukelow.' My father coughed and laughed. 'Amn't I right she could claim the best, Henry? Couldn't Bridie have any husband she put her eye on?'

'I'll carry over the chops to Mrs Ashe,' said Mr Dukelow, getting up from the table.

My father laughed. 'Henry Dukelow wouldn't be interested,' he said. 'D'you understand me, Dicey?'

'Oh, now, why wouldn't Henry be interested?' inquired Mr Dicey, interested himself.

Mr Dukelow washed his hands at the sink. He dried them on a towel that hung on the back of the kitchen door, a special towel that only he and my father used.

'He's not a marrying man,' said my father. 'Amn't I right, Henry?'

Mr Dukelow smiled at my father and left the kitchen without speaking. Mr Dicey began to say something, but my father interrupted him.

'He's not a marrying man,' he repeated. He pressed a piece of bread into the grease on his plate. He cleaned the plate with it, and then ate it and drank some tea. Mr Dicey put his cup and saucer on to the table, telling Bridget she was a marvel at making tea. There wasn't better tea in the town, Mr Dicey said, than the tea he drank in this kitchen. He wanted to remain, to hang around in case something happened: he was aware of a heavy atmosphere that morning and he was as puzzled as I was.

My mother was still reading the letter, my father was still staring at her head. Was he trying to hurt her? I wondered: was he attempting to upset her by saying that Bridget could have anyone she wanted as a husband?

She handed the letter to me, indicating that I should pass it on to him. I saw that it was from my sister Sheila, who had married, two Christmases before, a salesman of stationery. I gave it to my father and I watched him reading.

'Bedad,' he said. 'She's due for a baby.'

When I heard my father saying that I thought for only a moment about what the words signified. Bridget exclaimed appropriately, and then there was a silence while my father looked at my mother. She smiled at him in a half-hearted way, obliged by duty to do that, reluctant to share any greater emotion with him.

'Is it Sheila herself?' cried Mr Dicey in simulated excitement. 'God, you wouldn't believe it!' From the way he spoke it was evident that he had known the details of the letter. He went on to say that it seemed only yesterday that my sister was an infant herself. He continued to talk, his squinting eyes moving rapidly over all of us, and I could sense his interest in the calm way my mother had taken the news, not saying a word. There was a damper on the natural excitement, which no one could have failed to be aware of.

My father tried to make up for the lack of commotion by shouting out that for the first time in his life he would be a grandfather. My mother smiled again at him and then, like Mr Dukelow, she rose and left the kitchen. Reluctantly, Mr Dicey took his leave of us also.

Bridget collected the dishes from the table and conveyed them to the sink. My father lit a cigarette. He poured himself a cup of tea, humming a melody that often, tunelessly, he did hum. 'You're as quiet as Henry Dukelow this morning,' he said to me, and I wanted to reply that we were all quiet except himself, but I didn't say anything. Sometimes when he looked at me I remembered the time he'd said to me that he wondered when I was grown up if I'd take over his shop and be a butcher like he was. 'Your brothers didn't care for that,' he'd said, speaking without rancour but with a certain sorrow in his voice. 'They didn't fancy the trade.' He had smiled at me coaxingly, saying that he was a happy man and that he had built up the business and wouldn't want to see it die away. At the time I felt revulsion at the thought of cutting up dead animals all day long, knifing off slices of red steak and poking for kidneys. I had often watched him at work since he encouraged me to do that, even offering me the experience as a treat. 'Well, mister-me-buck,' he would shout at me, bustling about in his white apron, 'is there a nice piece of liver there for Mrs Bourke?' He would talk to his customers about me as he weighed their orders, remarking that I was growing well and was a good boy when I remembered to be. 'Will you be a butcher like your daddy?' a woman often asked me and I could feel the tension in him without at the time understanding it. It wasn't until I saw Mr Dukelow going about the business in his stylish way that I began to say to the women that I might be a butcher one day. Mr Dukelow didn't make me feel that he was cutting up dead animals at all: Mr Dukelow made it all seem civilised.

I didn't leave the kitchen that morning until my father had finished his cup of tea and was ready to go also, in case he'd kiss Bridget when they were alone together. He told me to hurry up and go and help my mother, but I delayed deliberately and in the end I shamed him into going before me. Bridget went on cleaning the dishes in the sink, standing there silently, as if she didn't know what was happening.

I went to my parents' bedroom, where my mother was making their bed. She asked me to take the end of a sheet and to pull it up so that she wouldn't have to walk around the bed and do it herself. She had taught me how to help her. I seized the end of the sheet and then the end of a blanket. I said:

'If you go away I will go with you.'

She looked at me. She asked me what I'd said and I said it again. She didn't reply. We went on making the bed together and when it was finished, she said:

'It isn't me who's going away, love.'

'Is it Bridget?'

'There's no need for Bridget – '

'I saw him – '

'He didn't mean any harm.'

'Did you see him too?'

'It doesn't matter at all. Sheila's going to have a little baby. Isn't that grand?'

I couldn't understand why she was suddenly talking about

my sister having a baby since it had nothing to do with my
father kissing Bridget.

'It's not he who's going away?' I asked, knowing that for my
father to go away would be the most unlikely development of
all.

'Bridget was telling me yesterday,' my mother said, 'she's
going to marry the porter at the Munster and Leinster Bank.
It's a secret Bridget has: don't tell your father or Mr Dicey or
anyone like that.'

'Mr Dukelow – '

'It is Mr Dukelow who will be going away.'

She covered the big bed with a candlewick bedspread. She
pointed a finger at the side of the bedspread that was near me,
indicating that I should aid her with it.

'Mr Dukelow?' I said. 'Why would – '

'He moves around from one place to another. He does
different kinds of work.'

'Does he get the sack?'

My mother shrugged her shoulders. I went on asking questions, but she told me to be quiet. I followed her to the
kitchen and watched her making potato cakes, while Bridget
went in and out. Occasionally they spoke, but they weren't
unfriendly: it wasn't between them that there was anything
wrong. I remembered Bridget saying to me one time that my
mother was always very good to her, better than her own
mother had ever been. She had a great fondness for my
mother, she said, and I sensed it between them that morning
because somehow it seemed greater than it had been in the
past, even though the night before my father had been kissing
Bridget in the hall. I kept looking at my mother, wanting her
to explain whatever there was to explain to me, to tell me why
Mr Dukelow, who'd said he never wanted to leave my father's
shop, was going to leave now, after only six months. I
couldn't imagine the house without Mr Dukelow. I couldn't

imagine lying in my bed without anyone to come and tell me about Vasco da Gama. I couldn't imagine not seeing him lighting a Craven A cigarette from the little lighter I'd bought him.

'Well, isn't that terrible?' said my father when we were all sitting down again at the kitchen table for our dinner. 'Henry Dukelow's shifting on.'

Mr Dukelow looked nervous. He glanced from me to my mother, not knowing that my mother had guessed he would be going, not knowing she'd suggested it to me.

'We thought he might be,' my mother said. 'He's learnt the business.'

My father pressed potatoes into his mouth and remarked on the stew we were eating. His mood was wholly different now: he wagged his head at my mother, saying she'd cooked the meat well. There wasn't a woman in the country, he tediously continued, who could cook stew like my mother. He asked me if I agreed with that, and I said I did. 'You'll be back at school tomorrow,' he said, and I agreed with that also. 'Tell them they'll have an uncle in the class,' he advised, 'and give the teacher a few smiles.'

Releasing an obstreperous laugh, he pushed his plate away from him with the stumps of two fingers. 'Will we go down to Keogh's,' he suggested to Mr Dukelow, 'and have a talk about what you will do?'

'You can talk here,' said my mother with severity. I could see her saying to herself that it was the half-day and if my father entered Keogh's he'd remain there for the afternoon.

'Hurry up, Henry,' said my father, scraping his chair as he pushed it back on the flagged floor. 'A tip-top stew,' he repeated. He made a noise in his mouth, sucking through his teeth, a noise that was familiar to all of us. He told Mr Dukelow he'd be waiting for him in Keogh's.

'Keep an eye on him,' my mother murmured when he'd gone, and Mr Dukelow nodded.

'I would have told you that tonight,' he said to me. 'I didn't want to say a thing until I'd mentioned it to your father first.'

'Mr Dukelow'll be here a month yet.' My mother smiled at me. 'He can tell you a good few stories in that time.'

But Mr Dukelow in fact did not remain in our house for another month. When he returned with my father later that day, my father, in a better mood than ever, said:

'We've come to a good agreement. Henry's going to pack his traps. He'll catch the half-seven bus.'

But Mr Dukelow didn't say anything. He walked from the kitchen without swaying like my father was swaying.

My father had his hat on and he didn't take it off. He took his turnip watch from his waistcoat pocket and examined it. 'I can't see without my glasses,' he said to me. 'Will you take a gander at it, boy?'

He never wore glasses, but he often made the joke when he'd been down to Keogh's for a while. I told him it was twenty past six. He put the stumps of two fingers on my head and said I was a great boy. Did I know, he asked me, that in six months' time I'd be an uncle? He had a way of touching me with his stumps instead of with the fingers that remained with him, just as he had a way of pushing from him a plate from which he'd eaten a meal. 'Don't forget to tell the teacher,' he said. 'It's not every day he has an uncle to instruct.'

My mother took a barm brack from a tin and began to butter it for Mr Dukelow before he went. Bridget moved a kettle on to the hot area of the stove. It boiled at once. 'Will I fry him something?' she asked my mother.

'There's rashers there,' said my mother, 'and a bit of black pudding. Do him eggs, Bridget, and a few potato cakes.'

'He's going,' repeated my father. His face, redder than

usually it was, had sweat on the sides of it. 'He's going,' he said again.

I was sitting at the end of the table with a comic spread out in front of me. While I gazed at my father half my vision retained the confused mass of cartoon characters.

'Well, that's that,' said my father.

He stood there swaying, his feet rooted to the kitchen floor, like a statue about to topple in a wind. He was wearing the blue-striped suit that he always wore on the half-day; his hands were hanging by his sides.

'You should be bloody ashamed of yourself,' he said suddenly, and I thought he was talking to me. He wasn't looking at any of us; his eyes were turned upwards, regarding a corner of the ceiling. 'A chancer like that,' he said, 'that gives a young fellow two-bob pieces.' Instinctively I knew then that he was speaking to my mother, even though she did not acknowledge his remarks.

'Sent up from Satan,' he said. 'Sent up to make wickedness. I'm sorry about that thing, Bridget.'

Bridget shook her head, implying that it didn't matter, and I knew they were referring to what had happened in the hall last night.

'Tell Henry Dukelow I'll see him at the bus.' He moved to the back door, adding that he was returning to Keogh's until it was time to say good-bye to Mr Dukelow. 'He'll never make a butcher,' he said, 'or any other bloody thing either.'

I closed the comic and watched my mother and Bridget preparing Mr Dukelow's last meal in our house. They didn't speak and I was afraid to, now. I still couldn't understand why this series of events was taking place. I tried to connect one occurrence with another, but I failed. I felt forgotten in the house: I might have been dead at the table for all they considered me: they were assuming I had no mind.

Mr Dukelow came into the silence, carrying the suitcase he

had first carried into the kitchen six months ago, bound up with what looked like the same piece of string. He ate in silence, and Bridget and my mother sat at the table, not saying anything either. I pretended to read the comic, but all the time I was thinking that I'd rather have Mr Dukelow for my father. I couldn't help thinking it and I began to imagine my father sitting on the Bantry bus and Mr Dukelow staying where he was, running the shop better than my father had ever run it, cutting the meat better. I thought of Mr Dukelow in the big bed with my mother, lying asleep beside her. I saw his hands on the white sheets, the thin clever hands instead of hands that made you turn your head away. I saw Mr Dukelow and my mother and myself going out for a walk together on a Sunday afternoon, and Mr Dukelow telling us about Vasco da Gama and Columbus. Mr Dukelow could spend the afternoon in Keogh's and not sway and lurch when he came back. There was no need for Mr Dukelow to go kissing the maid.

'I'm sorry I upset him,' said Mr Dukelow suddenly. 'He's a decent man.'

'It has nothing to do with anything,' said my mother. 'He's in a bad way with drink.'

'Yes,' said Mr Dukelow.

As out of a fog the truth came in pieces to me, and some of the pieces as yet were missing. In six months Mr Dukelow had become a better butcher than my father and my father was jealous of that. Jealousy had caused him to see Mr Dukelow as a monster; jealousy had spread from him in different directions until it wrapped my mother and myself, and tortured my father's pride until he felt he must get his own back and prove himself in some way.

'I'll say good-bye,' said Mr Dukelow, and I hated my father then for his silly pettiness. I wanted Mr Dukelow to go to my mother and kiss her as my father had kissed Bridget. I wanted him to kiss Bridget too, in a way more elegant than the way of my father.

But none of that happened, nor did I ask why, in the face of everything, my father was being described as a decent man. Mr Dukelow left the kitchen, having shaken hands with the three of us. I sat down again at the table while my mother and Bridget prepared the tea. They did not say anything, but I thought to myself that I could see in Bridget's flushed face a reflection of what was passing in her mind: that Mr Dukelow was a nicer man than the porter at the Munster and Leinster Bank. My mother's face was expressionless, but I thought to myself that I knew what expression would be there if my mother cared to permit its presence.

Again I pretended I was reading the comic, but all the time I was thinking about what had silently occurred in our house and how for no sensible reason at all my father's rum-bustiousness had spoilt everything. No one but my father could not love Mr Dukelow: no one in the wide world, I thought, except that red-faced man with stumps on his hands, who fell over chairs when he'd been down in Keogh's, who swayed and couldn't read the time. I thought about the ugliness of my father's jealous nature and the gentleness it had taken exception to. 'Sent up from Satan,' his stumbling voice had ridiculously announced. 'Sent up to make wickedness.' How could it be, I wondered, that I was the child of one instead of the other?

'Well, mister-me-buck,' said my father, returning to the kitchen after a time. When I looked at him I began to cry and my mother took me up to bed, saying I was tired.

Kinkies

'Look,' said Mr Belhatchet in the office one Thursday afternoon, 'want you back in Trilby Mews.'

'Me, Mr Belhatchet?'

'Whole stack new designs. Sort them out.'

A year ago, when Eleanor had applied for the position at Sweetawear, he'd walked into Mr Syatt's office, a young man with a dark bush of hair. She'd been expecting someone much older, about the age of Mr Syatt himself: Mr Belhatchet, a smiling, graceful figure, was in his mid-twenties. 'Happy to know you,' he'd said in an American manner but without any trace of an American accent. He'd been sharply dressed, in a dark grey suit that contained both a blue and a white pinstripe. He wore a discreetly jewelled ring on the little finger of his left hand. 'Mr Belhatchet,' Mr Syatt had explained, 'will be your immediate boss. Sweetawear, of which he is in command, is one small part of our whole organisation. There is, as well, Lisney and Company, Harraps, Tass and Grady Designs, Swiftway Designs, Dress-U, et cetera, et cetera.' There was a canteen in the basement, Mr Syatt had added; the Christmas bonus was notably generous. Mr Syatt spoke in a precise, rather old-fashioned manner, punctuating his sentences carefully. 'Use these?' Mr Belhatchet had more casually offered, holding out a packet of Greek cigarettes, and she, wearing that day a high-necked blouse frilled with lace, had smilingly replied that she didn't smoke.

'All righty, Eleanor?' pursued Mr Belhatchet a year later,

referring to his suggestion that she should help him sort out dress designs in Trilby Mews. 'Okayie?'

'Yes, of course, Mr Belhatchet.'

Trilby Mews was where Mr Belhatchet lived. He'd often mentioned it and Eleanor had often imagined it, seeing his flat and the mews itself as being rather glamorous. Occasionally he telephoned from there, saying he was in bed or in the bath. He couldn't bear a room that did not contain a telephone.

They left the office at a quarter-past six, having finished off what work there was. Eleanor was wearing a pale blue suit in tweed so fine that it might have been linen, and a pale blue blouse. Around her neck there was a double row of small cultured pearls. Her shoes, in darker blue, were square-toed, as current fashion decreed.

That evening she was due to attend the night-school where, once a week, she learned Spanish. It wouldn't matter missing a class because she never had in the past. Several of the other girls missed classes regularly and it never seemed to matter much. They'd be surprised not to see her all the same.

In the taxi Mr Belhatchet lit a Greek cigarette and remarked that he was exhausted. He'd had an exhausting week, she agreed, which was true, because he'd had to fly to Rome in order to look at designs, and then to Germany. In the taxi he said he'd spent all of Tuesday night examining the Italian designs, discussing them with Signor Martelli.

'Dog's Head,' he suddenly ordered the taxi-driver, and the taxi-driver, who appeared to know Mr Belhatchet personally, nodded.

'Join us, Bill?' Mr Belhatchet invited as he paid the fare, but the taxi-driver, addressing Mr Belhatchet with equal familiarity, declined to do so on the grounds that the delay would cost him some trade.

'Two gin, tonic,' Mr Belhatchet ordered in the Dog's Head.

'Large, Dorrie,' he said to the plump barmaid. 'How keeping?'

The barmaid smiled at Eleanor even though the bar was full and she was busy. She was keeping well, she told Mr Belhatchet, whom she addressed, as the taxi-driver had, as Andy.

A Mr Logan, who taught golf at the night-school, had asked Eleanor to have a drink a few times and he'd taken her to a place that wasn't unlike the Dog's Head. She'd quite liked Mr Logan at first, even though he was nearly thirty years older than she was. On the third occasion he'd held her hand as they sat in a corner of a lounge-bar, stroking the back of it. He'd confessed then that he was married – to a woman who'd once dropped, deliberately, a seven-pound weight on his foot. He wanted to leave her, he said, and had then suggested that Eleanor might like to accompany him to Bury St Edmunds the following Saturday. They could stay in a hotel called the Queen's Arms, he suggested, which he'd often stayed in before and which was comfortable and quiet, with excellent food. Eleanor declined, and had since only seen Mr Logan hurrying through the corridors of the night-school. He hadn't invited her to have another drink with him.

Mr Belhatchet consumed his gin and tonic very quickly. He spoke to a few people in the bar and at one point, while speaking to a man with a moustache, he put his arm round Eleanor's shoulders and said that Eleanor was his secretary. He didn't introduce her to any of the others, and he didn't reveal her name to the man with the moustache.

'Feel better,' he said when he'd finished his drink. He looked at hers and she drank the remainder of it as quickly as she could, finding it difficult because the ice made her teeth cold. She wanted to say to Mr Belhatchet that she was just an ordinary girl – in case, later on, there should be any misunderstanding. But although she formed a sentence to that

effect and commenced to utter it, Mr Belhatchet didn't
appear to be interested.

'I just thought – ' she said, smiling.

'You're fantastic,' said Mr Belhatchet.

They walked to Trilby Mews, Mr Belhatchet addressing
familiarly a newsvendor on the way. The flat was much as she
had imagined it, a small, luxuriously furnished apartment
with green blinds half drawn against the glare of the evening
sun. The sitting-room was full of small pieces of Victorian
furniture and there was a large sofa in purple velvet, fashion-
ably buttoned. The walls were covered with framed pictures,
but in the green gloom Eleanor couldn't see what any of them
were of.

'Want loo?' suggested Mr Belhatchet, leading her down a
short passage, the walls of which also bore framed pictures
that couldn't be properly seen. ' 'Nother drink,' he said,
opening the lavatory door and ushering her into it. She said
she'd better not have another drink, not really if she was to
keep a clear head. She laughed while she spoke, realising that
her head was far from clear already. 'Fix you one,' said Mr
Belhatchet, closing the door on her.

The lavatory had a telephone in a nook in the wall and the
seat was covered in brown and white fur. There were framed
picture postcards on the walls, seaside cards with suggestive
messages. They didn't seem the kind of thing that should be
so expensively framed, Eleanor considered, and was surprised
to see them there, especially in such numbers. One or two, she
noticed, were in German.

'Same 'gain,' said Mr Belhatchet in the sitting-room. 'Sit
yourself, Ellie.'

She couldn't see the designs he'd spoken of: she'd imagined
they'd be spread all over the place, propped up on chairs,
even on the walls, because that was the way he liked to sur-
round himself with designs when he was making a selection in

the office. She couldn't even see a pile anywhere, but she put this down to the gloom that pervaded the sitting-room. It surprised her, though, that he'd addressed her as Ellie, which he'd never done before. Nobody, in fact, had ever called her Ellie before.

'Know Nick's?' asked Mr Belhatchet. 'Nick's Diner? Okayie?'

He smiled at her, blowing out Greek cigarette smoke.

'What about the designs?' she asked, smiling at him also.

'Eat first,' he said, and he picked up a green telephone and dialled a number. 'Belhatchet,' he said. 'Andy. Table two, nine-thirty. All righty?'

She said it was very kind of him to invite her to dinner, thinking that it couldn't be more than half-past seven and that for almost two hours apparently they were going to sit in Trilby Mews drinking gin and tonic. She hoped it was going to be all right.

Besides Mr Logan, many men – most of them much younger than Mr Logan – had taken Eleanor out. One called Robert had repeatedly driven her in his yellow sportscar to a country club on the London–Guildford road called The Spurs. At half-past three one morning he'd suggested that they should walk in the wood behind the country club: Eleanor had declined. Earlier that evening he'd said he loved her, but he never even telephoned her again, not after she declined to walk in the woods with him.

Other men spoke of love to her also. They kissed her and pressed themselves against her. Occasionally she felt the warm tip of a tongue exploring one of her ears and she was naturally obliged to wriggle away from it, hastily putting on lipstick as a sign that the interlude was over. She was beautiful, they said, men she met at the night-school or men employed in Sweetawear or Lisney and Company or Dress-U. But when she resisted their ultimate advances they didn't again say she was beautiful; more often than not they didn't say anything further to her at all. She'd explained a few times that she didn't want to anticipate marriage because she believed that marriage was special. But when it came to the point, although stating that they loved her, not one of them proposed marriage to her. Not that any of them had ever been right, which was something she felt most strongly after they'd made their ultimate advances.

'Use grass?' inquired Mr Belhatchet and for a moment, because of his economical manner of speech, she didn't know what he was talking about: use grass for what? she wondered, and shook her head.

'Mind?' asked Mr Belhatchet, breaking open a fresh cigarette and poking what looked like another kind of tobacco among the leaves that were already there. He fiddled around for some time, adding and taking away, and then placed the untidy-looking cigarette between his lips. She asked again about the designs, but he didn't seem to hear her.

Eleanor didn't enjoy the next two hours, sipping at her drink while Mr Belhatchet smoked and drank and asked her a series of economically-framed questions about herself. Later, while they waited for a taxi, he said he felt marvellous. He put his arm round her shoulders and told her that the first day he saw her he'd thought she was fabulous.

'Fabulous,' he said in Nick's Diner, referring to a bowl of *crudités* that had been placed in front of them. He asked her then if she liked him, smiling at her again, smoking another Greek cigarette.

'Well, of course, Mr Belhatchet.'

'Andy. What like 'bout me?'

'Well – '

'Ha, ha, ha,' said Mr Belhatchet, hitting the table with the palm of his left hand. He was smiling so much now that the smile seemed to Eleanor to be unnatural. Nevertheless, she tried to keep smiling herself. None of the girls at Sweetawear had ever told her that there was anything the matter with Mr Belhatchet. She'd never thought herself that there might be something the matter with him: apart from his mode of speech he'd always seemed totally normal. His mother had set him up in Sweetawear, people said, occasionally adding that he'd certainly made a go of it.

'Fabulous,' said Mr Belhatchet when a waiter served them with fillet steak encased in pastry.

They drank a red wine that she liked the taste of. She said, making conversation, that it was a lovely restaurant, and when he didn't reply she said it was the best restaurant she'd ever been in.

'Fabulous,' said Mr Belhatchet.

At eleven o'clock she suggested that perhaps they should return to Trilby Mews to examine the designs. She knew, even while she spoke, that she shouldn't be going anywhere that night with Mr Belhatchet. She knew that if he was anyone else she'd have smiled and said she must go home now because she had to get up in the morning. But Mr Belhatchet, being her office boss, was different. It was all going to be much harder with Mr Belhatchet.

'Age you now, Ellie?' he asked in the taxi, and she told him she'd become twenty-seven the previous Tuesday, while he'd been in Rome.

'Lovely,' he said. 'Fabulous.'

He was still smiling and she thought he must be drunk except that his speech was in no way slurred.

'It's really so late,' she said as the taxi paused in traffic. 'Perhaps we should leave the designs for tonight, Mr Belhatchet?'

'Andy.'

'Perhaps, Andy – '

'Take morning off, Ellie.'

As they entered the flat he asked her again if she'd like to use the lavatory and reminded her where it was. While she was in there the telephone in the nook beside her rang, causing her to jump. It rang for only a moment, before he picked up one of the other extensions. When she entered the sitting-room he was speaking into the receiver, apparently to Signor Martelli in Rome. 'Fabulous,' he was saying. 'No, truly.'

He'd turned several lights on and pulled the green blinds fully down. The pictures that crowded the walls were more conventional than those in the lavatory, reproductions of drawings mainly, limbs and bones and heads scattered over a single sheet, all of them belonging to the past.

' *'vederci*,' said Mr Belhatchet, replacing his green telephone.

In the room there was no pile of designs and she said to herself that in a moment Mr Belhatchet would make a suggestion. She would deal with it as best she could; if the worst came to the worst she would naturally have to leave Sweetawear.

'Fancy drop brandy?' offered Mr Belhatchet.

'Thanks awfully, but I really think I'd better – '

'Just get designs,' he said, leaving the sitting-room.

He returned with a stack of designs which he arrayed around the room just as he would have done in the office. He asked her to assess them while he poured both of them some orange juice.

'Oh, lovely,' she said, because she really felt like orange juice.

The designs were of trouser-suits, a selection of ideas from four different designers. One would be chosen in the end and Sweetawear would manufacture it on a large scale and in a variety of colours.

'Fancy that,' he said, returning with the orange juice and pointing at a drawing with the point of his right foot.

'Yes. And that, the waistcoat effect.'

'Right.'

She sipped her juice and he sipped his. They discussed the designs in detail, taking into consideration the fact that some would obviously be more economical to mass-produce than others. They whittled them down to three, taking about half an hour over that. He'd come to a final decision, he said, some time tomorrow, and the way he said it made her think that he'd come to it on his own, and that his choice might even be one of the rejected designs.

She sat down on the buttoned sofa, feeling suddenly strange, wondering if she'd drunk too much. Mr Belhatchet, she saw, had pushed a few of the designs off an embroidered arm-chair and was sitting down also. He had taken the jacket of his suit off and was slowly loosening his tie.

'Okayie?' he inquired, and leaned his head back and closed his eyes.

She stood up. The floor was peculiar beneath her feet, seeming closer to her, as though her feet had become directly attached to her knees. It moved, like the deck of a ship. She sat down again.

'Fantastic,' said Mr Belhatchet.

'I'm afraid I've had a little too much to drink.'

'God, those days,' said Mr Belhatchet. 'Never 'gain. Know something, Ellie?'

'Mr Belhatchet – '

'Mother loved me, Ellie. Like I was her sweetheart, Mother loved me.'

'Mr Belhatchet, what's happening?'

She heard her own voice, as shrill as a bird's, in the bright, crowded room. She didn't want to move from the sofa. She wanted to put her feet up but she felt she might not be able to move them and was frightened to try in case she couldn't. She closed her eyes and felt herself moving upwards, floating in the room, with a kaleidoscope in each eyelid. 'Mr Belhatchet!' she cried out. 'Mr Belhatchet! Mr Belhatchet!'

She opened her eyes and saw that he had risen from his chair and was standing above her. He was smiling; his face was different.

'I feel,' she cried, but he interrupted her before she could say what she felt.

'Love,' he murmured.

He lifted her legs and placed them on the sofa. He took her shoes off and then returned to the chair he'd occupied before.

'You made us drunk,' she heard her own voice crying, shrill again, shrieking almost in the room. Yet in another way she felt quite tranquil.

'We're going high,' he murmured. 'All righty? We had it in our orange juice.'

She cried out again with part of her. She was floating above the room, she said. The colours of the trouser-suits that were all around her were vivid. They came at her garishly from the paper; the drawn heads of the girls were strange, like real people. The purple of the buttoned sofa was vivid also, and the green of the blinds. All over the walls the pictures of limbs and bones were like glass cases containing what the pictures contained, startling on a soft background. Bottles gleamed, and silver here and there, and brass. There was polished ebony in the room, and ivory.

'You're riding high, Ellie,' Mr Belhatchet said and his voice seemed a long way away, although when she looked at him he seemed nearer and more beautiful than before. He was insane, she thought: there was beauty in his insanity. She never wanted to leave the vivid room above which and

237

through which she floated, depending on the moment. She closed her eyes and there were coloured orchids.

Eleanor slept, or seemed to sleep, and all through her dreams Mr Belhatchet's voice came to her, speaking about his mother. At the same time she herself was back at school, at Springfield Comprehensive, where Miss Whitehead was teaching Class 2 French. The clothes of Miss Whitehead were beautiful and the hairs on her face were as beautiful as the hair on her head, and the odour of her breath was sweet.

'Mother died,' said Mr Belhatchet. 'She left me, Ellie.'

He talked about a house. His voice described a house situated among hills, a large house, remote and rich, with an exotic garden where his mother walked in a white dress, wearing dark glasses because of the sunshine.

'She left me the little business,' he said. 'The pretty little business. Flair: she had flair, Ellie.'

He said he could remember being in his mother's womb. She'd taught him to remember, he said. They read novels together. His mother's hand took his and stroked the flesh of her arm with it.

He took off his shirt and sat in the embroidered chair with the upper half of his body naked. His feet, she saw, were naked also.

'I loved her too,' he said. 'She's back with me now. I can taste her milk, Ellie.'

He was like a god in the embroidered chair, his bushy hair wild on his head, his pale flesh gleaming. His eyes seemed far back in his skull, gazing at her from the depths of caverns. Time did not seem to be passing.

In the house among the hills there were parties, he said, and afterwards quiet servants gathered glasses from the lawns. Cars moved on gravel early in the morning, driving away. Couples were found asleep beneath trees.

She wanted to take some of her own clothes off as Mr Belhatchet had, but her arms were heavy and in time, she guessed, he would take them off for her and that would be beautiful too. His eyes were a rare blue, his flesh was like the flesh of flowers. The room was saturated with colours that were different now, subtly changing: the colours of the trouser-suits and the purple of the sofa and the coloured threads of the embroidered chair and the green blinds and telephone. The colours were liquid in the room, gently flowing, one into another. People stood on banks of foliage, people at Mrs Belhatchet's parties. Mrs Belhatchet stood with her son.

She would like to have children, Eleanor said; she would like to be married. She'd noticed a house once, in Gwendolyn Avenue in Putney, not far from where her bed-sitting-room was: she described it, saying she'd once dreamed she lived there, married to a man with delicate hands.

'I love you,' she said, knowing that she was speaking to that man, a man she had always imagined, who would marry her in a church and take her afterwards to Biarritz for a honeymoon.

'I love you,' she said again, with her eyes closed. 'I've waited all my life.'

She wanted him to come to her, to lie beside her on the sofa and gently to take her clothes off. In the room they would anticipate marriage because marriage was certain between them, because there was perfection in their relationship, because in every detail and in every way they understood each other. They were part of one another; only death could part them now.

'Come to me,' she said with her eyes still closed. 'Oh, come to me now.'

'Mother,' he said.

'No, no – '

'Up here you can be anyone, Ellie. Up here where everything is as we wish it.'

He went on speaking, but she couldn't hear what he said, and it didn't matter. She murmured, but she didn't hear her own words either. And then, a long time later it seemed, she heard a voice more clearly.

'The truth is in this room,' Mr Belhatchet was saying. 'I couldn't ravish anyone, Mother.'

She opened her eyes and saw Mr Belhatchet with his bushy hair, still looking like a god.

'My friend,' she said, closing her eyes again.

She spoke of her bed-sitting-room in East Putney and the posters she'd bought to decorate its walls, and the two lamps with pretty jade-coloured shades that she'd bought in the British Home Stores. She'd said to her landlady that she was determined to make a home of her bed-sitting-room and the landlady said that that sounded a first-class idea. Her landlady gave her a brass gong she didn't want.

In the room their two voices spoke together.

'I put my arms around her,' he said. 'With my arms around her and hers round me, it is beautiful.'

'It is beautiful here,' she said. 'The foliage, the leaves. It is beautiful in the garden of your mother's house.'

'Yes,' he said.

'I am waiting here for a tender man who wouldn't ever hurt me.'

'That's beautiful too,' he said. 'Your clothes are beautiful. Your blue clothes and the pearls at your neck, and your shoes. We are happy in this present moment.'

'Yes.'

'We have floated away.'

They ceased to speak. Time, of which as they dreamed and imagined neither of them was aware, passed normally in the room. At half-past six Eleanor, still feeling happy but by now

more in control of her limbs, slowly pushed herself from the
sofa and stood up. The floor swayed less beneath her feet; the
colours in the room, though vivid still, were less so than they
had been. Mr Belhatchet was asleep.

Eleanor went to the lavatory and when she returned to the
sitting-room she did not lie down on the sofa again. She stood
instead in the centre of the room, gazing around it, at Mr
Belhatchet with bare feet and a bare chest, asleep in his embroidered chair, at the designs of trouser-suits and the pictures of limbs and bones. 'Mother,' murmured Mr Belhatchet
in his sleep, in a voice that was a whisper.

She left the flat, moving slowly and gently closing the door
behind her. She descended the stairs and stepped out into
Trilby Mews, into fresh early-morning air.

Police Constable Edwin Lloyd found Eleanor an hour later.
She was lying on the pavement outside a betting-shop in Garrad Street, W.1. He saw the still body from a distance and
hurried towards it, believing he had a death on his hands. 'I
fell down,' Eleanor explained as he helped her to rise again.
'I'm tired.'

'Drugs,' said Police Constable Lloyd in Garrad Street
police station, and another officer, a desk sergeant, sighed.
'Cup of tea, miss?' Constable Lloyd offered. 'Nice hot
tea?'

A middle-aged policewoman searched Eleanor's clothing in
case there were further drugs on her person.

'Pretty thing like you,' the woman said. 'Shame, dear.'

They brought her tea and Eleanor drank it, spilling some
over her pale blue suit because her hands were shaking. Constable Lloyd, returning to his beat, paused by the door.

'Will she be O.K.?' he asked, and his two colleagues said
that they considered she would be.

In the police station the colours were harsh and ugly, not at all like the colours there'd been in Mr Belhatchet's flat. And the faces of the desk sergeant and the policewoman were unpleasant also: the pores of their skin were large, like the cells of a honeycomb. There was something the matter with their mouths and their hands, and the uniforms they wore, and the place they occupied. The wooden seat was uncomfortable, the pages of a book in front of the desk sergeant were torn and grubby, the air stank of stale cigarette smoke. The man and the woman were regarding her as skeletons might, their teeth bared at her, their fingers predatory, like animals' claws. She hated their eyes. She couldn't drink the tea they'd given her because it caused nausea in her stomach.

The noise in the room, a distant fuzziness, was her voice. It spoke of what her mind was full of: Mrs Belhatchet and her son in the garden he had described. Servants collected glasses that were broken and jagged; their hands had blood on them. Couples were found dead beneath trees. The garden was all as ugly as the room she was in now, as dirty and as unpleasant.

And then it was different. In the garden they came at her, Mr Logan of the night-school, Robert in his yellow sportscar, and all the others. The touch of their hands was hard, like metal; she moaned in distress at their nakedness. They laughed because of that, pressing her apart, grunting with the passion of beasts. Through blood she screamed, and the voices of the men said that her tortured face was ecstasy to them. They longed for her cries of pain. They longed to wrap her in the filth of their sweat.

Their voices ceased and she heard the fuzziness again, and then it ceased also.

'Eh now,' murmured the desk sergeant soothingly.

'I can't help it,' she said, weeping. 'I'm frightened of it, and disgusted. I can't help it; I don't know why I'm like this.'

'Just drink your tea and stop quiet, dear,' the policewoman suggested. 'Best to stop quiet, dear.'

Eleanor shook her head and for a moment her vision was blurred. She closed her eyes and forgot where she was. She opened them and found that her vision had cleared: she saw that she was in a grimy police station with two ugly people. Tea was spilt over her suit and there were drops of tea on her shoes. Her office boss had given her a drug in orange juice: she had experienced certain dreams and fantasies and had conducted with him a formless conversation. She'd never be able to return to the offices of Sweetawear.

'He floats away,' she heard a voice crying out and realised that it was her own. 'He lies there entranced, floating away from his fear and his disgust. "The truth's in this room," he says – when what he means is the opposite. Poor wretched thing!'

She wept and the policewoman went to her and tried to help her, but Eleanor struck at her, shrieking obscenities. 'Everywhere there's ugliness,' she cried. 'His mother loved him with a perverted passion. He floats away from that.'

Tears fell from her eyes, dripping on to her clothes and on the floor by her feet. She wanted to be dead, she whispered, to float away for ever from the groping hands. She wanted to be dead, she said again.

They took her to a cell; she went with them quietly. She lay down and slept immediately, and the desk sergeant and the policewoman returned to their duties. 'Worse than drink,' the woman said. 'The filth that comes out of them; worse than a navvy.'

'She's hooked, you know,' the desk sergeant remarked. 'She's hooked on that floating business. That floating away.'

The policewoman sighed and nodded. They sounded like

two of a kind, she commented: the girl and the chap she'd been with.

'Kinkies,' said the desk sergeant. 'Extraordinary, people getting like that.'

'Bloody disgraceful,' said the policewoman.

O Fat White Woman

Relaxing in the garden of her husband's boarding-school, Mrs Digby-Hunter could not help thinking that it was good to be alive. On the short grass of the lawn, tucked out of sight beneath her deck-chair, was a small box of Terry's All Gold chocolates, and on her lap, open at page eight, lay a paper-backed novel by her second-favourite writer of historical fiction. In the garden there was the pleasant sound of insects, and occasionally the buzzing of bees. No sound came from the house: the boys, beneath the alert tutelage of her husband and Mr Kelly, were obediently labouring, the maids, Dympna and Barbara, were, Mrs Digby-Hunter hoped, washing them-selves.

Not for the moment in the mood for reading, she surveyed the large, tidy garden that was her husband's pride, even though he never had a moment to work in it. Against high stone walls forsythia grew, and honeysuckle and little pear-trees, and beneath them in rich, herbaceous borders the garden flowers of summer blossomed now in colourful var-iety. Four beech-trees shaded patches of the lawn and roses grew, and geraniums, in round beds symmetrically arranged. On either side of an archway in the wall ahead of Mrs Digby-Hunter were two yew-trees and beyond the archway, in a wilder part, she could see the blooms of rhododendrons. She could see as well, near one of the yew-trees, the bent figure of Sergeant Wall, an ex-policeman employed on a part-time basis by her husband. He was weeding, his movements slow

in the heat of that June afternoon, a stained white hat on his
hairless head. It was pleasant to sit in the shade of a beech-
tree watching someone else working, having worked oneself
all morning in a steamy kitchen. Although she always considered herself an easy-going woman, she had been very angry
that morning because one of the girls had quite clearly
omitted to make use of the deodorant she was at such pains to
supply them with. She had accused each in turn and had got
nowhere whatsoever, which didn't entirely surprise her.
Dympna was just fifteen and Barbara only a month or two
older; hardly the age at which to expect responsibility and
truthfulness. Yet it was her duty to train them, as it was her
husband's duty to train the boys. 'You'll strip wash, both of
you,' she'd commanded snappishly in the end, 'immediately
you've done the lunch dishes. From top to toe, please, every
inch of you.' They had both, naturally, turned sulky.

Mrs Digby-Hunter, wearing that day a blue cotton dress
with a pattern of pinkish lupins on it, was fifty-one. She had
married her husband twenty-nine years ago, at a time when
he'd been at the beginning of a career in the army. Her
father, well-to-do and stern, had given her away and she'd
been quite happy about his gesture, for love had then possessed her fully. Determined at all costs to make a success of
her marriage and to come up to scratch as a wife, she had
pursued a policy of agreeableness: she smiled instead of
making a fuss, in her easy-going way she accepted what there
was to accept, placing her faith in her husband as she believed
a good wife should. In her own opinion she was not a clever
person, but at least she could offer loyalty and devotion, instead of nagging and arguing. In a bedroom of a Welsh hotel
she had disguised, on her wedding night, her puzzled disappointment when her husband had abruptly left her side,
having lain there for only a matter of minutes.

Thus a pattern began in their marriage and as a result of it

Mrs Digby-Hunter had never borne children although she had, gradually and at an increasing rate, put on weight. At first she had minded about this and had attempted to diet. She had deprived herself of what she most enjoyed until it oc-curred to her that caring in this way was making her bad-tempered and miserable: it didn't suit her, all the worrying about calories and extra ounces. She weighed now, although she didn't know it, thirteen stone.

Her husband was leaner, a tall man with bony fingers and smooth black hair and eyes that stared at other people's eyes as if to imply shrewdness. He had a gaunt face and on it a well-kept though not extensive moustache. Shortly after their marriage he had abandoned his career in the army because, he said, he could see no future in it. Mrs Digby-Hunter was surprised but assumed that what was apparent to her husband was not apparent to her. She smiled and did not argue.

After the army her husband became involved with a firm that manufactured a new type of all-purpose, metal step-ladder. He explained to her the mechanism of this article, but it was complicated and she failed to understand: she smiled and nodded, murmuring that the ladder was indeed an ingeni-ous one. Her husband, briskly businesslike in a herring-bone suit, became a director of the step-ladder company on the day before the company ran into financial difficulties and was obliged to cease all production.

'Your father could help,' he murmured, having imparted to her the unfortunate news, but her father, when invited to save the step-ladder firm, closed his eyes in boredom.

'I'm sorry,' she said, rather miserably, feeling she had failed to come up to scratch as a wife. He said it didn't matter, and a few days later he told her he'd become a vending-machine operator. He would have an area, he said, in which he would daily visit schools and swimming-pools, launder-ettes, factories, offices, wherever the company's vending-machines were sited. He would examine the machines to see that they were in good trim and would fill them full of powdered coffee and powdered milk and a form of tea, and minerals and biscuits and chocolate. She thought the work odd for an ex-army officer, but she did not say so. Instead, she listened while he told her that there was an expanding market for vending-machines, and that in the end they would make a considerable amount of money. His voice went on, quoting percentages and conversion rates. She was knitting him a blue pullover at the time. He held his arms up while she fitted it about his chest; she nodded while he spoke.

Then her father died and left her a sum of money.

'We could buy a country house,' her husband said, 'and open it up as a smart little hotel.' She agreed that that would be nice. She felt that perhaps neither of them was qualified to run an hotel, but it didn't seem worth making a fuss about that, especially since her husband had, without qualifications, joined a step-ladder firm and then, equally unskilled, had gone into the vending-machine business. In fact, their abilities as hoteliers were never put to the test because all of a sudden her husband had a better idea. Idling one evening in a saloon bar, he dropped into conversation with a man who was in a state of depression because his son appeared to be a dunce.

'If I was starting again,' said the man, 'I'd go into the cramming business. My God, you could coin it.' The man talked on, speaking of parents like himself who couldn't hold their heads up because their children's poor performances in the Common Entrance examination deprived them of an association with one of the great public schools of England. The next day Mrs Digby-Hunter's husband scrutinised bound volumes of the Common Entrance examination papers.

'A small boarding-school,' he later said to her, 'for temporarily backward boys; we might do quite nicely.' Mrs

Digby-Hunter, who did not immediately take to the notion of being surrounded day and night by temporarily backward boys, said that the idea sounded an interesting one. 'There's a place for sale in Gloucestershire,' her husband said.

The school, begun as a small one, remained so because, as her husband explained, any school of this nature must be small. The turn-over in boys was rapid, and it soon became part of the educational policy of Milton Grange to accept not more than twenty boys at any one time, the wisdom of which was reflected in results that parents and headmasters agreed were remarkable: the sons who had idled at the back of their preparatory school classrooms passed into the great public schools of England, and their parents paid the high fees of Milton Grange most gratefully.

At Milton Grange, part ivy-clad, turreted and baronial, Mrs Digby-Hunter was happy. She did not understand the ins and outs of the Common Entrance examination, for her province was the kitchen and the dormitories, but certainly life at Milton Grange as the headmaster's wife was much more like it than occupying half the ground floor of a semi-detached villa in Croydon, as the wife of a vending-machine operator.

'Christ, what a time we're having with that boy for Harrow,' her husband would say, and she would make a sighing noise to match the annoyance he felt, and smile to cheer him up. It was extraordinary what he had achieved with the dullards he took on, and she now and again wondered if one day he might even receive a small recognition, an OBE maybe. As for her, Milton Grange was recognition enough: an apt reward, she felt, for her marital agreeableness, for not being a nuisance, and coming up to scratch as a wife.

Just occasionally Mrs Digby-Hunter wondered what life would have been like if she'd married someone else. She wondered what it would have been like to have had children of her own and to have engaged in the activity that caused, eventually, children to be born. She imagined, once a year or so, as she lay alone in her room in the darkness, what it would be like to share a double bed night after night. She imagined a faceless man, a pale naked body beside hers, hands caressing her flesh. She imagined, occasionally, being married to a clergyman she'd known as a girl, a man who had once embraced her with intense passion, suddenly, after a dance in a church hall. She had experienced the pressure of his body against hers and she could recall still the smell of his clothes and the dampness of his mouth.

But Milton Grange was where she belonged now: she had chosen a man and married him and had ended up, for better or worse, in a turreted house in Gloucestershire. There was give and take in marriage, as always she had known, and where she was concerned there was everything to be thankful for. Once a year, on the last Saturday in July, the gardens of the school were given over to a Conservative fête, and more regularly she and her husband drove to other country houses, for dinner or cocktails. A local Boy Scout group once asked her to present trophies at a sports because she was her husband's wife and he was well regarded. She had enjoyed the occasion and had bought new clothes specially for it.

In winter she put down bulbs, and in spring she watched the birds collecting twigs and straw for nests. She loved the gardens and often repeated to the maids in the kitchen that one was 'nearer God's Heart in a garden than anywhere else on earth'. It was a beautiful sentiment, she said, and very true.

On that June afternoon, while Mrs Digby-Hunter dropped into a doze beneath the beech-trees and Sergeant Wall removed the weeds from a herbaceous border, the bearded Mr Kelly walked between two rows of desks in a bare attic room.

Six boys bent over the desks, writing speedily. In the room next door six other boys wrote also. They would not be idling, Mr Kelly knew, any more than the boys in the room across the corridor would be idling.

'*Amavero, amaveris, amaverit,*' he said softly, his haired lips close to the ear of a boy called Timpson. '*Amaverimus, Timpson, amaveritis, amaverint.*' A thumb and forefinger of Mr Kelly's seized and turned the flesh on the back of Timpson's left hand. '*Amaveritis,*' he said again, '*amaverint.*' While the flesh was twisted this way and that and while Timpson moaned in the quiet manner that Mr Kelly preferred, Dympna and Barbara surveyed the sleeping form of Mrs Digby-Hunter in the garden. They had not washed themselves. They stood in the bedroom they shared, gazing through an open, diamond-paned window, smoking two Embassy tipped cigarettes. 'White fat slug,' said Barbara. 'Look at her.'

They looked a moment longer. Sergeant Wall in the far distance pushed himself from his knees on to his feet. 'He's coming in for his tea,' said Barbara. She held cigarette smoke in her mouth and then released it in short puffs. 'She can't think,' said Dympna. 'She's incapable of mental activity.' 'She's a dead white slug,' said Barbara.

They cupped their cigarettes in their hands for the journey down the back stairs to the kitchen. They both were thinking that the kettle would be boiling on the Aga: it would be pleasant to sit in the cool, big kitchen drinking tea with old Sergeant Wall, who gossiped about the village he lived in. It was Dympna's turn to make his sandwich, turkey paste left over from yesterday, the easy-to-spread margarine that Mrs Digby-Hunter said was better for you than butter. 'Dead white slug,' repeated Barbara, laughing on the stairs. 'Was she human once?'

Sergeant Wall passed by the sleeping Mrs Digby-Hunter

and heard, just perceptibly, a soft snoring coming from her partially open mouth. She was tired, he thought; heat made women tired, he'd often heard. He removed his hat and wiped an accumulation of sweat from the crown of his head. He moved towards the house for his tea.

In his study Digby-Hunter sat with one boy, Marshalsea, listening while Marshalsea repeated recently acquired information about triangles.

'Then DEF,' said Marshalsea, 'must be equal in all respects to – '

'Why?' inquired Digby-Hunter.

His voice was dry and slightly high. His bony hands, on the desk between himself and Marshalsea, had minute fingernails.

'Because DEF – '

'Because the triangle DEF, Marshalsea.'

'Because the triangle DEF – '

'Yes, Marshalsea?'

'Because the triangle DEF has the two angles at the base and two sides equal to the two angles at the base and two sides of the triangle ABC – '

'You're talking bloody nonsense,' said Digby-Hunter quietly. 'Think about it, boy.'

He rose from his position behind his desk and crossed the room to the window. He moved quietly, a man with a slight stoop because of his height, a man who went well with the room he occupied, with shelves of text books, and an empty mantelpiece, and bare, pale walls. It was simple sense, as he often pointed out to parents, that in rooms where teaching took place there should be no diversions for the roving eyes of students.

Glancing from the window, Digby-Hunter observed his wife in her deck-chair beneath the beeches. He reflected that in their seventeen years at Milton Grange she had become expert at making shepherd's pie. Her bridge, on the other hand, had not improved and she still made tiresome remarks to parents. Once, briefly, he had loved her, a love that had begun to die in the bedroom of a Welsh hotel, on the night of their wedding day. Her nakedness, which he had daily imagined in lush anticipation, had strangely repelled him. 'I'm sorry,' he'd murmured, and had slipped into the other twin bed, knowing then that this side of marriage was something he was not going to be able to manage. She had not said anything, and between them the matter had never been mentioned again.

It was extraordinary, he thought now, watching her in the garden, that she should lie in a deck-chair like that, unfastidiously asleep. Once at a dinner-party she had described a dream she'd had, and afterwards, in the car on the way back to Milton Grange, he'd had to tell her that no one had been interested in her dream. People had quietly sighed, he'd had to say, because that was the truth.

There was a knock on the door and Digby-Hunter moved from the window and called out peremptorily. A youth with spectacles and long, uncared-for hair entered the sombre room. He was thin, with a slight, thin mouth and a fragile nose; his eyes, magnified behind the tortoiseshell-rimmed discs, were palely nondescript, the colour of water in which vegetables have been boiled. His lengthy hair was lustreless.

'Wraggett,' said Digby-Hunter at once, as though challenging the youth to disclaim this title.

'Sir,' replied Wraggett.

'Why are you moving your head about like that?' Digby-Hunter demanded.

He turned to the other boy. 'Well?' he said.

'If the two angles at the base of DEF,' said Marshalsea, 'are equal to the two angles at the base of – '

'Open the book,' said Digby-Hunter. 'Learn it.'

He left the window and returned to his desk. He sat down. 'What d'you want, Wraggett?' he said.

'I think I'd better go to bed, sir.'

'Bed? What's the matter with you?'

'There's a pain in my neck, sir. At the back, sir. I can't seem to see properly.'

Digby-Hunter regarded Wraggett with irritation and dislike. He made a noise with his lips. He stared at Wraggett. He said:

'So you have lost your sight, Wraggett?'

'No, sir.'

'Why the damn hell are you bellyaching, then?'

'I keep seeing double, sir. I feel a bit sick, sir.'

'Are you malingering, Wraggett?'

'No, sir.'

'Then why are you saying you can't see?'

'Sir – '

'If you're not malingering, get on with the work you've been set, boy. The French verb to drink, the future conditional tense?'

'*Je boive* – '

'You're a cretin,' shouted Digby-Hunter. 'Get out of here at once.'

'I've a pain, sir – '

'Take your pain out with you, for God's sake. Get down to some honest work, Wraggett. Marshalsea?'

'If the two angles at the base of DEF,' said Marshalsea, 'are equal to the two angles at the base of ABC it means that the sides opposite the angles – '

His voice ceased abruptly. He closed his eyes. He felt the small fingers of Digby-Hunter briefly on his scalp before they grasped a clump of hair.

'Open your eyes,' said Digby-Hunter.

Marshalsea did so and saw pleasure in Digby-Hunter's face.

'You haven't listened,' said Digby-Hunter. His left hand pulled the hair, causing the boy to rise from his seat. His right hand moved slowly and then suddenly shot out, completing its journey, striking at Marshalsea's jaw-bone. Digby-Hunter always used the side of his hand, Mr Kelly the ball of the thumb.

'Take two triangles, ABC and DEF,' said Digby-Hunter. Again the edge of his right hand struck Marshalsea's face and then, clenched into a fist, the hand struck repeatedly at Marshalsea's stomach.

'Take two triangles,' whispered Marshalsea, 'ABC and DEF.'

'In which the angle ABC equals the angle DEF.'

'In which the angle ABC equals the angle DEF.'

In her sleep Mrs Digby-Hunter heard a voice. She opened her eyes and saw a figure that might have been part of a dream. She closed her eyes again.

'Mrs Digby-Hunter.'

A boy whose name escaped her stood looking down at her. There were so many boys coming and going for a term or two, then passing on: this one was thin and tall, with spectacles. He had an unhealthy look, she thought, and then she remembered his mother, who had an unhealthy look also, a Mrs Wraggett.

'Mrs Digby-Hunter, I have a pain at the back of my neck.'

She blinked, looking at the boy. They'd do anything, her husband often said, in order to escape their studies, and although she sometimes felt sorry for them she quite understood that their studies must be completed since that was the

reason for their presence at Milton Grange. Still, the amount
of work they had to do and their excessively long hours, half-
past eight until seven at night, caused her just occasionally to
consider that she herself had been lucky to escape such pres-
sures in her childhood. Every afternoon, immediately after
lunch, all the boys set out with Mr Kelly for a brisk walk,
which was meant to be, in her husband's parlance, twenty
minutes of freshening up. There was naturally no time for
games.

'Mrs Digby-Hunter.'

The boy's head was moving about in an eccentric manner.
She tried to remember if she had noticed it doing that before,
and decided she hadn't. She'd have certainly noticed, for the
movement made her dizzy. She reached beneath the deck-
chair for the box of All Gold. She smiled at the boy. She
said:

'Would you like a chocolate, Wraggett?'

'I feel sick, Mrs Digby-Hunter. I keep seeing double. I
can't seem to keep my head steady.'

'You'd better tell the headmaster, old chap.'

He wasn't a boy she'd ever cared for, any more than she'd
ever cared for his mother. She smiled at him again, trying to
make up for being unable to like either himself or his mother.
Again she pushed the box of chocolates at him, nudging a
coconut caramel out of its rectangular bed. She always left the
coconut caramels and the blackcurrant boats: the boy was
more than welcome to them.

'I've told the headmaster, Mrs Digby-Hunter.'

'Have you been studying too hard?'

'No, Mrs Digby-Hunter.'

She withdrew her offer of chocolates, wondering how long
he'd stand there waggling his head in the sunshine. He'd get
into trouble if the loitering went on too long. She could say
that she'd made him remain with her in order to hear further

details about his pain, but there was naturally a limit to the amount of time he could hope to waste. She said:

'I think, you know, you should buzz along now, Wraggett–'

'Mrs Digby-Hunter – '

'There's a rule, you know: the headmaster must be informed when a boy is feeling under the weather. The headmaster comes to his own conclusions about who's malingering and who's not. When I was in charge of that side of things, Wraggett, the boys used to pull the wool over my eyes like nobody's business. Well, I didn't blame them, I'd have done the same myself. But the headmaster took another point of view. With a school like Milton Grange, every single second has a value of its own. Naturally, time can't be wasted.'

'They pull the hair out of your head,' Wraggett cried, his voice suddenly shrill. 'They hit you in a special way, so that it doesn't bruise you. They drive their fists into your stomach.'

'I think you should return to your classroom – '

'They enjoy it,' shouted Wraggett.

'Go along now, old chap.'

'Your husband half murdered me, Mrs Digby-Hunter.'

'Now that simply isn't true, Wraggett.'

'Mr Kelly hit Malcolmson in the groin. With a ruler. He poked the end of the ruler – '

'Be quiet, Wraggett.'

'Mrs Digby-Hunter – '

'Go along now, Wraggett.' She spoke for the first time sharply, but when the boy began to move she changed her mind about her command and called him back. He and all the other boys, she explained with less sharpness in her voice, were at Milton Grange for a purpose. They came because they had idled at their preparatory schools, playing noughts and crosses in the back row of a classroom, giggling and disturbing everyone. They came to Milton Grange so that, after the skilled teaching of the headmaster and Mr Kelly, they might succeed at an examination that would lead them to one of England's great public schools. Corporal punishment was part of the curriculum at Milton Grange, and all parents were apprised of that fact. If boys continued to idle as they had idled in the past they would suffer corporal punishment so that, beneath its influence, they might reconsider their behaviour. 'You understand, Wraggett?' said Mrs Digby-Hunter in the end.

Wraggett went away, and Mrs Digby-Hunter felt pleased. The little speech she had made to him was one she had heard her husband making on other occasions. 'We rap the occasional knuckle,' he said to prospective parents. 'Quite simply, we stand no nonsense.'

She was glad that it had come so easily to her to quote her husband, once again to come up to scratch as a wife. Boys who were malingering must naturally receive the occasional rap on the knuckles and her husband, over seventeen years, had proved that his ways were best. She remembered one time a woman coming and taking her son away on the grounds that the pace was too strenuous for him. As it happened, she had opened the door in answer to the woman's summons and had heard the woman say she'd had a letter from her son and thought it better that he should be taken away. It turned out that the child had written hysterically. He had said that Milton Grange was run by lunatics and criminals. Mrs Digby-Hunter, hearing that, had smiled and had quietly inquired if she herself resembled either a lunatic or a criminal. The woman shook her head, but the boy, who had been placed in Milton Grange so that he might pass on to the King's School in Canterbury, was taken away. 'To stagnate,' her husband had predicted and she, knitting another pullover for him, had without much difficulty agreed.

Mrs Digby-Hunter selected a raspberry and honey cream.

She returned the chocolate-box to the grass beneath her deck-chair and closed her eyes.

'What's the matter, son?' inquired Sergeant Wall on his way back to his weeding.

Wraggett said he had a pain at the back of his neck. He couldn't keep his head still, he said; he kept seeing double; he felt sick in the stomach. 'God almighty,' said Sergeant Wall. He led the boy back to the kitchen, which was the only interior part of Milton Grange that he knew. 'Here,' he said to the two maids, who were still sitting at the kitchen table, drinking tea. 'Here,' said Sergeant Wall, 'have a look at this.'

Wraggett sat down and took off his spectacles. As though seeking to control its wobbling motion, he attempted to shake his head, but the effort, so Barbara and Dympna afterwards said, appeared to be too much for him. His shoulders slipped forward, the side of his face struck the scrubbed surface of the kitchen table, and when the three of them settled him back on his chair in order to give him water in a cup they discovered that he was dead.

When Mrs Digby-Hunter entered the kitchen half an hour later she blinked her eyes several times because the glaring sunshine had affected them. 'Prick the sausages,' she automatically commanded, for today being a Tuesday it would be sausages for tea, a fact of which both Barbara and Dympna would, as always, have to be reminded. She was then aware that something was the matter.

She blinked again. The kitchen contained people other than Barbara and Dympna. Mr Kelly, a man who rarely addressed her, was standing by the Aga, Sergeant Wall was endeavouring to comfort Barbara, who was noisily weeping.

'What's the matter, Barbara?' inquired Mrs Digby-Hunter, and she noticed as she spoke that Mr Kelly turned more of his back to her. There was a smell of tobacco smoke in the air: Dympna, to Mrs Digby-Hunter's astonishment, was smoking a cigarette.

'There's been a tragedy, Mrs Digby-Hunter,' said Sergeant Wall. 'Young Wraggett.'

'What's the matter with Wraggett?'

'He's dead,' said Dympna. She released smoke through her nose, staring hard at Mrs Digby-Hunter. Barbara, who had looked up on hearing Mrs Digby-Hunter's voice, sobbed more quietly, gazing also, through tears, at Mrs Digby-Hunter.

'Dead?' As she spoke, her husband entered the kitchen. He addressed Mr Kelly, who turned to face him. He said he had put the body of Wraggett on a bed in a bedroom that was never used. There was no doubt about it, he said, the boy was dead.

'Dead?' said Mrs Digby-Hunter again. '*Dead?*'

Mr Kelly was mumbling by the Aga, asking her husband where Wraggett's parents lived. Barbara was wiping the tears from her face with a handkerchief. Beside her, Sergeant Wall, upright and serious, stood like a statue. 'In Worcestershire,' Mrs Digby-Hunter's husband said. 'A village called Pine.' She was aware that the two maids were still looking at her. She wanted to tell Dympna to stop smoking at once, but the words wouldn't come from her. She was asleep in the garden, she thought: Wraggett had come and stood by her chair, she had offered him a chocolate, now she was dreaming that he was dead, it was all ridiculous. Her husband's voice was quiet, still talking about the village called Pine and about Wraggett's mother and father.

Mr Kelly asked a question that she couldn't hear: her husband replied that he didn't think they were that kind of people. He had sent for the school doctor, he told Mr Kelly, since the cause of death had naturally to be ascertained as soon as possible.

'A heart attack,' said Mr Kelly.

'Dead?' said Mrs Digby-Hunter for the fourth time.

Dympna held towards Barbara her packet of cigarettes. Barbara accepted one, and the eyes of the two girls ceased their observation of Mrs Digby-Hunter's face. Dympna struck a match. Wraggett had been all right earlier, Mr Kelly said. Her husband's lips were pursed in a way that was familiar to her; there was anxiety in his eyes.

The kitchen was flagged, large grey flags that made it cool in summer and which sometimes sweated in damp weather. The boys' crockery, of hardened primrose-coloured plastic, was piled on a dresser that almost reached the ceiling. Through huge, barred windows Mrs Digby-Hunter could see shrubs and a brick wall and an expanse of gravel. Everything was familiar and yet seemed not to be. 'So sudden,' her husband said. 'So wretchedly out of the blue.' He added that after the doctor had given the cause of death he himself would motor over to the village in Worcestershire and break the awful news to the parents.

She moved, and felt again the eyes of the maids following her. She would sack them, she thought, when all this was over. She filled a kettle at the sink, running water into it from the hot tap. Mr Kelly remained where he was standing when she approached the Aga, appearing to be unaware that he was in her way. Her husband moved. She wanted to say that soon, at least, there'd be a cup of tea, but again the words failed to come from her. She heard Sergeant Wall asking her husband if there was anything he could do, and then her husband's voice said that he'd like Sergeant Wall to remain in the house until the doctor arrived so that he could repeat to the doctor what

Wraggett had said about suddenly feeling unwell. Mr Kelly spoke again, muttering to her husband that Wraggett in any case would never have passed into Lancing. 'I shouldn't mention that,' her husband said.

She sat down to wait for the kettle to boil, and Sergeant Wall and the girls sat down also, on chairs near to where they were standing, between the two windows. Her husband spoke in a low voice to Mr Kelly, instructing him, it seemed: she couldn't hear the words he spoke. And then, without warning, Barbara cried out loudly. She threw her burning cigarette on the floor and jumped up from her chair. Tears were on her face, her teeth were widely revealed, though not in a smile. 'You're a fat white slug,' she shouted at Mrs Digby-Hunter.

Sergeant Wall attempted to quieten the girl, but her fingernails scratched at his face and her fingers gripped and tore at the beard of Mr Kelly, who had come to Sergeant Wall's aid. Dympna did not move from her chair. She was looking at Mrs Digby-Hunter, smoking quietly, as though nothing at all was happening.

'It'll be in the newspapers,' shouted Barbara.

She was taken from the kitchen, and the Digby-Hunters could hear her sobbing in the passage and on the back stairs. 'She'll sell the story,' said Dympna.

Digby-Hunter looked at her. He attempted to smile at her, to suggest by his smile that he had a fondness for her. 'What story?' he said.

'The way the boys are beaten up.'

'Now look here, Dympna, you know nothing whatsoever about it. The boys at Milton Grange are here for a special purpose. They undergo special education – '

'You killed one, Mr Digby-Hunter.' Still puffing at her cigarette, Dympna left the kitchen, and Mrs Digby-Hunter spoke.

'My God,' she said.

'They're upset by death,' said her husband tetchily. 'Naturally enough. They'll both calm down.'

But Mr Kelly, hearing those remarks as he returned to the kitchen, said that it was the end of Milton Grange. The girls would definitely pass on their falsehoods to a newspaper. They were telling Sergeant Wall now, he said. They were reminding him of lies they had apparently told him before, and of which he had taken no notice.

'What in the name of heaven,' Digby-Hunter angrily asked his wife, 'did you have to go engaging creatures like that for?'

They hated her, she thought: two girls who day by day had worked beside her in the kitchen, to whom she had taught useful skills. A boy had come and stood beside her in the sunshine and she had offered him a chocolate. He had complained of a pain, and she had pointed out that he must make his complaint to the headmaster, since that was the rule. She had explained as well that corporal punishment was part of the curriculum at Milton Grange. The boy was dead. The girls who hated her would drag her husband's boarding-school through the mud.

She heard the voice of Sergeant Wall saying that the girls, one of them hysterical but calming down, the other insolent, were out to make trouble. He'd tried to reason with them, but they hadn't even listened.

The girls had been in Milton Grange for two and a half months. She remembered the day they had arrived together, carrying cardboard suitcases. They'd come before that to be interviewed, and she'd walked them round the house, explaining about the school. She remembered saying in passing that once a year, at the end of every July, a Conservative fête was held, traditionally now, in the gardens. They hadn't seemed much interested.

'I've built this place up,' she heard her husband say. 'Month by month, year by year. It was a chicken farm when I bought it, Kelly, and now I suppose it'll be a chicken farm again.'

She left the kitchen and walked along the kitchen passage and up the uncarpeted back stairs. She knocked on the door of their room. They called out together, saying she should come in. They were both packing their belongings into their cardboard suitcases, smoking fresh cigarettes. Barbara appeared to have recovered.

She tried to explain to them. No one knew yet, she said, why Wraggett had died. He'd had a heart attack most probably, like Mr Kelly said. It was a terrible thing to have happened.

The girls continued to pack, not listening to her. They folded garments or pressed them, unfolded, into their suitcases.

'My husband's built the place up. Month by month, year by year, for seventeen years he has built it up.'

'The boys are waiting for their tea,' said Dympna. 'Mrs Digby-Hunter, you'd better prick the sausages.'

'Forget our wages,' said Barbara, and laughed in a way that was not hysterical.

'My husband – '

'Your husband,' said Dympna, 'derives sexual pleasure from inflicting pain on children. So does Kelly. They are queer men.'

'Your husband,' said Barbara, 'will be jailed. He'll go to prison with a sack over his head so that he won't have to see the disgust on people's faces. Isn't that true, Mrs Digby-Hunter?'

'My husband – '

'Filth,' said Dympna.

She sat down on the edge of a bed and watched the two girls

packing. She imagined the dead body in the bedroom that was never used, and then she imagined Sergeant Wall and Mr Kelly and her husband in the kitchen, waiting for the school doctor to arrive, knowing that it didn't much matter what cause he offered for the death if these two girls were allowed to have their way.

'Why do you hate me?' she asked, quite calmly.

Neither replied. They went on packing and while they packed she talked, in desperation. She tried to speak the truth about Milton Grange, as she saw the truth, but they kept interrupting her. The bruises didn't show on the boys because the bruises were inflicted in an expert way, but sometimes hair was actually pulled out of the boys' scalps, small bunches of hair, she must have noticed that. She had noticed no such thing. 'Corporal punishment,' she began to say, but Barbara held out hairs that had been wrenched from the head of a boy called Bridle. She had found them in a wastepaper basket; Bridle had said they were his and had shown her the place they'd come from. She returned the hairs to a plastic bag that once had contained stockings. The hairs would be photographed, Barbara said, they would appear on the front page of a Sunday newspaper. They'd be side by side with the ex-headmaster, his head hidden beneath a sack, and Mr Kelly skulking behind his beard. Milton Grange, turreted baronial, part ivy-clad, would be examined by Sunday readers as a torture chamber. And in the garden, beneath the beech-trees, a man would photograph the deck-chair where a woman had slept while violence and death occurred. She and her husband might one day appear in a waxworks, and Mr Kelly, too; a man who, like her husband, derived sexual pleasure from inflicting pain on children.

'You are doing this for profit,' she protested, trying to smile, to win them from the error of their ways.

'Yes,' they said together, and then confessed, sharing the

conversation, that they had often considered telephoning a Sunday newspaper to say they had a story to tell. They had kept the hairs in the plastic bag because they'd had that in mind; in every detail they knew what they were going to say.

'You're making money out of – '

'Yes,' said Dympna. 'You've kept us short, Mrs Digby-Hunter.'

She saw their hatred of her in their faces and heard it in both their voices; like a vapour, it hung about the room.

'Why do you hate me?' she asked again.

They laughed, not answering, as though an answer wasn't necessary.

She remembered, although just now she didn't wish to, the clergyman who had kissed her with passion after a dance in a church hall, the dampness of his lips, his body pressed into hers. The smell of his clothes came back to her, across thirty years, seeming familiar because it had come before. She might have borne his children in some rectory somewhere. Would they have hated her then?

Underclothes, dresses, lipsticks, Woolworth's jewellery, unframed photographs of male singing stars were jumbled together in the two cardboard suitcases. The girls moved about the room, picking up their belongings, while Mrs Digby-Hunter, in greater misery than she had ever before experienced, watched them from the edge of the bed. How could human creatures be so cruel? How could they speak to her about being a figure in a waxworks tableau when she had done nothing at all? How could they so callously propose to tell lies to a newspaper about her husband and Mr Kelly when the boy who had so tragically died was still warm with the memory of life?

She watched them, two girls so young that they were not yet fully developed. They had talked about her. In this room, night after night, they had wondered about her, and in the end had hated her. Had they said in their nightly gossiping that since the day of her marriage she had lived like a statue with another statue?

It was all her fault, she suddenly thought: Milton Grange would be a chicken farm again, her husband would be examined by a psychiatrist in a prison, she would live in a single room. It was all her fault. In twenty-nine years it had taken violence and death to make sense of facts that were as terrible.

The girls were saying they'd catch a bus on the main road. Without looking at her or addressing her again they left the bedroom they had shared. She heard their footsteps on the back stairs, and Dympna's voice asking Barbara if she was all right now and Barbara saying she was. A white slug, the girl had called her, a fat white slug.

She did not leave the room. She remained sitting on the edge of the bed, unable to think. Her husband's face appeared in her mind, with its well-kept moustache and shrewd-seeming, dark eyes, a face in the bedroom of a Welsh hotel on the night of her wedding day. She saw herself weeping, as she had not wept then. In a confused way she saw herself on that occasion and on others, protesting, shaking her head, not smiling.

'I'm leaving the army for a step-ladder firm,' he said to her, and she struck his face with her hands, tormented by the absurdity of what he said. She cried out in anger that she had married an army officer, not a step-ladder salesman who was after her father's money. She wept again when ridiculously he told her that he intended to spend his days filling machines full of powdered coffee. He had failed her, she shrilled at him, that night in the Welsh hotel and he had failed her ever since. In front of boys, she accused him of ill-treating those who had been placed in his care. If ever it happened again, she threatened, the police would be sent for. She turned to the boys and ordered them to run about the gardens for a while. It was ludicrous that they should be cooped up while the sun shone, it was ludicrous that they should strive so painfully simply to pass an examination into some school or other. She banged a desk with her hand after the boys had gone, she spat out words at him: they'd all be in the Sunday papers, she said, if he wasn't careful, and she added that she herself would leave Milton Grange for ever unless he pursued a gentler course with the boys who were sent to him, unless he at once dismissed the ill-mannered Mr Kelly, who was clearly a sinister man.

In the room that had been the maids' room Mrs Digby-Hunter wept as her mind went back through the years of her marriage and then, still weeping, she left the room and descended the back stairs to the kitchen. To her husband she said that it was all her fault, she said she was sorry. She had knitted and put down bulbs, she said, and in the end a boy had died. Two girls had hated her because in her easy-going way she had held her peace, not wanting to know. Loyalty and devotion, said Mrs Digby-Hunter, and now a boy was dead, and her husband with a sack over his head would be taken from Milton Grange and later would have sessions with a prison psychiatrist. It was all her fault. She would say so to the reporters when they came. She would explain and take the blame, she would come up to scratch as a wife.

Her husband and Sergeant Wall and Mr Kelly looked at Mrs Digby-Hunter. She stood in the centre of the kitchen, one hand on the table, a stout woman in a blue and pink dress, weeping. The tragedy had temporarily unhinged her, Sergeant Wall thought, and Mr Kelly in irritation thought that if she could see herself she'd go somewhere else, and her husband thought that it was typical of her to be tiresomely stupid at a time like this.

She went on talking: you couldn't blame them for hating her, she said, for she might have prevented death and hadn't bothered herself. In a bedroom in Wales she should have wept, she said, or packed a suitcase and gone away. Her voice continued in the kitchen, the words poured from it, repetitiously and in a hurry. The three men sighed and looked away, all of them thinking the same thing now, that she made no sense at all, with her talk about putting down bulbs and coming up to scratch.